JORY STRONG

ROPING SAVANNAH

FALLON MATES

ELLORA'S CAVE
ROMANTICA PUBLISHING

*W*hat the critics are saying...

&

"*Roping Savannah* is a fast-paced, energetic read, with Savannah's personality and energy being the best part of the story." ~ *The Romance Studio*

"The plot line and characters were interesting and make the book a recommended read." ~ *Novelspot*

"*Fallon Mates: Roping Savannah* is fabulous. An attention grabbing mystery mixed with a stirring ménage romance and characters you will not forget." ~ *A Romance Review*

"This was a great story." ~ *Euro Reviews*

"*Roping Savannah* is a great mixture of romantic suspense and sci-fi elements, plus some really hot sexual scenes." ~ *Love Romances*

"The pages of this book were set on fire by the livable constant force magnetism, and the delicate yet binding anticipation of love." ~ *Coffee Time Romance*

An Ellora's Cave Romantica Publication

www.ellorascave.com

Roping Savannah

ISBN 9781419956997
ALL RIGHTS RESERVED.
Roping Savannah Copyright © 2006 Jory Strong
Edited by Sue-Ellen Gower.
Cover art by Syneca.

This book printed in the U.S.A. by Jasmine–Jade Enterprises, LLC

Electronic book publication May 2006
Trade paperback publication November 2009

ROPING SAVANNAH

�

Trademarks Acknowledgement

ℰↄ

The author acknowledges the trademarked status and trademark owners of the following wordmarks mentioned in this work of fiction:

Advil: Boots Company PLS

Beamer (BMW): Bayerische Motoren Werke Aktiengesellschaft

Chevy: General Motors Corporation

Formica: The Diller Corporation

iPod: Apple Computer, Inc.

Kool-Aid: Kraft Foods

Lincoln Town Car: Ford Motor Company

The Twilight Zone: CBS Inc.

Viagra: Pfizer Inc

Victoria's Secret: Victoria's Secret

Prologue

ഇ

Draigon d'Amato of the Baraqijal stood at the window of his clan's house. In the distance were desolate red mountains, a place of gorges and danger. Of death. A place as inhospitable as the miles of gold-yielding-to-red desert that separated Shiksa from the mountains, and past them, from the jungles of Belizair.

His body might be on his world, but his mind was on Earth. His thoughts on Adan, a childhood friend, a fellow bounty hunter, a law-keeper, an Amato who had done what Draigon had yet to bring himself to do. Accept not only a human female as a mate, but a Vesti as a co-mate.

Even though Adan's female was actually a match to Lyan, any who knew the two men knew the outcome would be the same, regardless of which man had Council law behind them when it came to claiming the human. If Krista Thomas of Earth had been Adan's mate, it would still be Lyan and Adan bonding with her.

No doubt the Council members were beside themselves that Lyan, one who had so often found himself at risk of being sanctioned, now had the benefit of their law and blessing. That in fact, his success was important to all of them.

Tension made Draigon roll his shoulders and stretch his white, feathered wings. Their veins and edges a fiery red interlaced with gold, the coloring a match to his hair, a reflection of the coal-hot knot that burned in his gut.

He was the oldest son and he knew why his father had asked him to return home when his assignment on Sinnett was completed. He had seen it in his mother's eyes when she greeted him. He had seen it in the face of his cousin Zantara.

And as always, her plight had ripped into Draigon's heart and soul. Made him curse the Hotalings for their virus. Made him curse the Araqiel clan-house of the Vesti for bringing it to Belizair where it had wrought unparalleled devastation. Where it still might lead to the extinction of both the Vesti and the Amato.

His stomach churned. Long ago the Vesti and the Amato had warred and nearly destroyed themselves. Even before the Hotaling virus, pockets of distrust and long-held memories, hidden hostilities remained between the two races. Now the situation on Belizair threatened to pierce the wall keeping those prejudices contained even as it required the two races to work together to avoid extinction. Required unmated males to form alliances and share a mate.

Draigon sighed as he heard his father's voice in another part of the house. It would not be long now.

He had thought when the time came to settle and raise a family that he would share a mate with the brother closest to him in age. Or perhaps be part of a foursome if their female wanted a second to join with them. The Amato had always bonded in whatever arrangement was agreeable to those involved. But to pursue that vision of the future now meant there would be no children.

Draigon rubbed his chest even as he knew nothing would remove the tightness there. If only one of his younger brothers had been matched...

Like many of the unmated males on Belizair, when news of the first successful pregnancies spread across their world, his brothers had gone to the Council scientists and provided a sample of their DNA. Draigon had not gone. Had never intended to go. But as his father's footsteps drew nearer, Draigon mentally prepared himself for the inevitability of his fate. The desolate and harsh scene in front of him mirroring the reality of the path laid out for him. A Vesti co-mate. A human female. He would do what was required of him.

Chapter One

๛

Savannah Holden grimaced as she opened her locker and started stripping out of her uniform. Her ears were already starting to burn, her skin starting to chafe in anticipation of the captain catching up with her before she could get out of the building. She knew he'd be looking for her now that he was back from his conference, but that didn't mean she intended to make it easy for him to find her. She was in for a lecture again, about passing on whatever tips she came across and then letting others—in this case, the guys in Vice—take it from there.

Damn. The captain just didn't get it. Or if he did then he was doing a fine job of ignoring it.

When she joined the police force, she'd actually had visions of taking down the bad guys. Yeah, she took them down all right. But if she'd wanted to wrestle drunk and disorderlies to the ground every day as part of her job description, then she'd have found a job as a bouncer at a bar, or chaperoned rowdy ranch hands on their days off.

She wanted to be a detective. She wanted to use her brain to solve crime. Not that she thought being a beat cop was a lowly profession. No way. But... She'd always been great at puzzles and she was a killer at board games. A mind like that should be put to use, right? She was more than just a warm body filling a uniform, right?

Hell yeah!

She pulled on her jeans and checked her watch. Plenty of time to get to The Dive.

Savannah grinned. Yeah, that place brought back a lot of memories. Most of them involving Krista Thomas. They were more like sisters than friends. Months could pass, even years, but whenever they saw each other, it was like no time had passed at all.

The theme music from *The Twilight Zone* moved through Savannah's head and she laughed softly. She'd been thinking more and more about Krista lately. Which meant she'd be seeing her soon. It had always been like that, some kind of weird sixth sense letting her pick up on things that couldn't be explained. Too bad that sixth sense couldn't lead her to a detective's title. *Detective Savannah Holden.* Yeah, she liked the sound of that.

Definitely better than Rancher Savannah Holden. Or Rancher's Wife Savannah Holden. Not that she didn't know ranching from planting the corn to shoveling the shit that came out of the cow further along toward the end of the food chain cycle. She'd been born and raised on the Bar None Ranch so she knew for a fact that ranching was hard work, with longer hours than a cop put in and only slightly less danger.

But the rancher's life didn't call to her, and besides, despite the fact she could ride, rope, doctor livestock and castrate bulls just as well as any of her brothers, they didn't really need her. *And there it is in a nutshell,* she admitted to herself. She wanted her work to have meaning. She wanted her life to have meaning. She wanted to be needed.

Savannah checked her watch again. Plenty of time to meet The Ferret. Damn. She had to try and remember his real name. Dale? Or was it Ricky? Crap. She was terrible with real names. She'd given him a nickname and never thought of him any other way afterward.

Her thoughts ranged over the phone conversation she'd had with him earlier. "I've got a tip for you," he'd said.

"I'm listening."

"Not here. It's too big to talk about over the phone. You break it wide open, the brass will be kissing your ass and begging you to take a detective shield."

"Where?"

"You know a place called The Dive?"

"Sure."

"I'll see you there." And they'd agreed on a time.

Savannah's cell phone rang. She laughed when she answered it and heard Krista's voice, *The Twilight Zone* theme song returning to play briefly in her mind as soon as Krista told her she was nearing Reno. "Do you remember where that hole-in-the-wall place called The Dive is?" Savannah asked.

Krista laughed. "You know I do. That's the only place in town that used to let us in with our obviously fake IDs when we were sixteen."

"I'll take the fifth on that. Why don't you meet me at The Dive? It's a safe enough place these days and as soon as I change clothes I'm heading there anyway. I'm supposed to meet a snitch but my business with him shouldn't take too long."

"Okay, see you there."

Savannah put the phone in the holder on her belt and quickly changed her shirt, then bent over and slipped on her tennis shoes, a good choice over her usual cowboy boots because she was feeling an intense urge to bolt before the captain could catch up to her.

"Hey, Holden, wait up," a male voice said as she left the locker room.

Savannah cringed in reaction before her brain processed who was calling her. She turned, watching as Fowler, the golden boy of Vice, closed the distance between them and put a companionable arm around her shoulders.

"You got a career death wish?" Fowler asked.

She grimaced. "It probably looks that way. You sure you want to be seen with me?"

He laughed. An infectious sound that was impossible to resist. Then again, he was GQ material. The embodiment of every secretarial fantasy and quite a few officer fantasies—hers included—since he'd transferred in from Vegas.

They began walking down the hall, his arm still slung around her shoulder. Savannah tried to keep it in perspective. He'd never hit on her. Never given her reason to think he was interested. And even if he was… Dating a cop was a bad idea. She'd tried it a couple of times and sworn off it.

They turned a corner and Savannah cursed silently at the sight of the two cops walking in their direction. Fowler gave her shoulder a little squeeze in silent support. "Hey, Creech, Mastrin," he said as they passed.

"You sure you don't have a career death wish?" Savannah joked a minute later. "Creech and Mastrin are not part of my fan club. It was their case I just interfered with."

She hadn't meant to get tangled up in a Vice operation. And in her defense, she had passed on the tip she got about a couple of underage prostitutes. If someone had just said, *We're on it* or *Back off, it's part of an active investigation*, then she'd have been happy to leave it to them. She wasn't interested in working Vice.

But instead of a satisfying response to her tip, all she'd gotten was a vague okay. And she couldn't leave it alone. Not after she'd done a drive-by and seen one of the girls hanging out in front of the residential hotel. The kid hadn't been openly soliciting, so Savannah hadn't been able to act—then.

Damn, even now she couldn't get the kid out of her mind. The haunted, disillusioned eyes in a small pixie-face.

Fowler pulled his arm from Savannah's shoulder. "Look, you want to work Vice, I'll put in a word for you."

"I don't think I'm cut out for Vice."

"You kidding me? People talk to you. That's a big part of the equation. Take those girls you hauled in, somebody came to you with the information. Right?"

"Right," Savannah said, though it wasn't exactly the truth. She'd gone to the information source—for fried chicken and a side of coleslaw—rather than the information source coming to her.

"See what I mean?" He laughed and cut her a hopeful look. "Want to share the snitch?"

Savannah grinned. "I think it's safe to say this was a one-time deal. The guy heard rumors and he's got young daughters of his own."

Fowler winked and flashed a smile that could melt stone. "Okay, okay. You don't want to share, that's fine." He fished a small notebook and a pen out of his pocket, wrote something and then tore off the sheet, handing it to Savannah. "This is my cell number. You get another tip and want someone to take it seriously, call me."

She stuffed the paper in her back pocket. He started to put the notebook away then hesitated. "You got a cell number?" Savannah gave it to him. He shoved the notebook and pen in his pocket. "I've got to get going. But I'm serious, you ever want to try Vice, I'll do what I can to help you. Just let me know."

"Thanks," she said, and he peeled away, heading back in the direction of the locker rooms as she turned the corner and came face-to-face with the captain. Great! What was this, happy hour in the halls of the police station?

"Holden. Any reason you think the guys in Vice can't handle their job? Any reason why you've got to take it on yourself to do a stakeout while you're off the clock?"

She grimaced. "No, Captain, but—"

He held up his hand and she thought his face had turned an unhealthy shade of red. "Stop while you're ahead, Holden. I know you grew up listening to your grandfather's outrageous tales and watching westerns where the guy in the white hat charged in and saved the day, shooting up the place in the process and being made sheriff. But we don't work that way here. You pay your dues, maybe kiss a little ass even if it sours you, and you wait your time. You'll get your detective's

15

shield — maybe — if you can keep from pissing off the higher-ups and stepping on other people's toes."

Savannah ducked her head, knowing what the captain was saying was right. The trouble was, she'd always been a little…impetuous. A little unrestrained. But hell, how could she be any different after growing up with rowdy, hell-raising brothers and ranch hands who worked hard and played equally hard? It was keep up or get left behind, and she wasn't about to miss the action.

The captain glanced at his watch, signaling the end of his lecture. Savannah breathed a sigh of relief — until his eyes locked on hers and he said, "Try to stay out of trouble for the rest of the day, Holden."

Her thoughts flashed to The Ferret and she had to work hard at controlling her expression so she wouldn't look as guilty as she suddenly felt. She knew the captain was trying to help her, and for a second, the temptation to tell him about The Ferret's call hovered at the tip of her tongue.

She suppressed it, taking the edge off her conscience by promising herself that if the tip was a good one, she'd try to rein in her impulsiveness. She'd try to work the system, maybe even go to the captain and get his advice. "I'll try," she muttered and felt the captain's gaze on her back until she rounded the corner and escaped the building.

Krista was already at The Dive when she got there. "Sorry I'm late," Savannah said as she hugged her friend. "The captain had to give me my weekly dressing-down about investigating while off-duty."

Krista laughed. "As in meeting a snitch tonight?"

Savannah rolled her eyes. "Don't even go there! With any luck the captain won't find out about it." *Unless it pans out.* She looked around. "We might as well go in. The Ferret will know where to find me."

"The Ferret?"

16

"Looks like a weasel, smells like a weasel and acts like a weasel—so I call him The Ferret, though I think his real name is something like Dale or Ricky."

Damn. She'd memorized his address but she kept blanking on his legal name. She'd intended to pull The Ferret's rap sheet before meeting him, but after encountering the captain she didn't have any choice but to get out of the building and do nothing suspicious. Shit. The captain meant well, so it was hard to be mad at him, but... Savannah shrugged it off as she and Krista took a back booth.

"What were you investigating that got you in trouble?" Krista asked.

"I got a tip about a couple of underage girls involved in prostitution. My source didn't know who was running them, but he gave me an address and a description of the girls. I did a drive-by then passed the information on, but...I just couldn't get one of the girls out of my mind. Holland." Savannah looked at Krista and realized that part of the reason the kid had gotten to her was because Holland reminded her of Krista and she'd been thinking about Krista more often lately.

"You arrested the girls?" Krista asked.

"I went back and staked the place out. Along comes an older girl, she's nineteen and goes by the name Camryn, I know that now. Anyway, she's got a guy with her who has *perv* radiating off him. Holland and another girl her age are outside, sharing an iPod. Camryn and the scumbag stop. There's talking. Pointing. The sicko john gives a belly laugh and then disappears into the residential hotel with Holland and the other underage kid. To make a long story short. I call for backup and then go in. The perv's down to his boxers. Holland's in the bathroom. The other girl is naked on the bed."

Krista frowned. "And *you* got in trouble?"

"It turns out Vice has been looking at an escort service these girls have some connection to. But the perv I brought in was a freelance job. Not that any of the participants are admitting anything."

"So what's going to happen to them?"

"The perv will probably get lewd conduct with a minor — if he gets that." Savannah shrugged. "I didn't see any money change hands. I didn't actually catch them in the act. But there was no way I could drive away once I saw them go inside."

"And the girls?"

"I don't know. I was planning on following up. I still am as soon as I can manage it without the guys in Vice ripping me a new one. The one kid is already pretty hardened, but the other, Holland—" Savannah shrugged. "You'd think the job would toughen me up, but something about her still seems vulnerable, like it's not too late to turn it around for her." A waitress stopped by the table. Once she'd taken their orders and moved on, Savannah changed the topic. "So what brings you to Reno?"

"I thought it'd be nice to get away for a while, maybe use the cabin if it's available."

"Man trouble?" Savannah asked, watching as a wide range of emotions washed over Krista's face. "Oh boy, you have it bad. Want to tell me about the asshole who broke your heart? Maybe he's got an outstanding warrant or something and I can make sure the wheels of justice turn."

Krista laughed. "What you really mean is, make sure the wheels of justice roll over the guy and flatten him."

Savannah grinned. "That too." Then on a more serious note she added, "Feel free to use the cabin for as long as you need to. I'm all ears if you want to talk."

The waitress arrived and placed their drinks and food on the table, then left. Krista cleared her throat and reached for a nacho, her face flushing with color before saying, "It's not just one guy, it's two. And they didn't break my heart exactly. I want to be with them, but I can't."

18

Savannah's eyebrows lifted. She grabbed a nacho and dug it into a pot containing hot cheese. "Oh boy. Are you talking both at the same time, or two different boyfriends in two different locations?"

"Both at the same time."

Savannah made a show of waving air onto her face. "Is this your idea or theirs?"

Krista's blush deepened. "We're all okay with it."

"I am speechless."

"That's a first."

Savannah grinned. "Yeah, my captain would say that too." Her face went serious. "So what's holding you back? Are you afraid it'd get back to your principal and you'd get canned on a morals clause?"

"Yeah, something like that."

Savannah reached for Krista's arm and gave a little squeeze. "So go on a trip somewhere and enjoy the fantasy. That's what I'd do."

Surprise chased across Krista's face and Savannah laughed. "What, you don't think I have fantasies too?" Her eyebrows went up and down in a comical manner. "I have a very active imagination."

Krista laughed. "So you'd take on two guys at once?"

"Oh yeah. And I'd bring out the lariat."

"No!"

Savannah grinned. "You know how much I love to rope and tie things. Now tell me about these two guys."

"The word gorgeous doesn't do them justice. They look like..." Krista laughed. "I'm embarrassed to even say this. But I will. They look like warriors, the kind you picture on the cover of a very steamy erotic romance novel. Tanned, muscled. Alike but different." She wrinkled her nose. "They complement each other and I get the idea that they've been friends for a long time."

Savannah snorted. "Not a lot of time was spent on conversation I take it."

Krista gave a small, husky laugh and admitted, "No." She hesitated. "Do you still believe love can happen a few heartbeats after lust at first sight?"

"Yeah. I think it's possible to recognize someone you can spend your life with at the same time your hormones are in overdrive and you want to jump his body." Savannah sighed. "I can only dream. So besides gorgeous, what do they look like?"

"Both have shoulder-length hair, but Adan's is golden and Lyan's is black." Krista's expression could only be described as dreamy. "They're like walking fantasies. It's crazy. The first time they both touched me, I felt...like it was more than lust. And then when I was...in bed with them..."

Savannah held her hand in front of her. "Stop. Do not pass GO. Do not collect your two hundred dollars. Tell me if they have any gorgeous friends, then find a room and lock the three of you in it!"

Krista laughed. "I take it there aren't any fantasy men in your life right now."

"Not even close. The only guys I see are cops and crooks—not exactly prime candidates in the relationship department."

"What about the cowboys on your parents' ranch? The way I remember it, that's where all the great-looking guys could be found."

Savannah rolled her eyes. "Now that my brothers have taken over so my parents can travel, any guy they catch looking my way gets to check fences. I've been told that riding the fence line with a raging hard-on is very painful. These days all I have to do to clear a room of cowboys is to walk into it! And yeah, you're right—the Bar None bunkhouse is still full of eye candy."

Krista snickered. "So close and yet so far away."

"You've got that right," Savannah said as she checked her watch and frowned.

"Is your snitch late?"

"Yeah, by about ten minutes. The Ferret is the nervous type. He usually arrives early, lurks in the shadows until he makes sure it's safe then slinks out. It's not like him to be late." She rose from her chair. "I think I'll check outside, just in case."

Krista stood up too. "I'll go with you."

"No way, this is police business."

"Official police business?"

Savannah shook her head ruefully. "That's the trouble with confessions — they always come back to haunt you. Come on. These days The Dive is a pretty quiet place. I don't really expect trouble. The Ferret probably got a better offer and that's why he's a no-show, but I'd kick myself if I found out later that he was hanging around outside."

"What kind of information is he selling?"

"I don't know." She wasn't even sure if The Ferret expected to be paid for it.

"You don't know!"

Savannah grimaced. "All he said was that it was something big. Something big enough that if I break it wide open, the brass will have to give me a detective shield, and my days as a beat cop will be over." They stepped out of the bar and Savannah said, "That looks like The Ferret's car."

The car was parked down the street, on the other side of an alleyway. The brand new black Beamer was one of the expensive models. "This feels bad," Krista said. "Why didn't he park here?"

"I don't know. But there's one way to find out."

"Shouldn't you call for backup or something?"

Savannah shook her head but didn't say anything as she stopped at the truck long enough to retrieve her weapon before heading toward the Beamer. At the alleyway she held up a hand to signal a halt, then crouched low with her gun in the ready position before she eased around to check the alley.

* * * * *

Kye d'Vesti's cock came to a rapid and throbbing attention when he saw the flame-haired woman step out of the bar with Krista Thomas, the bond-mate his cousin Lyan shared with Adan d'Amato. By the stars, the flame-haired beauty was the one. She was his mate.

He didn't need the Council and its scientists to confirm it. The blood pouring into his shaft, the fire racing through his veins, the need that made him want to leave his hiding place and stride over to claim her were all the proof he needed. She was his.

She was also armed and dangerous.

Kye shook his head as though to clear the images being transmitted from his eyes to his brain. Had his soon-to-be-mate just pulled one of their primitive weapons from a holster at her side? Was she even now moving away from him in the manner of a hunter tracking prey?

She was.

Kye didn't know whether to laugh or to yell in rage as he quickly determined a destination and transported to it. Now that he'd found his mate, there was no way he would allow anything to happen to her. She was his only hope to sire children, not that the desire for offspring was on his mind at the present time—though fucking was. Oh yes, he definitely had fucking on his mind.

But first he needed to stop this foolishness of inviting danger into her life. She was far, far too valuable—to him, to his race—to one of the unmated Amato he would need to share her with. Kye frowned at the thought then pushed it away, his heart jerking in his chest as he saw Krista grab her flame-haired friend and jerk her into an alley just as the car they were approaching exploded in a blast that rocked the area and sent metal and glass and pieces of brick flinging like deadly projectiles in all directions.

Chapter Two

໕ව

In a heartbeat Kye was there, rage and deadly resolve swirling through him in a wild rush. Until this moment, he had never felt the primitive emotions that so often overtook Vesti males. But now, as he looked down at his debris-covered mate, they poured through him, turning him into a deadly opponent. He wanted to find whoever had done this to her and make them pay—slowly and painfully. He wanted to carry his mate home and ensure her life was never in danger again.

Kye's eyes traveled to Lyan's mate and love for her swelled in his heart. If not for Krista, his own mate would be dead.

"Lyan?" Krista asked, frowning in puzzled confusion.

"No, I am Kye."

Krista slowly sat up, her attention shifting to her friend. "Savannah, are you okay?"

Savannah groaned and rolled to her side before also sitting up. "Yeah, nothing that some Advil and hydrogen peroxide won't take care of." She brushed a hand over her hair, sending small pieces of glass and brick to the concrete. "Man, I knew I wasn't going to like what was in that Beamer!"

Her grin sent a wave of fury through Kye. Didn't his mate realize that someone had been waiting for her? Was trying to kill her?

Krista shook her head and shuddered. "Maybe you should leave town for a while, Savannah. Somebody set you up."

Savannah rubbed her hands together, quelling the riot of emotions roaring through her with a show of bravado. "Where there's smoke, there's fire. This could be my big break. What'd you see before the explosion? What tipped you off?"

"Did you see the car pull away from the curb as we were heading toward the Beamer?"

"Yeah." Savannah frowned. Had she missed something obvious?

"The window came down and then something like an antenna came out. I just had a bad feeling..."

Shit! She'd been so focused on the Beamer... "Good thing for both of us that you did."

Kye's nostrils flared with fury. The purple crystals in his wristbands swirled and pulsed as his emotions threatened his control. The need to take his woman and get her to safety was almost overwhelming. "Who wants to hurt you?" he demanded.

Green fire flashed in his mate's eyes and sent blood roaring to his cock. When he got her away from here, she'd feel the sting of his hand on her ass before he mounted her.

"And you are?" his defiant mate—Savannah—had the nerve to ask in a challenging tone.

"Kye d'Vesti, cousin to Lyan d'Vesti."

Savannah's eyes grew round and her lips formed a small *o*. To Krista she said, "Wow."

Krista flushed with heightened color before her attention shifted to Kye. "Did Lyan and Adan send you? How did they know I was here?"

"Lyan does not yet know where you are. He told me of you and I was curious so I followed you here from Las Vegas."

Krista stiffened. "Why were you curious?"

Kye grinned, amusement temporarily displacing the killing fury and wild possessiveness battling inside him. "It is not every day that my fierce cousin is brought to his knees. I wanted to see the female who had tamed him." He shook his head. "Be warned, once Lyan returns to his senses, he'll come after you."

"Are you going to tell him that I'm here?"

The range of emotions warring on Krista's face—the longing and despair—made Kye more curious than ever as to what was going on between Adan and Lyan and their beautiful bond-mate, but he shook his head and set her mind at ease by saying, "No, you have my word that I will say nothing to him."

Of course, he had no need to tell his cousin. The serum Lyan injected into Krista's bloodstream when he sunk his mating teeth into her had forged a connection that allowed him to sense where she was. Once claimed, it was impossible for a Vesti mate to escape.

Kye's eyes darkened momentarily as his attention moved to his own mate. He didn't intend to make the same mistake with her as Lyan had made initially with Krista. As soon as Savannah was underneath him, he intended to sink his mating fangs into her. She would never be able to disappear from his life after he had done so.

A siren sounded in the distance and Savannah scrambled to her feet. "Damn, we need to get out of here. Let's go out the alley and around. The fewer people that see us, the better."

Krista frowned. "Shouldn't you stick around and make a report or something?"

"Trust me, it'll do more harm than good if my captain gets word of this. And until I know more about what's going on, I'm going to play this one close to the chest. The Ferret said he was on to something big. I don't know how long it's going to take for them to find out who the car belonged to, but I need to get to The Ferret's place and see if there's something there that'll help me make sense of this thing."

"I'll go with you," Krista said as she and Kye followed Savannah to the end of the alley and around the corner.

Savannah shook her head. "No. It'd be safer if you didn't. Please, go to the cabin. I'll call you to let you know I made it home."

Krista's face grew determined. "I'm not letting you go by yourself. I'm going, even if I have to wait in the car."

Kye's jaw clenched. His mate would soon learn that putting herself in danger was unacceptable. Despite his promise to Krista, he sent out a mental probe to determine if Lyan and Adan were near. Relief washed through him when he found they were rapidly approaching the city. Soon they would be here to take charge of their female.

Kye and the two women slipped into The Dive's parking lot unnoticed. A crowd was gathered around the remains of the black Beamer. Savannah used the remote on her key chain to unlock the doors of her truck. Krista said, "I'm not letting you go alone, I'll follow you in my car."

"No," Kye said. He could not allow anything to happen to Lyan and Adan's mate. "I will go with Savannah."

Savannah stiffened. "I don't believe you were invited."

Kye's attention was immediately drawn to his mate. He took her arm and tried to retrieve the keys. When she didn't yield, he pulled her against his body. The smell of her filling his nostrils and imprinting itself on his soul.

"Back off," she growled, trying to escape his arms.

Savannah's struggles only served to press her hard-tipped breasts against his chest. He smiled. She was not immune to him. But if looks could kill, his mate would even now be facing charges for his murder.

"No. We have much to discuss." Kye didn't bother to keep the growl out of his voice as he forced the keys from her hand then opened the door and urged Savannah into the truck. Once she was inside, he turned to Krista and cupped her face in his hand. "You have my word that I will keep your friend safe. She is my bond-mate. Those who would harm her will pay with their lives."

Krista's eyes widened. Kye smiled and pressed his lips to hers, sucking and teasing until she opened her mouth to him. His tongue rubbed over hers, offering comfort and reassurance—as well as the taste and memory of him for Lyan to find—and react to. It was foolish, baiting his cousin in such a manner, but he couldn't help himself.

"Leave now. Do not worry for your friend," he said when the kiss ended.

Krista got into her car. Reluctantly. And he could feel his own mate's hostile glare boring into his back and sending even more blood to his cock as he stood in the parking lot and watched Krista drive away. When she was out of sight he turned and climbed into the truck, feeling his control threatened by the heady scent and beauty of Savannah.

"All right, Batman," she said, "I humored you for Krista's sake. But we need to get a few things straight." She paused to look at the growing crowd of people around the Beamer. "After we get out of here."

A ripple of shock moved through Kye. *Bat-man?* Had she glimpsed his true form? His heart soared. Only those humans who carried the Fallon gene markers could see the Vesti and the Amato as they truly were.

His mate's frown deepened. "Get moving, or get out of the truck."

Kye grinned at her command. Oh yes, he and his mate definitely had a few things to get straight. Not the least of which was that from this moment on, it would be *his* commands that would be followed, *not* hers. She belonged to him now, and she would no longer put herself in danger, nor do as she pleased without regard to her own safety.

He started the truck's engine and escaped the parking lot, moving away from the area just as police cars roared in with their sirens blaring and their lights flashing. Next to him Savannah whipped around, a frown settling on her face as she looked out the back window. Frustration moved through Kye.

If they were already mated then he would know Savannah's thoughts, but since they weren't yet connected in that manner, he had to ask, "Why do you frown?"

She turned back to him, scowling, though he sensed it was directed at herself and not at him. "I wasn't thinking straight. I should have at least checked the car to see if The Ferret's body was in it." She leaned over and turned on a police radio, its static and squawking stretching Kye's nerves even further.

"And who is this Ferret?"

"A snitch." When Kye frowned, she said, "An informant."

"He takes money for information?"

"Sometimes."

Outrage flashed through Kye. Primitive and hot, and directed at his soon-to-be-mate. "You trusted such a man!"

Temper flared in her eyes, a challenge that tightened Kye's body with need. "Look, Batman, the only reason I'm not dropping you off at the nearest bus station so you can buy a ticket and head back to your cave is because I don't have time at the moment. Now take a left at the next light."

A shock of laughter filled Kye's chest at his fiery mate's words, at her boldness and confidence. At her audacity to threaten him with exile even as *he* was driving her primitive vehicle!

But he turned as she'd directed, arguing with himself as to the wisdom of letting her go to this Ferret's living quarters, though he feared he had little choice. She would be in no mood to accept his advances until this matter was attended to, and he could not afford to part from her until after he'd mounted her and pierced her with his fangs.

Kye's hands tightened on the steering wheel in anticipation of that moment. His cock protesting the delay, surging painfully against the uncomfortably tight pants he was forced to wear while in Savannah's world.

The need to mate with her was almost unbearable. The pheromones her body was assaulting him with making every moment in her presence a battle for control. The Vesti mating fever was upon him, had been from the moment he first saw her.

By the stars, he had not expected this to happen. Had not even hoped for it. In truth, he had not wanted it — yet.

He had offered his services to the Council because he believed the only way to overcome the devastation wrought by the cursed Hotalings was to work together, to change and accept the unavoidable. That both races weren't doomed to extinction was a miracle, though right now it was only human women with the Fallon gene sequence who provided the hope and promise of children. Even so, Kye had not completely reconciled himself to sharing a mate with anyone. He still could not envision it — especially with the Vesti mating fever burning through his veins and pooling in his cock and testicles.

Once the Vesti and Amato had been a single great race of winged shapeshifters. But arrogance and jealousy, pride and prejudice had destroyed it, splintering it into a multitude of races that were lesser than what they had once been.

And then the Hotalings had struck. Unleashing their bio-gene weapons, thinking to kill all those on Belizair and gain possession of the Ylan power stones, or perhaps simply to hold the threat of extinction over the heads of the Vesti and Amato in order to gain what they desired.

A few on Belizair had died as a result of the virus, mainly the weak, the old. Their passing painful, but not a festering wound. Far more devastating had been the miscarriages by women who were early in their pregnancies, followed by the realization there would be no new pregnancies.

Kye turned his attention to Savannah and felt his heart expand. She was a gift he hadn't asked for, or expected, but one he wouldn't refuse. He'd been content to use his skills as a bounty hunter — a law enforcer — to track and watch over those women the Council scientists discovered carrying the Fallon genes. Lyan and Adan's mate was one of those women.

Kye frowned, thinking of all the cities Krista had traveled to, never staying more than a few days in any one of them. She'd first been found in San Francisco, where she was a teacher. But before the scientists could match the marker in her genes with a Vesti or Amato mate, she'd disappeared.

He had chosen to risk censure and ridicule by implanting a tiny tracking chip in her without being told to do so by the Council scientists. Usually the chip was implanted only when the scientists feared they might lose track of a potential bond-mate. It was done at a distance, with a special device, so the female was not frightened or forewarned. The sting was no more painful than the bite of an insect and the chip was easily destroyed once the female was claimed and mated.

If it were left to him, then *all* potential mates would be tagged. Why risk losing them? Especially now, when old jealousies and long-held grudges threatened to surface and take over in the wake of the Hotalings attack.

True, the Amato were sticklers for following the law when compared to the more hot-tempered Vesti. But neither race had allowed the hostility of its own members to escalate to the point of bloodshed. And now each race needed the other — desperately.

Kye shook his head, glad he had tagged Krista. Had he not done so, he might never have found her again. Her movements across the country had been unpredictable, except for the fact she appeared to gain what money she needed by visiting the gambling hells.

Kye shifted in his seat, trying to relieve some of the pressure from his too-full cock. *Thank the stars Krista was now Lyan and Adan's responsibility!* His own mate was going to require all his attention.

"Park in that spot right there," Savannah said, sending his pulse spiking upward a few moments later when she got out of the truck, striding away before he'd even cut the engine. Leaving him scrambling after her like a *banzit* after dropped fruit.

He entered the building seconds past when she did, but still there was only time to see one of the elevators close. Fear for her safety clashed with anger as he stood helpless, waiting to see which floor the elevator stopped on even as he hoped it was indeed the floor where she exited.

Despite the show of bravado in front of Krista and Kye, adrenaline-laced wariness raced through Savannah as she took the final few steps to the fourth floor. She'd had a lot of close calls during her life — the time she flipped her ATV while chasing an ornery bull, the time a visiting cousin had found a loaded rifle in the bunkhouse and fired at her — not realizing it *was* loaded, the time she'd ended up in the hospital when a drunk driver she'd pulled over put his car in reverse and mowed her down. But she'd never had someone want her dead seriously enough to plant a bomb and then detonate it.

She shivered, easing the stairwell door open. What could The Ferret have known? And why call her instead of someone higher up in the force? Though the answer was obvious when she thought about it. Maybe he'd just figured she was good for her word. She'd let him slip on a minor infraction a time or two in exchange for information — well, maybe more than a time or two.

Her stomach tightened. It'd crossed her mind that maybe it was a setup. But she couldn't think of anything she'd seen, done, or said that would warrant a car explosion.

Damn! She should have taken the time to see if there was a body in the car. It might help if she knew whether or not the information The Ferret had was hot enough for someone to stick around and see who showed up to meet him. Though of course, if they recognized her *before* they tried to blow her up, things could get a little dicey once they realized they'd missed her. Savannah doubted Krista had seen anything in those first seconds after the car had blown, but when she called and checked in with Krista later she'd ask her if she'd noticed whether the black car and its occupants had stuck around long enough to see the results of the explosion.

Savannah cocked her head, surprised she didn't hear footsteps in the stairwell. Then again, she'd gotten lucky when an elderly couple had stepped into the elevator and the door had closed just as she was coming through the front door. That might divert Kye for a few minutes. She had a bad feeling she was already going to be in enough trouble without involving a civilian in this—even if said civilian was the most gorgeous man she'd ever met.

Just her luck to encounter him today, when Krista was in town—and after Krista's blushing confession of being with two men at once. It was one of Savannah's favorite fantasies, even without the rope she'd joked about.

She looked at the number on the door across from the stairwell. Depending on how many units were on each floor, The Ferret's apartment was toward the other end, on the same side as she was unless it was around either corner where the hallway formed a "T" with another section. She couldn't guess how those units were numbered.

Savannah double-checked that the safety on her gun was off before moving forward. Chances were that whoever had blown up The Ferret's car had already been to his apartment and gone. But she wasn't going to be stupid.

Impatience crawled over Kye's skin, adding to the jangling clamor of nerve endings left raw by the disappearance of his bond-mate. When he got his hands on her…

His attention shifted to the numbers displayed above the elevator and he knew immediately that he'd erred in waiting to see which floor it stopped on. She wouldn't have taken the elevator to the second one.

He retraced his steps and found a stairway, cursing himself as he moved upward, pausing at the door to the second floor. There was no choice but to open it. To sprint down the empty hall and check around the corner, then dash into the stairwell again and repeat the process on the next floor. And then the next.

His training as a law-keeper served him well, as did his instinct. Though he was also willing to credit luck and the faint hint of his elusive mate's perfume for drawing him down a hallway and around a corner to where a door stood open, Savannah's curses finding him in the hallway.

Kye closed the distance between them, promising himself things would change once he got her to a private location and claimed her. He intended to ride her so fiercely, to pleasure her so thoroughly she wouldn't find it easy to get farther away from the bed than the kitchen or the bathroom.

He stepped into The Ferret's living quarters and into chaos. The place had been ransacked and in the middle, surrounded by debris, stood Savannah.

Kye actually found amusement in the sight. He could well imagine that his fiery-haired bond-mate was capable of such fury, though he doubted she could have rendered the apartment inhabitable in so short a period of time.

"It would appear someone was here before us," Kye said. "I doubt anything useful remains to be found."

"Shit! What was The Ferret involved in?"

She moved deeper into the apartment and Kye followed, both of them stopping in the doorway to the small bedroom. Seeing the slashed mattress, the dresser drawers tossed on the floor, their contents scattered everywhere.

Chapter Three

Ꮹ

"I'm going to have to bring the captain up to speed on this and he's going to nail my ass to a desk-chair. If I'm lucky," Savannah said, wading into the bedroom but not touching anything.

Kye nodded in approval then stilled when Savannah whipped her head around and glared at him.

"If you're going to ride with me, Batman, you'd better start paying attention to your surroundings."

Kye laughed, undaunted by his feisty bond-mate, though his gaze went immediately to the mirror where his face and expressions were captured. Revealed.

He grinned. Unrepentant. Her Earth-days were numbered and he would prefer she not work at all. But if she must, then he would gain a measure of peace by knowing she was guarding a desk, safely entombed in one of the cave-like buildings the humans seemed to feel safest in.

He needed to get a sample of her DNA to the Council scientists so they could confirm what his cock and his instinct already knew. She was his. Once it had been confirmed by the scientists, then he needed only to choose a co-mate from among the Amato and make arrangements for lodging in Winseka, the Bridge City where all those newly mated to humans lived.

True, there was the small matter of getting her to agree to go through the binding ceremony and return home with her bond-mates—their destination and true form not revealed until they were in the transport chamber—but Kye didn't doubt his ability to convince Savannah her future lay with him…and another.

His chest tightened in protest at the thought of sharing Savannah. It was not the way of the Vesti to share their mates. From the very beginning it had always been one male, one female.

The thought of another man covering Savannah's body, thrusting his cock into her, had Kye gritting his teeth. It went against his nature, his instinct, drove the heat of the mating fever into a raging inferno, an insistent demand that he hoard her, guard her, keep her for himself.

Kye forced the thoughts away. There was no choice but to choose a co-mate. To form a threesome.

So far the Council scientists had found only one way to defeat the Hotaling virus. Now the Council's agents searched among the humans in order to identify those females who had the genetic marker of one of the Fallon—the shared ancestor race of the Amato and Vesti.

All hope to avoid extinction rested on the unmated males, yet each male carried both the fear there would be no match and the knowledge it required a Vesti or Amato co-mate in order to produce offspring. Though the scientists couldn't reproduce the results in the laboratory with either an Amato or Vesti female, when it came to the human females carrying the Fallon gene, they theorized the serum a Vesti male injected while mating somehow changed the female's chemistry, allowing for both the Vesti and Amato sperm to fertilize her eggs.

They'd stumbled on it accidentally, when an Amato in an experimental program was matched to a human but elected to share her with his best friend, a Vesti. She'd become pregnant, the test results confusing as to whether her children would be Vesti or Amato since the twins she carried contained the distinctive markers for both races.

Still, it was the first conception, the first time a woman on Belizair had managed such a feat since the Hotaling virus had struck. And since none of the earlier "experimental" matches between a human female and a Vesti or Amato had produced children, the scientists had gone to those pairs and urged them to take a co-mate. It had been a difficult undertaking, but eventually all of the couples had expanded to include another partner in their union, and now all were expecting children. Twins. The test results on the fetuses equally confusing, but the scientists were predicting a child of each race. Guessing that perhaps the Hotaling virus had mutated the males' sperm in such a way that both needed to be present in a human womb of one carrying the Fallon gene and that she also needed to be injected with the Vesti mating serum.

So the unmated males on Belizair who had reconciled themselves to sharing a mate, to taking a human female, submitted samples of their DNA and waited for a match to be made as they considered who they would choose for a co-mate.

Kye had not given the choice of a co-mate much thought. He had presented himself to the Council instead and asked to be sent to Earth as one of those aiding the scientists in finding the females with the Fallon gene markers, monitoring and protecting the women then minimizing the impact of their disappearance after they were taken to Belizair.

It was satisfying work. Fun for the most part, and he'd become fond of Savannah's homeworld.

His bond-mate turned toward him, a frown on her face. "Let's get out of here."

"A good plan."

The frown deepened, gathering the skin between her eyebrows and making Kye want to reach out and smooth the wrinkles down. He resisted, afraid that if he began touching her he wouldn't be able to stop.

His cock was killing him with its demands, its need to sink into wet heat and glorious feminine mystery. Even the thought of it had him clenching his buttocks as fingers of white-hot desire speared through his shaft and up his spine.

Something in his expression gave him away. Savannah's eyes widened. Her face flushed slightly as her tongue peeked out between lips meant to pleasure a mate. "Let's get out of here," Kye said, echoing her earlier statement. Afraid he would soon be forced to decide between two bad choices—to take her here, where others might arrive and interfere, or to take his own cock in hand.

Savannah stepped forward, the heat deepening in her face. She couldn't believe this! She should be concentrating on what to do next, how to dodge the captain's disciplinary bullet so she could blow the lid off whatever it was The Ferret knew. Instead she was having a hard time drawing her attention away from her swollen cunt lips and standing-at-attention clit. Each step sent a small explosion of sensation through her. Engorged flesh fighting the restraint of a g-string and meeting the resistance of stiff denim.

Damn. She couldn't remember ever reacting to a man the way she was reacting to the one currently standing in front of her. The one bristling with macho intention, his cock an exclamation mark to his belief that he would be the one in charge.

Oh yeah. He could try and they'd both have a good time. After the day she'd had she was more than ready to blow off some steam. And right now a stiff drink wasn't nearly as interesting to her as a stiff cock—Kye's.

If she hadn't already promised herself she was going to try to rein in her impulsiveness and work the system, then she would pore over this crime scene until she either found something or was convinced there was nothing to find. But there was no use making things worse for herself. The planned meet with The Ferret shouldn't land her in too much trouble. Leaving the scene of the destroyed Beamer might. And then this—coming here instead of calling it in. She sighed and hoped the captain had taken his blood pressure medicine.

She moved from the center of the bedroom to the doorway, stiffening when two armed men entered the apartment, their weapons drawn, their bodies signaling an intent to shoot if provoked.

Only Kye's training as a bounty hunter kept him from using the Ylan stones at his wrists to dematerialize the men in The Ferret's apartment. Only the knowledge that a quick movement might endanger Savannah kept him from reaching out and shoving her behind him.

"What are you guys doing here?" Savannah asked and the men lowered their arms, holstering the primitive weapons though Kye didn't drop his guard.

"We could ask the same about you," one of the men said. His face hardened, his lip lifting in a slight sneer as his gaze flickered to Kye. "And who's the pretty boy?"

Savannah frowned. "None of your business, Mastrin. So Vice has an interest in The..." she stumbled, threw out a name Kye didn't recognize, "in Ricky?"

"On a first-name basis with the low-lifes, Holden?" the other man asked, shifting his bulk from one foot to the other, his gaze moving to take in the trashed living room. "Has *Ricky* got something that belongs to you? That why you tore up his place?"

Savannah stiffened. "This is the way I found it after he was a no-show. What's your interest in him?"

The cop named Mastrin smiled, the flash of his teeth reminding Kye of the sharks he'd seen when he was guarding Krista and she'd visited an aquarium. "That's on a need-to-know basis, Holden. Last time I looked, your name wasn't on the list."

"Last time I looked," the other cop chimed in, "this isn't your beat. Your captain know you're dealing with snitches like Nowak?"

"That's on a need-to-know basis, Creech," Savannah shot back, moving into the other cops' personal space.

They stepped out of her way at the last minute, giving her a clear path to the exit.

"You calling this in or you want me to?" she asked from the doorway.

Kye's eyes narrowed as he watched the two men exchange glances. The one named Creech said, "We'll handle it. You see anything? Touch anything? Find anything?"

"No, no and no."

Kye moved to stand next to Savannah.

"What about him?" Mastrin asked.

"No," Kye said, keeping the distrust out of his voice, feeling compelled to warn the two men that Savannah wasn't unprotected. "I am also involved in law-enforcement and trained in dealing with these situations."

Mastrin laughed, an unfriendly sound. "You a rent-a-cop?"

"A bounty hunter."

Creech glanced at Kye and frowned. "Nowak jump bail somewhere?"

Amusement moved through Kye. He suspected he'd pay for it with a lecture from his mate, but he couldn't resist. "As your partner said earlier, *That's on a need-to-know basis and your name isn't on the list.*"

Creech's face flushed an angry red. "Where can we find you?"

"With me," Savannah said, taking Kye's wrist. "And we're smoke."

Kye congratulated his mate on holding her temper until they got inside the elevator. He even managed to keep his reflection somber in the shiny metal walls as Savannah ranted and cursed in frustration, though he also heard the underlying worry for this snitch whose car had been blown up. When she finally lapsed into silence, he said, "I don't trust those two."

Savannah frowned and he once again had the urge to smooth her skin back into place. "Creech and Mastrin? They're still pissed at me for mucking up their investigation."

"What happened?" Kye asked as the elevator doors opened and they stepped out into the hallway.

Savannah sighed, her shoulders slumping slightly, and Kye found it impossible not to reach for her, to pull her into his arms and hold her against his body, their faces only inches apart. Their eyes locked.

Joy raced through Kye at the way she relaxed against him, instinctively accepting the protection and caring he offered. Acknowledging, at least for the moment, that she recognized the natural order of things, the way it was supposed to be between mates. He would see that no harm came to her. In fact, as soon as possible, he would see her safely housed on Belizair.

"What happened?" he asked again.

"I hauled in a couple of underage girls for prostitution and stepped on some toes in Vice, including Creech and Mastrin's." She pulled out of his arms. "Time to face the music."

He allowed himself a small smile. Earth sayings amused him and his mate's earlier exit line, *We're smoke,* was one he intended to remember and use just prior to dematerializing and transporting.

They left the building, Kye's training taking over, his eyes scanning the area, looking for danger to his mate. It bothered him that he'd had to leave her truck unprotected, but there'd been no choice but to do so. Unwelcome realization intruded. A co-mate might prove useful while Savannah remained on Earth.

He shook the thought off. Pride filling him when he saw Savannah scanning the area around them as they moved forward. It pleased him that his mate was a warrior—though she would not be allowed to pursue such a calling on Belizair. She was already important *to him,* and if she had the Fallon gene marker as he suspected, then she would be too valuable to the survival of their world to risk.

Kye scanned the area again, sensing danger. Though he didn't have the wealth of experience his cousin Lyan did, Kye had been to his share of primitive planets and hostile, alien cities. Before he began his service for the Council, he had protected both Amato and Vesti alike as they worked on other worlds.

A shiver of warning streaked up Kye's spine. He whirled, instinct and training converging in a smooth action as his wrist lifted, his mind already commanding the Ylan stones so that in the blink of an eye, in the instant he saw the sniper sighting on Savannah from the upper story of a nearby garage, the stones reacted, reducing the killer and his weapon to particles so small that neither a healer nor Amato priest would be able to re-form him.

"You see something?" Savannah asked and Kye turned toward her, his heart thundering in his ears, adrenaline charging through his body like a series of lightning strikes. At her quizzical expression he lowered his wrist. The sense of being watched, of danger, gone.

"No," Kye said, closing the distance, both of them checking her truck for signs of tampering or explosives before climbing in. Kye once again in the driver's seat.

Savannah called the station but wasn't surprised to learn Creech and Mastrin had already set the wheels in motion for her to get reamed by the captain. "Get your ass in here, Holden," he said when her call was put directly through to him.

"You'll stay with the truck?" Savannah asked a short time later as they parked in the lot reserved for police department employees.

Kye frowned but nodded. He hated the idea of letting her out of his sight but his presence would only complicate matters for her and he knew she would be safe inside her workplace.

Savannah squared her shoulders and went in, rehearsing arguments in her mind, though guilt pooled in her stomach as she remembered the earlier conversation with the captain and her stifled impulse to tell him about The Ferret's call. He was going to be pissed, and she knew he had a right to be.

"Sit down, Holden," he barked as soon as she walked into his office.

She sat. "Captain, I'm—"

"Getting ready to use up some of your vacation time."

Her heart jerked, the pool of guilt turning into a lake of icy water. Was she going to lose her job over this? She'd rather know than guess. "And when I come back from vacation?"

"Hopefully things will have cooled off and the guys in Vice will have forgotten your name." He shot her a hard look. "And you won't do anything else to bring it to their attention. Now tell me what you did after you left the station. After we had our last little chat and agreed you were going to stay out of trouble." There was no mistaking the sarcasm and anger in his voice.

"I met a friend at a place called The Dive."

A muscle jumped in the captain's cheek. "The same place where a Beamer belonging to Ricky Nowak just happened to blow up?"

"I was supposed to meet him there but he was a no-show. I was going to tell you about it after I talked to him, when I had something to pass on."

The captain closed his eyes and massaged his eyelids. "What'd he have?"

"All I could get out of him was that he knew something too big to talk about over the phone. But like I said, I met a friend. She came into town unexpectedly and then The Ferret...Ricky Nowak...was a no-show. Next thing I knew, the Beamer was blowing up." She paused, wondering if she should mention the black car Krista saw, then decided against it. Krista was running from something. Her men—maybe—but Savannah's instinct said it was something else.

She'd intended to badger the truth out of Krista when she paid a "friendly" visit to the cabin later on. But given the nature of her own set of problems, Savannah knew she was going to have to put that on hold. She couldn't risk going anywhere near her family or Krista until she could figure out whether the bomb was meant for her or whether the bomber just got tired of waiting around and decided to blow The Ferret's car, maybe as a warning.

Savannah decided to risk a question, given how the Captain seemed relatively calm. "Did they find him in the car?"

The captain's hands stopped moving—a bad sign. He pulled them away from his face and gave her another hard look. "You haven't gotten to the good part of your story yet, Holden. Why Vice found you in Nowak's apartment. Why there was no call-in from you, not even a one-liner stating your intentions, suspicions or the fact you might need backup." He slammed his fist on the desk. "Oh, that's right. You *had* backup. A bounty hunter!"

Guilt weighed Savannah down, bending her spine slightly and pulling her shoulders in. "Sorry, Captain. I got caught up in the heat of the moment." She decided to embellish a little bit in the hopes of giving the captain some peace of mind. "And the bounty hunter isn't working a case. He's my friend's boyfriend's cousin. He's kind of a last minute hook-up."

The captain sighed, a long, tortured, why-me sound that actually made Savannah feel hopeful. "Here's what's going to happen, Holden. First you're going to tell me whether or not you found anything of interest in Nowak's apartment."

"Nothing, sir."

"Good. Next you're going to get your ass out of my office, out of this station house and, if you're smart, out of the city for a while. As of now, you're on vacation. Repeat after me, Holden, I am on vacation."

"I'm on vacation," Savannah dutifully repeated. "For how long?"

"A week minimum."

"What about…"

The captain held up his hand. "I'll handle the paperwork. I'll handle the explanations. I'll even handle Vice." He paused. "Holden, do I look like I enjoy kissing ass?"

Savannah grimaced. "No, sir."

"Do you want to know why I'm willing to do it?"

She was tempted to say no, just to avoid feeling worse about not mentioning the meet with The Ferret earlier, when she'd had a chance to come clean about it. "Yes, sir."

The captain snorted. "Not likely. But I'm going to tell you anyway. Pride, Holden. In my officers—who sometimes get a little too full of themselves but who are good cops. And because your uncles and I go back a long way. Now get out of here."

Savannah stood. Hesitated. Wanted to ask again whether The Ferret's body had been in the car. Decided against it. Then decided she'd never be able to duck out of sight if she didn't know the answer. "About The…about Ricky Nowak. Did they find him in the Beamer?"

Captain Holden sighed. "Far as I know, the car was empty."

"Thanks, Captain. For everything."

"Yeah, when you come back from vacation you can show your appreciation by bringing me some of that salsa your grandfather makes. It's going to take something hot and spicy to get rid of the bad taste in my mouth from kissing ass."

Savannah laughed but quickly suppressed it when she saw he wasn't ready to let go of his "mad" yet.

"One last thing, Holden," the captain said as she got to his door. "I want you to check in daily. My direct line. And just to be on the safe side, use a pay phone. And don't use the same one twice."

"Sure thing, Captain."

He sighed, worry flickering on his face for an instant. "Get out of here." And she left his office and the police station with a lighter heart and a resolve not to put him in a bad position again—though as soon as the resolve formed, she wondered what she was going to do about The Ferret.

Nothing, she forced herself to answer. Nothing. Though the answer chafed like a pair of ill-fitting cowboy boots.

Chapter Four

ஐ

Savannah spotted her banged-up Chevy and the sight of the truck had never looked so good. She snickered. Of course that just might have something to do with the man casually leaning against the hood. Wow! Who'd have guessed a man with long hair would be such a turn-on? She'd grown up with cowboys and that was the look she usually went for, but right now the thought of spearing her fingers through all that silky blackness and using it to hold Kye down to the mattress while she rode him to a mind-blowing orgasm nearly had her panting.

Of course, turnaround was fair play, and if he wanted to do the same to her, she was willing. Savannah grinned. After the day she'd had, the week she'd had, hell the last year of what she *hadn't* had, she was more than willing—and he was a safe bet—related to one of Krista's boyfriends, so not exactly a stranger.

Too bad he hadn't brought a friend with him. Oh yeah, taking on two guys at once was a big fantasy of hers. But then again, he was gorgeous and she was sure he could help her find ways to keep occupied and therefore stay out of trouble until things died down and the guys in Vice weren't gunning for her. Savannah laughed. It was probably just as well Kye was alone. He was a lot like her brothers and despite the fact she could rope, ride, doctor, brand and castrate with the best of them, the men in her family all seemed to think women needed to be protected—not just from possible outside dangers but from themselves.

Savannah's thoughts flashed back to The Dive parking lot and how Kye had taken her keys from her, then opened the door and forced her into the truck. How he'd yet to relinquish her keys.

Yep, he was a lot like her brothers, which therefore meant he was going to take some work. Her gaze traveled up his body, lingering on the clear outline of his erection before moving to tight abs, a muscled chest and a face that could stop traffic. Damn, he was gorgeous. She met his eyes and her cunt spasmed at the heat she saw in them, the possessive confidence. Oh yeah, he was going to need some serious work and she was just the woman to take him on.

Kye straightened away from the truck as Savannah approached. The spring in her step told him she wasn't in too much trouble with her captain. The look in her eyes told him she was ready to get down to the important business of mating.

He grinned even as his cock tried to force its way out of the uncomfortable Earth clothing. It was probably a good thing his mate had no idea what was in store for her. A permanent bond. A change of address, as the people on her world liked to say.

By the stars, she was a vision. A tigress not unlike the large cats found in the jungles of Belizair. And he could hardly wait to mount her, to claim her, to sink his mating fangs into her.

"Keys, Batman," she said, coming to a stop in front of him and holding her hand out, challenging him and firing his blood, fanning the flames of the Vesti mating fever.

"I will continue to drive," he said, enjoying the narrowing of her green eyes, the thought of taming her.

He was torn between wishing she'd assault him—as the fire in her eyes predicted—and hoping she'd wait until they had some privacy. As bold as his mate was, he doubted she'd like to be spanked publicly. Though he had little doubt her behavior would soon warrant the feel of his hand across her bare buttocks.

Kye grimaced, only barely restraining himself from grasping his erection as his cock jerked in anticipation of being pressed against her as she lay across his lap to receive her punishment. He turned away from her, deciding it was better to avoid further confrontation by simply getting into the driver's seat and leaving her no choice but to be a passenger.

Savannah gave him directions to an apartment building that had him frowning with dismay. "Yeah, I know," she said. "But I'm not home much and I can't see paying a fortune in rent for something nicer."

They climbed out of the truck, both of them stopping to look at it, no doubt thinking about the informant's destroyed car. Savannah scowled, glancing up and down the street. "Why don't you stay here while I grab some of my things? Maybe I'll spend a couple of days in Tahoe while things chill out."

Kye had no intention of letting her out of his sight again. "Where is your apartment?"

"Fifth floor."

"On this side?"

She pointed upward and to the left. "On the corner."

"If we get there quickly then I can guard the truck from there."

Savannah hesitated for only a second before nodding. "Fine." She held out her hand. "Keys."

This time Kye relinquished them, only barely managing to suppress a smile. His mate might think she now held the upper hand, but he was confident he could retrieve the keys from her in the privacy of her apartment.

They caught the elevator, getting to her apartment in record time, with Kye going directly to the window.

"Shit," Savannah said, still standing just inside the door and scanning the tiny apartment. Sniffing, catching just a hint of aftershave. The scent familiar, though it didn't set off any alarm bells. "Someone's been here."

Kye's entire body stiffened. "Gather your things," he said, his tone making her glance at him. Making her think that despite his cockiness and quick laugh, he was probably a damn fine bounty hunter.

She didn't argue. She didn't have a death wish. Instead she moved around the apartment, making a quick check, noticing that whoever had been there had been careful. They'd searched her desk, gone through the things on her kitchen counter and coffee table, but tried to put it back the way they'd found it.

Same guys who'd been to The Ferret's place but a different MO? Or different guys with the same agenda?

She'd had every intention of taking a vacation. She'd even halfway convinced herself that she and Krista had just been in the wrong place at the wrong time—maybe a case of mistaken identity or criminal impatience when the Beamer blew up. But this raised the stakes. This told her whatever The Ferret was involved in, she was now involved too.

Fuck! Only the fact that the majority of her possessions were still at the Bar None made it easy for her to tell someone had been through what few things she kept in town. Not that any of it would be of interest to anyone but her—which was a good thing.

At least she didn't have to freak about something sensitive getting out. It would hardly be headline news if someone leaked the fact she liked thong underwear, was sometimes guilty of looking through *Playgirl* magazine and yeah, she had a few porno DVDs because desperate times sometimes called for desperate measures.

Savannah retrieved a gym bag and packed some clothing. There were definite advantages to favoring jeans and casual shirts. It cut down on what she considered essential.

She grinned, managing to find some humor as she cut a glance over at Kye. There was no point in packing anything to sleep in. First, because she didn't intend to do much sleeping.

Second, because from the look of his hard-on, he didn't need anything from Victoria's Secret to inspire him to action.

"Ready," she said, moving to the door.

Kye joined her, grabbing her wrists and pinning them to the door, immobilizing her with his grip and his weight as he freed one hand in order to tunnel into the pocket of her jeans and retrieve the keys. He was so smooth and efficient that it was done within seconds—leaving her admiration warring with her outrage.

"I'll remember this, Batman," she said when he released her. They moved out into the hallway. "And for the record, I don't get mad, I get even."

Behind her, Kye grinned, committing her words to memory. *I don't get mad, I get even.* He would share it with his brothers and cousins. Such a saying could come in handy for a bounty hunter. Perhaps it would even become the motto of their clan-house—though no doubt the Amato, who were sticklers for justice served in a somber, orderly manner, would find offense in it.

They checked the truck for explosives before climbing in and driving away, Kye once again asking for directions.

Savannah sighed. The moment of truth had arrived and the truth for the moment was that she couldn't hightail it to Tahoe. That left two viable options. A hotel. Or the line cabin on her great-uncle's ranch—a once-upon-a-time shack that had been seriously enhanced by her brothers so it would be suitable for their little sexcapades.

She knew for certain the cabin was well-stocked with canned goods, and it should be unoccupied. Her parents were traveling so her brothers had full use of the ranch house. And since her great-uncle's cattle had been trucked to different grazing lands there was no reason for ranch hands to be in the cabin.

Oh yeah. The line cabin won hands down. It was in the middle of nowhere. Easy to defend. And there was no way in hell anyone after her would either know it existed or guess she was there.

She glanced at the man next to her and smiled. Not to mention, the cabin was the perfect place to get rowdy and blow off some steam.

Her gaze dropped to Kye's erection and her smile widened. He was definitely packing some serious heat and it was time to take him out to the range and pull his trigger.

Kye gripped the steering wheel and willed himself to remain in control. If his mate had any idea how fiercely the Vesti mating fever rode him, she wouldn't be smiling so smugly and filling the interior of the truck with the heady scent of her arousal. By the stars, it took every bit of his training to resist the urge to pull to the side of the road and take her there—an act frowned upon in his world and against the law in hers.

With great effort he limited his breathing to shallow pants and tilted his head slightly to benefit from the open window as he fantasized about what he would do when they got to this "cabin" she spoke of.

He would strip first, before the Earth clothing made a gelding of him. And then he would insist that Savannah strip.

He didn't feel like playing with her. Didn't feel like drawing it out in a game of seduction.

He wanted to mate. To tumble her onto her hands and knees and mount her. To thrust his cock in and out of her and hear her hoarse cries of pleasure.

He wanted to bury his mating fangs in her shoulder in the moment of climax, something he'd never done before, and feel the sweet bliss of an enhanced release while gaining the security of knowing she could never escape him again. That he'd taken the first step in forming a bond with her.

There was protocol that should be followed. Rather than fuck her, he should see to her safety and then take a sample of her DNA to the Council scientists. He should wait for the match to be officially sanctioned. He should select a co-mate from among the Amato—a task he was reconciled to, though he preferred not to contemplate the reality of seeing another male cover his—*their* mate.

He grimaced. Then reminded himself that if Lyan could stomach such a thing, then he could do no less.

Kye's cock pulsed hungrily in the constricting garments and he knew the true reason why he would ignore protocol and take Savannah—riding her fiery body throughout the night. He wanted to hoard her screams of pleasure. He wanted memories that belonged only to the two of them. He wanted what his ancestors had always had. A mate that belonged only to him. And for this night, he would have it.

No doubt there would be lectures to endure, whispers he was like his cousin Lyan, who seemed to take pleasure in bending—if not completely breaking—the law. Many a time Kye had seen suspicion on some of the faces of the Council members and scientists. But he'd proven himself a man of honor. A man capable of keeping those human women identified as potential bond-mates safe until they could be claimed.

He hadn't taken liberties with *any* human female, even those who weren't found to carry the Fallon gene sequence. Not that he hadn't been tempted.

By the stars, he had been. His fantasies had been filled with women such as his mate, women with red tresses and flashing green eyes. He could hardly believe his own good fortune at finding Savannah.

On Belizair only a few of the Amato clan-houses boasted such coloring. And of those... Kye shuddered. He had little doubt the human images of vengeful angels came from encounters with the Amato who possessed flame-colored hair and fire-veined wings. He couldn't imagine aligning himself to such a clan-house, couldn't imagine sharing his bed with a female from one of them. Which made him cherish Savannah all the more and give thanks to the wandering god of the Vesti for leading him to her.

A small measure of relief found him when Savannah finally said, "There it is," though it took him a moment to see the small cabin surrounded by trees. It was perfect. Private. Reminding him of the transport chamber deep in the Sierras. The distance between the two not so great he couldn't use the Ylan stones to get there tomorrow. Then use the portal to take a sample of her DNA to the scientists in San Francisco.

But until then...anticipation roared through him. She was aroused and there was no one around. He would take her underneath the trees and sky if necessary. But he would take her. She was his.

Kye parked where Savannah directed, nearly took his cock in hand at the small smile she sent in his direction as she pulled her gym bag from the truck then grabbed one of the sacks of groceries she'd insisted they stop for. He retrieved the others, leaving the chest of ice and drinks as he followed her. Each step a painful reminder of how confining the Earth clothing was.

The cabin had the smell of a closed-up place, a situation easily remedied by opening windows. He wanted to pounce but forced himself to help Savannah put away the groceries and make the bed, to give her a few minutes to relax. In truth, he found he needed a few minutes to set aside the horror of both attempts on her life. To let the peacefulness of the setting seep into him.

He couldn't get her to Belizair fast enough. Earth was too violent, too dangerous, and he suspected his bond-mate was a magnet for trouble.

He knew it.

The smile she was directing at him was proof she had no idea of her peril.

Kye's nostrils flared as she moved into him. Her intention clear. Her aggression arousing, more potent than the strongest beverages in the Kotaka Gaming Sector. When she put her hands on his chest the blood roared in both his cock and his ears.

Savannah grinned. If he had a thought left in his head, then she should be kicked off the force for not being able to see a situation clearly. Damn, he was gorgeous. Hard muscle. An erection like a flagpole ready to burst out of his pants and wave the red, white and blue—all to the tune of the "Star-Spangled Banner".

His obvious lust—for her—was sexy as hell. And a real boost to her morale and her libido.

She closed her fingers, gripping his shirt and managing to capture the tiny male nipples underneath it at the same time. His face tightened and his head lowered. Without warning his arms went around her, jerking her against his body, trapping her there.

"From now on you will answer to me," he said, covering her mouth before she could comment or argue. Chasing away the outrageousness of his statement with the assault of his tongue against hers.

God. He knew how to kiss.

They were Savannah's last thoughts as the aggressive thrust of his tongue made her crave the feel of flesh against flesh, made her want to wrap her legs around his waist and feel his cock plunge into her channel.

She moaned, tangled her tongue with his, slid and rubbed against it as her pelvis did the same to his erection.

He growled in response, walked her backward until her thighs came up against the kitchen table. The obstacle irrelevant to him. He kept pushing, using his chest and arms, the solid muscles of his thighs to force her upper body to retreat until she was lying on the table, trapped there, the hard ridge of his jeans-covered cock now rubbing against her cloth-protected core.

Savannah battled with the buttons of his shirt, her hands still trapped between them. He made a hungry sound deep in his throat, his hands joining hers, ripping at clothing until skin touched skin.

He stilled then, lifted his mouth from hers. Met her eyes.

Her cunt clenched in reaction to the fierce desire she saw there. Sent another wave of arousal to panties already soaking in it.

His nostrils flared as though he could smell it. His breathing coming one short pant after another. "You are mine."

"Prove it."

With a growl he levered himself up, his hands pinning her wrists to the table next to her hips, his gaze roaming down her body, returning to her exposed breasts and turning molten.

Kye burned with the fever of his race. Hungered to taste every inch of Savannah. To claim every inch.

She was exquisite. Her fiery beauty unmatched by any woman who had come before her.

He'd thought to take her, to mate with her, but now he wanted to savor her. To suckle at her breasts until the nipples darkened and ached with pleasure. To bury his face between her thighs and bathe in the scent of her as his lips and tongue explored wet heat and feminine slickness.

It was a primitive call. A most basic need.

Kye leaned over and took her nipple into his mouth, attacked it as ruthlessly as he'd assaulted her mouth. He was no babe at its mother's breast and there was nothing gentle in the way he claimed her, in the message he conveyed with his tongue and his teeth, with the strong, fierce tugs to first one nipple and then the other.

Her body arched underneath his onslaught, her head tossed and her voice became a plea for more of what he had to offer. He freed her wrists and savage satisfaction rushed through him when her hands went to his hair, her grip as strong as any warrior's as she held him to her breast, pushed against him as if she wanted him to swallow her whole.

Kye freed the top button of her jeans and the zipper gave under the force with which he peeled them down her legs, tangling at her ankles until he rid her of her shoes, freeing the pants to fall to the floor. He shivered at the slick feel of arousal-soaked panties against his heated flesh.

He lifted his head and endured the sharp sting. Her fingers tightening on his long hair as she tried to pull him back to her breast. But there was no resisting the lure of her cunt now, not when it remained hidden by only a thin barrier of material.

Still, he was a man who'd survived working for the Council because he could compromise. He could do no less for the woman who would be his bond-mate.

He touched his lips to her breast, paid homage to one love-bruised nipple and then the other before traveling downward, leaving a wet trail of kisses and bites, pausing at her navel to test its depth with his tongue before moving lower, tormenting them both by nibbling at the elastic edge of her dark green panties, by running his mouth and nose over the erect clit, torturing it through the fabric, his breath adding to the heat and moistness.

Her buttocks tightened, lifting her, pressing her covered mound against his face. But when her hands went to her hips he grabbed them and kept her from pushing her panties down. By the stars, she'd tortured him from the first moment he'd seen her and now she would experience the same!

Chapter Five

ॐ

Kye sucked her clit into his mouth, the material covering it doing little to hide her arousal from him. He toyed with her engorged knob until she was writhing, begging for the pleasure of his mouth on her naked, burning flesh.

It was beyond anything he'd ever known with a woman. Anything he'd ever thought to experience.

Now he saw a purpose for the layers of clothing Earth women wore. To drive the lust higher. The ridiculous scraps of material turning a female into an erotic package to be unwrapped.

His cock pulsed and leaked. His balls were heavy and full and he cursed himself for not opening his own pants before he'd started his claiming of Savannah. But there was no way to free himself from the confines of his jeans, no way to take himself in hand without releasing Savannah's wrists. And so he endured, ached, suffered as he assaulted her with his mouth until he could no longer tolerate the barrier of cloth between them.

He released her wrists. Dragged her panties down so they joined her jeans on the floor. Paused. Capturing the image of her cunt so he would remember this first viewing for the rest of his life. The neat triangle of deep red pubic hair a sign-post arrowing downward, pointing to swollen lips, open and glistening, waiting for his kiss.

He needed no other urging.

With a groan he lowered his mouth to them, sucked and lapped, thrust his tongue into her channel as his nose rubbed against her clitoris, its hood pulled back to expose tender skin, an engorged knob designed for no other purpose than a woman's pleasure.

Desperately he freed his cock, taking it in a strangle-hold grip to prevent himself from spewing his seed on his abdomen, his other hand going to her belly, her mound, holding her to the table as he consumed her, lashed her with his tongue and made her scream in orgasm.

Kye straightened then, satisfaction roaring through him at the sight of her slick skin and limp form, at the way she struggled for breath, her eyes half closed, her body quivering from the force of her release.

He couldn't wait. He gathered her up, positioned her at the edge of the table, joy and happiness exploding in his chest when she laughed and curled her arms and legs around him. When her fingers chased his own away from his cock, when she guided him to her entrance and touched her lips to his as she welcomed him into her body.

Kye nearly came as unbearable pleasure flooded his senses. As her slick, heated inner muscles clamped down on his penis, a wet fist clenching and unclenching, resisting, enticing, drawing every blood cell to his engorged shaft so it throbbed in time with a heart racing, expanding, very nearly exploding with the intensity of sensation.

Savannah groaned, shifted, used his long hair like reins to guide his face where she wanted it so she could meld her lips to his and wrestle with his tongue again. He was killing her! But what a way to go!

He'd just about blown the top of her head off with the orgasm he'd given her and now… He was huge. His presence in her channel a painful pleasure, filling her, burning her, making her cunt squeeze against his invasion even as her legs were tightening around his waist to try and drive him deeper.

Fuck. Oh yeah —

She cried out when he thrust through the barrier of fisted muscle and gave her his full length and width. She started moaning when his fingers dug into her buttocks and he began moving in and out of her sheath, striking her clit with each inward stroke until her world revolved around him, the wet slide of tongue against tongue, the heady, indescribable heaven of a man's penis laying claim in the most intimate manner possible.

Savannah willingly gave up control, though her fingernails raked down his back and she swallowed his growls of pleasure, thrilled at the way his thrusts became more aggressive, more forceful until they were both panting for breath, straining for release. Their hands frantically racing over fevered, sweat-slick skin until she came and he followed her over the edge, his semen jetting toward her womb, his body jerking and shuddering between her thighs.

She didn't offer a protest when Kye eased her backward and rested his torso on hers, his cock still inside her, her legs still wrapped around his waist. He'd probably just ruined her for any other man and she didn't care.

A small laugh escaped. Sex on the kitchen table had never been one of her fantasies — but now she saw there were definite possibilities — once she recovered from this round. Savannah couldn't stop herself from saying, "I'm glad I brought you home for dinner."

Kye grinned, understanding her humor immediately.

By the stars she pleased him. Though life spans were much longer on Belizair than on Earth, they were still too short not to enjoy each moment and find pleasure in every day. He had surely found pleasure in *this* day.

He touched his mouth to hers, traced the seam of her lips in a gentle request for her to open for him. She did so and he tangled his tongue with hers in contentment, in a soft communication of satisfaction.

When the kiss ended he forced himself away from her, pulling from her feminine depths as he straightened and stepped back. She lingered for a moment, risking another ravishing as his gaze roamed over her body and his cock began to fill. As the Vesti mating fever threatened to roar to life again.

How could Lyan have let his mate drive away? It made even less sense to Kye now than it had before.

The thought of being away from Savannah... They weren't even truly mated and yet the idea of leaving her, of letting her out of his sight was unbearable.

He'd have to do it, but it would be a test of his endurance — rewarded by having the scientists confirm that she was his by Council law.

Kye's hand dropped to his cock and satisfaction rushed through Savannah at the way his face tightened. At the way he was starting to harden again.

He was something else, and if they'd been on the bed, she'd be all for it. But once on the table was enough — at least for today. And besides, she wanted him completely naked — not that standing with his shirt and fly open wasn't sexy as hell, but she wanted to see the entire picture.

Savannah laughed and forced herself to sit then slip over the edge of the table and onto her feet. "How about a shower, then some dinner, and after that... I'm sure we'll find a way to entertain ourselves."

Kye tightened his hold on his cock, warning it to subside until he could mount her on the bed or floor, in a place more conducive to hours of pleasure. Because the next time they made love it wouldn't stop until they were both exhausted, too weary to continue. And even then he had no intention of letting her escape his arms.

"A shower sounds good," he said, stripping where he stood, glad to be out of the clothing.

Her murmured *oh yeah* sent more blood coursing to his cock and when she reached out and touched his wristband he shuddered at the thought of seeing her wear the band he'd crafted in hopes of one day gaining a mate, shivered in anticipation of feeling the Ylan stones at his own wrists swell and multiply, pulse with a unique energy only experienced during bonding, and then separate and migrate even as he was merging and joining with Savannah.

His restraint disappeared in a heartbeat when the fingers of her free hand went to his other wristband. His intentions to delay mating forgotten in a surge of heat and need.

Kye paused only long enough to pull her open shirt and bra from her body and toss them to the floor before swooping her up in his arms and carrying her to the bed. She laughed when he dropped her onto the clean bedding, wrestled with him for the dominant position when he joined her there. But in end she was positioned on her elbows and knees, her legs spread to reveal swollen woman's flesh and damp arousal as he knelt behind her, cock in hand, entranced by the sight before him.

"By the stars, you're exquisite, Savannah," he said, rubbing his hand over her mound, leaning forward to kiss along her spine, to gently bite the sleek globes of her buttocks as his fingers found her clit and made her whimper.

"Please, Kye," she moaned, pushing against his hand, the sound of her voice filling his heart.

He closed his eyes, rubbed his cheek against her soft flesh, inhaled her. "Please what?"

"Fuck me."

With a groan he mounted her, drove his cock all the way in with a single thrust. She was so tight around him, so hot and wet that it felt as though his heart beat in his cock, as though their hearts beat in unison deep within her body. "Savannah," he panted, unable to remain still, the need to truly mate with her driving any hint of play or gentleness from his thoughts. And as if sensing what he wanted, what he needed, she pushed backward, forcing him deeper in an aggressive move that freed him from restraint, justified him taking her as he'd fantasized about from the first, rutting on her with the intensity of a Vesti male in the heat of the mating fever.

He wallowed in the heated scent of her arousal, soaked in her screams and cries of pleasure as he pinned her down, using more and more of his weight and strength in a demonstration of who was the more dominant partner. Until finally his mating fangs slipped from their sheaths and sank into her shoulder, causing her to climax wildly, to tighten on his cock until he thought his heart and mind and soul would explode in unparalleled ecstasy as his balls contracted violently, forcing his seed through his shaft as the serum rushed through his fangs in a Vesti's claiming of his mate.

* * * * *

Kye studied Savannah as she slept in a glorious cloud of red hair. He still couldn't believe his good fortune. They'd paused in their lovemaking the evening before only long enough to shower and eat before returning to bed. He should be tired, sated, and yet the craving had only grown.

He should be on his way to see the Council scientists. Instead he was still in bed with Savannah. Unable to resist the temptation of her soft skin.

Kye stroked her side, his cock jerking and filling when she rolled onto her back, reminding him again of the tiger-like cats found in the jungles of Belizair. And without hesitation his hand moved to his cock, enclosing it, pumping up and down slowly as he feasted on her beauty, the breasts that begged for a man's touch, a man's mouth. Her nipples large, softened in sleep.

On Belizair the women wore only thin trousers, the men only a loin covering. Neither wore shirts since their wings weren't transmuted when they were on their home world.

It was considered rude to stare at a woman's chest or a man's thinly disguised erection, and in truth, past the point in time when sexual stirrings first manifested themselves in

63

youth, most found it easy enough to notice partial nudity but not respond to it physically.

Kye tightened his grip on his penis, stroking upward until the tip pulsed against his palm, inhaling sharply at the hot-streaks of need that shot up his spine. His buttocks clenching as lust pooled in his testicles, making them heavy with seed.

The thought of other men seeing Savannah's full breasts with their pouty nipples had the mating fever of the Vesti stirring to life and Kye once again fantasizing about hoarding her for himself, as the Vesti had always done with their women.

He closed his eyes and forced himself to try to imagine seeing her body mounted by another male, one with the feathered wings of the Amato. But he gave up within seconds, envisioning instead the sight of her with two children at her breasts. One Amato, one Vesti.

It inflamed him. Sent more blood racing to his cock even as it tempered the mating fever.

He would share her with another. It was an unavoidable truth.

Kye opened his eyes, his gaze traveling downward, across flat, tanned skin, lingering on the hint of pubic hair, a small strip not hidden by the sheet. He used his leg and foot to push the cloth obstruction away, glad that on Belizair there would be no struggle with bed clothing. He would always wake to find her naked, her only covering the wings of her mates.

She stirred in her sleep, frowned, and Kye cursed himself for his lack of control. He needed to leave, to slip away, hopefully without her even being aware he was gone. He needed to get to the transport chamber, to use it in order to deliver a sample of her DNA to the scientists in San Francisco.

It should only take a short while for them to confirm what he already knew was true, that she was his bond-mate. And then he could return, could use the vacation her captain had imposed on her in order to get better acquainted, to contemplate the choice of a co-mate and to explore the idea with her, to prepare her for the experience of being taken by two men at the same time.

So far those who had claimed human mates had used the dual penetration as their wristbands touched in order to coax their Ylan stones into swelling, merging and migrating to the bands of their bond-mate. Perhaps it could be done another way. Kye didn't know and he wasn't willing to risk being wrong. He owed it to his clan-house, his line, to do everything in his power to claim her for Belizair.

With a groan he leaned forward. Unable to resist the temptation of her breast, her nipple. He should already be gone but his cock was hard and his balls were aching. There was no way he could leave the bed until he loved her again. Until he pinned her lithe body to the mattress and swallowed her cries of pleasure as he once again proved to her that she no longer belonged only to herself, was no longer free to do as she wanted. But now belonged to him, answered to him.

He laughed against her flesh, admitting to himself that despite the number of times he had mated with her the night before, despite injecting her with the serum of his kind and giving her pleasure no human male could give her, he didn't truly believe he'd succeeded in taming her or bringing her under his control. It might take a lifetime to achieve such a thing. But he was willing to take on such a long-term task, and on Belizair her safety would be assured.

Kye swirled his tongue over her nipple, sucked it into his mouth, then lifted his head and blew across it, watching as the soft crown hardened in a demand for more of his attention. It was a demand he readily answered, this time with stronger sucks, and when she awakened, moaning and arching into him, saying his name as her fingers went to his hair, he clamped down with his teeth, giving her the hint of pain he knew she liked.

She opened for him immediately. Wrapped her legs around his waist and tilted her pelvis. Made his cock throb when she said, "Kye, please," her voice a husky acknowledgement that she'd come to need and crave him as quickly as he did her.

One look, one touch, a word from her and he was desperate to be inside her body, to be one with her. "Admit you belong to me," he said.

She rubbed against him, wet him with her arousal. "Oh yeah, you can have me."

Kye groaned as his penis slid into sultry heat. Shuddered as he fought the urge to rut wildly on her.

He kissed across to her other nipple, gave it the same attention he'd given the first one as he forced himself to remain unmoving in her channel. His cock bathing in her slick, velvety heat. Pulsing in time to the fisting and unfisting of her sheath as he sucked and bit, wallowed in the sound of her moans and whimpered pleasure.

He held off for as long as he could. Resisted her pleas until the feel of her nails on his back and shoulders, the tugs she gave to his hair forced him upward to fuse his mouth to hers and storm its depths with his tongue, thrusting in and out as his penis was doing, his world narrowing, becoming one of movement, sensation, ecstasy—Savannah.

Even when he was empty of seed he had no desire to leave her body. No will to do anything other than remain with her. She was like the third sun on Belizair, a bright flame in his sky, scorching him, burning through all his protective layers in order to claim his heart, his soul.

She laughed against his shoulder, nipping him, making him smile when she demanded he roll over so she could breathe. He moved, taking her with him so they lay on their sides, still pressed against each other.

"Hmmm, very nice. I may just keep you around, Batman," she said, nuzzling his neck, kissing it before snuggling against him and drifting back to sleep.

He delayed, telling himself he wanted to make sure she had retreated into a deep slumber before leaving her. But in truth he knew he stayed in bed because he hated the idea of parting from her, of leaving her unguarded for even a second of the time she remained on Earth.

Kye rubbed his cheek against her hair, held her tightly to him as he wrestled with whether or not he should take her truck. He could use the need for fresh clothing as an excuse for his absence. And if he had the truck, she could not leave the cabin in pursuit of this Ferret.

Savannah may have been sent "on vacation" by her captain, but Kye wasn't convinced she would let the matter drop. And yet to take the truck was to leave her without a means of transportation should there be trouble before he could return.

In the end he forced himself from the bed and into the Earth clothing. Grimacing as he tugged the garments on, hating them all the more for having to wear them for a second day. But short of arriving naked for his visit with the scientists, there was little choice.

He checked the pocket of his jeans to ensure the strand of Savannah's hair he'd collected from her hairbrush the previous night was there. Then he left the cabin, habit and training leading him to a cluster of trees for cover. With a command to the embedded nanocomputers on his wristbands, the Ylan stones reacted, transporting him to the chamber deep in the Sierras. A place guarded at all times by at least one bounty hunter who watched from a small hidden residence.

Kye materialized in the chamber and paused for a moment, allowing the Ylan stones in his wristbands to absorb energy as he looked around, excitement filling him at the prospect of bringing Savannah here. They'd have to come by car, of course. Entering the sheltered adobe building and stopping in the vestibule to shed their Earth clothing before moving into the chamber itself — the intimate, terraced garden with its see-through ceiling and exquisite collection of flowering plants. Its floor a multitude of colorful stones arranged in exotic patterns, all leading to the center of the room.

Because of the Council edict that human women weren't allowed to see the true form of their bond-mates until they'd agreed to a binding ceremony, to returning home with their mates, and were in the transport chamber, many of those coming to Earth in order to claim their females were electing to finalize the match just before returning to Belizair. So in the center of the room, amid a spectacular pattern of Ylan crystals, was a thick mattress on a frame resting close to the ground.

Thoughts of lying on the bed as he bound Savannah to him made Kye's cock fill and press savagely against the confining clothing. He grimaced, cursing the garments yet again. They'd make him a gelding if he couldn't get Savannah to Belizair soon!

With a thought the stones on his wrists sang to those in the chamber, beginning a concert of light and color, of building energy and focused purpose until in the blink of an eye Kye moved from one place to another, though the chamber he arrived in looked like the one he'd just left, like the one on Belizair. The design and arrangement of the stones a legacy of their Fallon ancestors. The chambers on Earth moveable, the one in Winseka, permanent. The plants in each the only other thing that differed.

He stepped out of the circle and moved through the garden, leaving the room and coming face-to-face with Jeqon d'Amato. *So it is done?* Jeqon asked. *Lyan and Adan have taken charge of their mate?*

Chapter Six

ஸ

In a manner of speaking.

Jeqon's eyebrow lifted and Kye shook his head, grinning as he shared the scene he'd witnessed—his cousin and his cousin's co-mate walking Krista to her car, kissing her then letting her drive away. It still amazed him and he looked forward to teasing Lyan mercilessly, once Lyan and Adan had successfully returned to Belizair with their human bond-mate.

Jeqon frowned. *Is it safe to leave her unguarded?*

They followed Krista and have taken over the responsibility of attending to her safety.

So you are here for another assignment?

Kye's hand went to the pocket of his jeans. Excitement made his heart race and his blood thunder in his ears. He switched to the human manner of speaking. "I have found my mate. She is a friend of Krista's."

Surprise flashed in Jeqon's face, followed by concern. "Things are not the same with respect to the human women, you know that, Kye. A response from our Ylan stones, the filling of our cocks, even the Vesti mating fever of your race doesn't indicate the presence of a mate when it comes to those carrying the Fallon markers. The matching of genes is the only proof that matters. The only way to claim one of them and return to Belizair with her."

Kye stiffened, refusing to allow himself to doubt what he knew with every fiber of his being. "She calls me bat-man. She triggered the Vesti mating fever." And because they had worked together and he both liked and trusted Jeqon, Kye admitted to what he had done. "My mating fangs dropped when I took her. I have already injected her with the serum of my kind."

"You have a sample of her DNA?"

Kye nodded, pulling the strand of Savannah's hair from his pocket and handing it to Jeqon, who laughed despite the worried look on his face. "Why am I not surprised she has flame-colored hair?"

Kye laughed too, though some of the uneasiness he had been trying to evade settled into his chest as he followed Jeqon to the room used by the scientists to analyze and match the DNA.

In the past Kye had rarely joined the scientists in their laboratory. He was a bounty hunter, a law-keeper, and though science could be useful in the solving of crimes, most of those he was forced to hunt required tracking and capture abilities. *Not rocket science*, as the Earth inhabitants liked to say. And yet now it was science that held the key to Kye's fate. His happiness. His future.

He began pacing. Earning a sympathetic glance from Jeqon. "At least the Council has allowed us to modify the equipment available here," Jeqon said. "It is not fast, but it is tolerable."

When Jeqon moved to another piece of equipment, Kye joined him, so close that Jeqon sighed and looked backward. "Crowding me does not make the process go any faster."

Kye stepped to the side. "You have results?"

"No. I am retrieving your DNA information for comparison purposes."

Kye moved farther away, giving Jeqon additional room in which to work. And within seconds, he found himself pacing again. Thinking about Savannah. Worrying about her. Wondering if perhaps he should have taken her vehicle.

Surely she wouldn't go to town. But as soon as he thought it, his chest tightened and he caught himself rubbing it, remembering the sniper outside The Ferret's apartment.

He should investigate the garage and determine if the man he had transmuted into tiny particles had left anything of himself behind—a car, a phone, something written down. But to do so would mean a longer separation from Savannah. And if he transported to the garage and then to the cabin he would drain the Ylan stones of energy that might be necessary for their defense. The stones weren't native to Earth—each use came at an increased cost.

Frustration howled through Kye. Acceptance. He needed a co-mate. Not just for the continuance of his line but in order to keep Savannah safe. He didn't try to fool himself into believing she would agree to return home with him before the matter of The Ferret was resolved.

Jeqon returned to the work station where Savannah's DNA was being decoded. He adjusted the equipment, readjusted it, his body language filling Kye's with icy dread. There was sympathy in Jeqon's eyes when he finally looked up again and met Kye's. "She is not a match for you."

Pain ripped through Kye with the words. Pain such as he had never known. Pain so intense it took all of his control to keep from falling to his knees.

His mind and body screamed in denial. His heart felt as though a fist had plunged into his chest and encircled it in a fierce death grip.

For long moments he couldn't speak. Couldn't think.

* * * * *

Savannah woke to sunshine and deliciously aching muscles, to anticipation and then confusion when she realized Kye was gone. Her first action was to roll out of bed and check to make sure the truck was still there. Her second was to dress and try to track him.

She got nowhere. Which had her frowning and cursing and doubting the evidence of her own eyes.

Goddamn! He couldn't have vanished into thin air!

She stomped back into the cabin and made herself some coffee. Frustrated that a skill she'd developed and honed when she lived on the Bar None and had to chase down stray cattle seemed to have disappeared along with Kye.

Shit! She couldn't believe it.

Then again, he'd said he was a bounty hunter and she'd guessed he was pretty damn good at it. There was comfort in thinking maybe her inability to spot his track wasn't about her being bad but about him being excellent.

Savannah frowned as she looked at the tree and scrub-covered foothills framed in the window over the sink. Not that she'd had an endless string of lovers, but she'd never had one fuck her then decide to go commune with nature while she slept off the effects of great sex.

She went out to the truck and retrieved one of the ice chests they hadn't bothered with the day before, remembering as she did so just *why* they hadn't brought it in. Because they'd been immersed in a fog of lust.

Savannah rubbed her shoulder, her cunt spasming when her hand encountered the place Kye had bitten her more than once. God! How had he known that would do it for her?

She'd grown up on a ranch where the sight of stallions covering their mares had fed some fantasies—fantasies she'd definitely experienced with Kye. Man, she should have roped a man with a long mane of hair before!

A smile followed the thought. Then a laugh. If he was going to take to wandering off, she just might have to tie him to the bed. Oh yeah, now there was a fantasy to turn into a reality and savor for a lot of nights to come.

She wouldn't need the porno DVDs on nights when she was horny or stressed and all alone. All it would take would be memories of her *vacation* with Kye.

She retrieved the other cooler and put the food from the ice chests into the refrigerator, glad there was solar power and propane to make the cabin more than just a place to throw down a sleeping bag and camp. She poured some coffee and slathered cream cheese on a bagel. Polished both off within minutes then couldn't help herself, she went back outside, determined to find Kye's trail.

It ended in the same place it had before. In a grove of trees in back of the cabin.

She moved past the spot. Worked in ever increasing concentric circles until she was sweaty and tired of all the walking.

There wasn't a trace of him. And there should have been.

She'd even tried to hide her own track in places, and she'd managed it for short distances. But it was nearly impossible to cover as much ground as she'd covered, as much as Kye must have covered to be nowhere in sight—and leave no trace at all.

Savannah sat down on a smooth rock, frustrated, confused. Not sure whether or not she should be hurt, suspicious or worried by Kye's disappearance.

Men! It was coming back to her now why she didn't have a permanent one in her life.

She rubbed the spot over her heart. Grimacing as she did it and honest enough with herself to admit that rather than make her feel better, her attempt at humor had fallen flat and made her feel worse.

Yeah, she knew a night of wild sex did not make for a genuine connection between a man and a woman—the cowboys she'd grown up with were a walking, talking, fucking testament to that truth. But Kye...

Damn... It didn't even make sense to her, but he seemed so right.

Savannah sighed. Well, he was gone and she couldn't do anything about it. He'd just better hope he didn't encounter a bear or a mountain lion since he'd made sure she couldn't come to his rescue. But if he expected her to sit around the cabin waiting—well then, he had a rude awakening in store for him.

She stood and headed toward the cabin, forcing her mind away from Kye and sex and onto the events of the previous day. She grinned. It wasn't like she'd had a lot of time to contemplate what had happened. But now… Now she could actually *think*. Now, because Kye wasn't around to distract her, she could move from sex goddess to detective.

Savannah snickered at her own mental ramblings. But hey, if she couldn't laugh at herself, where did that leave her?

She scribbled a brief note for Kye telling him she was heading to town and would be back. And as the cabin disappeared from sight in the rearview mirror, she even decided she'd splurge and buy him some clothes—not that she intended he'd actually spend much time in them once they were both back at the cabin. But while she liked her men to be hard-working guys, she liked them to smell good and wear clean clothes, and he didn't have anything but the clothes on his back, so to speak. Which brought her full circle to The Ferret's car being blown up near The Dive and Kye's sudden appearance.

He'd told Krista he was following her, so that meant he probably had a car somewhere near The Dive—which wasn't useful at all since she had no intention of returning to the scene. At least today.

Savannah sighed, her eyebrows drawing together in concentration. Why a bomb? Why a car bomb in particular?

Was it supposed to say *terrorist*?

She didn't think so.

The Dive wasn't a cop or military hangout. It wasn't a "destination" for tourists. It was a dive. Literally.

She nibbled on her bottom lip as she replayed the conversation she'd had with The Ferret.

I've got a tip for you.

I'm listening.

Not here. It's too big to talk about over the phone. You break it wide open, the brass will be kissing your ass and begging you to take a detective shield.

Where?

You know a place called The Dive?

Sure.

I'll see you there.

The conversation made her think of a big-time crime. Something local. Maybe even something ongoing. Nothing in his words made her think terrorist plot. Hell, he hadn't even sounded really scared. Nervous, yeah, almost like he had a hustle going. He sure hadn't sounded freaked out in a somebody-wants-me-dead way.

So had he seen his car become a smoking wasteland of metal and glass and expensive leather? She bet he had.

Savannah tried to get into The Ferret's head, think like he would have thought. She tried to remember whether or not she'd seen the Beamer when she showed up at The Dive. She couldn't.

Damn, so much for making detective. She *should* have looked for it. But she'd been distracted by Krista being there. And she'd still been thinking about the run-in with Vice and about the kid, Holland. Not to mention feeling guilty for not coming completely clean with the captain. Plus she'd assumed The Ferret was already there somewhere. She'd figured on him arriving early, scoping the place out and coming to her when he was ready.

She sighed. Obviously she'd misread how rattled he was. She'd misjudged the situation and he'd probably freaked when he saw Krista. In his mind there was suddenly an unknown in the equation and The Ferret was the cautious type. Savannah knew that about him.

Krista didn't have *cop* written on her in any way, shape or form, so he had most likely hung around, observing, waiting, working up his courage or trying to figure out what to do next.

Savannah wanted to believe he hadn't watched someone turn his car into a death trap and then just left without warning her. She'd like to think she had a better read on people than that.

The Ferret was a hustler, a gambler. A guy whose lucky break was always right around the corner.

He wasn't someone she'd want as a personal friend. But she'd met him for the first time when she was on patrol and he'd flagged her down to tell her there was a bum bleeding to death in an alley. A lot of people had probably walked by and seen the same sight—and kept on walking.

So if she ruled out the bomb being planted while his car was parked down from The Dive. What did that tell her?

She didn't know. But a chill slid up her spine as she wondered just when her apartment had been searched. Before the bomb, or after?

She'd have to tell the captain about the search when she checked in with him. Then she'd have to pray he didn't get in touch with her uncles and brothers. And Gramps. God save her if Gramps came barreling into this mess with his rifle.

With a sigh she parked in front of a phone booth and got out of the car. The captain answered on the first ring.

* * * * *

It was a shock for Kye to realize how little difference there was between him and Lyan. How at his core, he too was willing to bend and even break the rules.

He would simply remain on Earth and make Savannah his wife. And though there would be no children, there would also be no need to share her.

As long as he fulfilled his obligation to the Council and continued to aid the scientists in whatever manner they required, there was no reason for any but Jeqon to know of his involvement with Savannah.

A heavy sickness rolled into Kye's chest, expanding and coiling in his stomach with the memory of the bomb that had exploded as Savannah and Krista approached The Ferret's car, of the sniper who had lain in wait for Savannah.

His work for the Council scientists sometimes required him to be gone for long periods of time. The thought of returning and finding Savannah had been killed... Pain returned to steal Kye's breath. He pushed it back and tried to find a solution.

If she knew what he was, why he'd come to her world, he could keep her with him. He could keep her safe.

And if the Council learned he had broken their rules... It could mean his exile from Belizair, though he would be made an example of and sent somewhere other than Earth. Or he might be restricted to his home planet until Savannah aged and died on her own.

Either way it would bring dishonor to his clan-house. Not as much as it once would have because many would understand the desperation he felt, the desire for a measure of happiness, a mate. But it would still bring dishonor, not just to himself but to his family.

And what of Savannah? What life would he be offering her?

"All is not lost," Jeqon said, interrupting the agonizing flow of Kye's thoughts. "She carries the Fallon marker. Both a Vesti and an Amato are needed in order to claim her."

Kye's gaze met Jeqon's. The sympathy remained, but there was also a measure of excitement in the Amato's eyes. Hope flared to life in Kye, along with fear. "You have found an Amato match?"

"No. But the good news is that with each match we discover, we gain information. Already we are starting to see patterns, hints as to which clan-houses might hold the most likely candidates."

Jeqon moved to where Kye was standing, placed his hand on Kye's shoulder in a gesture of support. "I will return to Belizair and begin searching among the Amato first. If a match is found, I will argue your case. The female already knows you, has already accepted your presence in her life and bed. That alone should add weight to the wisdom of choosing you as a co-mate."

"Or viewing me as an enemy and offering a complaint to the Council in order to make sure I am well out of Savannah's life."

Jeqon's hand tightened on Kye's shoulder in acknowledgement of the truth of Kye's statement. "Share what you know of her with me. Share some of what has happened between you so I can take the images with me to Belizair."

Kye nodded, seeing the wisdom of Jeqon's request as he documented the danger she was in by replaying those moments outside The Dive, the trip to The Ferret's ransacked apartment, the encounter with the policemen, the sniper, the searching of Savannah's apartment. He stopped short of sharing anything beyond the first rush of heat when she'd reached for *him*. When her eyes blazed with a desire every bit as hot as that of the Vesti mating fever.

Kye closed the curtain allowing Jeqon to view his memories and Jeqon laughed. *Ah, just when it was getting good!*

Find your own female.

Jeqon grinned. "Believe me. I am working on it and looking forward to it, though I am in no hurry. Unlike many of those from Belizair, I enjoy Earth and the humans. I would love nothing more than to be able to explore as you have done."

Kye sighed. "Despite the urgency of our mission here, it has been a great adventure and I will miss being here. Guarding Krista was a true learning experience and I can hardly wait for Lyan and Adan to secure their mate so I can hear the story and understand why she moved around so often. I would say she was being hunted, but..." He shrugged.

"If that was so, it would make no sense for Lyan and Adan to allow her to drive away after mating with her the first time."

From another part of the house, voices sounded. Jeqon said, "Unless you wish to explain your presence or risk gaining another assignment, you had better return to..."

"I found her in Reno, Nevada." Kye flashed an image of the cabin along with its coordinates to Jeqon. "You will leave for Belizair now?"

"After you use the transport chamber."

* * * * *

"Holden, you know why Ricky Nowak would be sending you an envelope full of chips from the Easy Times Casino?"

It took Savannah a second to translate Ricky Nowak into The Ferret. Another to get her head around what the captain was asking and to answer, "Not a clue. How much money?"

"Forty-five dollars worth. Three reds. Three yellows. The Easy Times uses ten-dollar chips like they do in Connecticut."

"Was there a note?"

"There was nothing. Envelope walked in by messenger service. Your name on the front. Nowak's fingerprints on the chips. And you're saying it doesn't mean anything to you?"

Savannah closed her eyes and tried to come up with an image of the Easy Times Casino but drew a blank. She didn't do a lot of gambling, not in casinos anyway. At home, sure, she'd join her brothers and the ranch hands for poker.

The chips were easier to envision. Most Nevada casinos went straight from red five-dollar chips, *nickels*, to *quarters*, green twenty-five-dollar chips. Still, she could picture the yellow chips The Ferret had sent to her. They'd be *dimes*.

He'd sent her nickels and dimes. Why?

"Holden, you going to answer my question anytime this century?" the captain's voice jarred her from her thoughts. "You sure this envelope doesn't mean anything to you?"

79

"The casino isn't ringing any bells with me. But the chips...I keep coming back to them being nickels and dimes, which doesn't make sense if you think about it as a saying. If something's *nickel-and-dime* it's *small time*, but The...Ricky said the information he had was too big to talk about over the phone." She sighed. "Maybe if I could come in, spend a little time—"

"Holden, I am ordering you back to wherever you're holed up. Right now and stay there. Check in again day after tomorrow. Before noon. Got it?"

"Yes, sir."

He hung up before she could tell him about her apartment being searched. She hesitated then shrugged, deciding against calling a second time. Day after tomorrow was soon enough, especially since she wasn't going anywhere near her place or The Ferret's.

She took a minute to check her voice mail. A couple of hang-ups. Maybe The Ferret, but no way of knowing for sure. Savannah's stomach tightened. Or maybe the underage prostitute. Before the guys from Vice arrived on the scene, Holland had pocketed Savannah's card when her friend wasn't looking.

Savannah dropped the receiver in the cradle, her good intentions to follow orders taking a detour. She'd do a drive-by of the residential hotel where Holland lived. Just in case.

Chapter Seven

✄

Savannah was gone!

Kye's stomach roiled as he paced the cabin in gut-churning disbelief, returning again and again to the note she'd left him. *Have to check in with the captain. Be back soon.*

The Ylan stones on his wrist pulsed in time to the fast beat of his heart, in wild synchronicity to the rage of his emotions. It was all he could do to keep from transporting to her location. But such an option was unavailable since she had yet to remain in one place and he could hardly explain his sudden appearance in her truck.

He forced a deep breath. Tried to calm himself. At least the link formed when he injected her with the serum of his kind provided information about her whereabouts, along with some assurance she was alive and well.

Kye studied the note again, trying to read her emotions from it, her thoughts. Uncertainty plagued him.

He realized now that it had been foolish not to take her truck. It had not occurred to him she would try to track his movements. But the evidence had been there for him to see upon his return. Her footsteps to the spot he had transported from. The ever-widening circle as she'd tried to determine where he had gone.

Was she suspicious of him now? Afraid of him?

Pride at her intelligence and cunning, her abilities, warred with a desperate fear inside him—that the note was a tactic meant to delay him.

They had talked...some. But he had no real knowledge of her beliefs. Whether she though it possible life existed on other planets. Whether or not she had ever wondered if human myth and legend might have sprung from contact with races more advanced than her own.

Kye rubbed his chest in an effort to reduce the crushing agony. The news Jeqon had presented him with had been nearly unbearable—and now this—she was gone. If he lost her...

* * * * *

Cop! The word screamed through Savannah as her gaze locked onto the man casually leaning against a bus stop a block away from the residential hotel where the two underage prostitutes had taken the pervert back to their room.

Savannah drove by, moving past where he stood and keeping her face in profile, stiffening when she looked in the side-view mirror and saw him pull a cell phone from his pocket.

It took her a block to calm down, to realize she'd never seen him before. To question her instincts, though her sour stomach told her he probably had something to do with the escort service investigation.

She was screwed. Big time. So there wasn't anything to lose by stopping in at the Easy Times Casino. Only as soon as she got there she realized that if The Ferret had sent the chips so she'd show up, then she needed to do it in something other than her truck. She needed to get another vehicle. One that couldn't be easily traced to her. She wasn't going to leave her truck unattended in a place someone might sabotage it. She wasn't that confident in her ability to spot a bomb, especially if it was a sophisticated device.

With a sigh of frustration Savannah decided to do a drive-by of her apartment building. She didn't really expect to see either The Ferret or Holland waiting on the street in front of it, but what she did see nearly made her slam on her brakes.

Another cop. This one dark-haired and leaning against a Town Car.

He straightened in surprised recognition when she rounded the corner. His body language giving him away though the dark glasses hid his expression.

Savannah hit the gas and shot past him, watching as he whipped his cell phone out of his pocket. Fuck, what was going on?

She almost raced back to the cabin...almost. But then she remembered her intention to buy some clothes for Kye. That slowed her down long enough to get her thinking. If she was going to obey the captain's orders and remain "on ice" until she had to call him again, then she sure as hell was going to take some time and do some research on the Easy Times Casino.

Savannah borrowed a phone book from the clerk at a clothing store on the edge of town. Located the nearest library with Internet access and a short time later took a seat in front of a computer.

Her thoughts flashed back to the two men she'd seen and she wondered if she should make a preemptive strike and call the captain before he heard about her drive-by activities. Instinct told her they were cops, but they could be private investigators and she wasn't in a hurry to get in trouble.

Savannah grimaced. She was good with faces but miserable with names. She knew she hadn't seen either man before. But that didn't mean anything. There were plenty of cops in Reno and surrounding areas she wouldn't know by sight. Plenty more in Nevada and the rest of the country, plus the Feds.

A sick feeling formed in the pit of her stomach with the image of the dark-haired man. He had the look of a Fed.

She tried to chase the queasiness away with hormones. Picturing the two men again, only this time seeing hard bodies that shouted *prime male specimen*—even with the short hair. Too bad about that. Kye had ruined her when it came to hair.

She frowned at the thought of Kye and his disappearance. A small worry settled in the pit of her stomach. If he wasn't at the cabin when she got back, she was going to have to decide whether or not to go to the Bar None for a horse or an ATV.

Or call her brothers and ask them to come over and help her look for him.

Or decide Kye had rolled out of bed and hit the road. Maybe walked back to the highway and thumbed a ride despite the way he'd demanded that she admit she belonged to him before he'd fucked her this morning.

Even the thought of him taking off like that made Savannah's chest go tight with threatened pain. Damn, no wonder she went for long stretches without a man in her life.

She forced her mind away from the cops and Kye, focusing instead on her search of the Internet for information regarding the Easy Times Casino.

It was a small casino—relatively speaking. She'd seen that for herself. And it was new. Opened by a dot-com millionaire named Steven Traynor.

There were pictures of him. A sixty-year-old man, a gorgeous thirty-year-old wife at his side. Him shaking hands with movers-and-shakers, politicians and businessmen, some local, some not. There were sports stars, actors and actresses, but no way of knowing who'd been hired to put in an appearance and who'd come on their own for their own reasons.

She expanded the search. But as far as she could see, there was nothing special about Traynor, nothing that rang any bells except for a tiny, one-liner about the wife—a former lingerie model from New Jersey who'd been a Las Vegas showgirl before she married Steven Traynor.

Savannah frowned. Didn't The Ferret come from Jersey? Didn't his rap sheet start there? If she could just swing by the station...

She left the computer and went to the periodicals section. It was a long shot but she scanned a week's worth of newspapers.

Nothing. Same old, same old. At least locally. And then a small, three-inch blurb in the international news caught her attention. *Prosecutor in Columbian drug lord trial killed when his car exploded.*

Her stomach dropped and her pulse jerked as realization spread through her. *Nickels and dimes.* Not just a way to describe casino chips or something small-time, but a way to describe quantities of drugs. A nickel bag. A dime.

Car bombs used to be a popular way to eliminate anyone trying to shut down the flow of drugs — not so much in the United States, but elsewhere, and borders didn't stop crime and terror from being imported.

If drugs were involved it would explain why Creech and Mastrin from Vice had shown up at The Ferret's apartment. It would explain the captain's hurried hang-up when she'd pointed out what the slang names for the chips were.

Savannah put the newspaper away, wondering how the guys she'd seen near the residence hotel and her apartment fit into it.

Then it clicked.

Casinos and prostitutes and money laundering. They went hand-in-hand despite all the rules in place.

Which meant she was right. Cops. Probably Feds.

Savannah grinned despite the nervousness curling in her stomach. She just might get a detective's shield after all — if she didn't get fired or killed.

She left the library. But not before she'd paused and scoped out the parking lot. Not before she'd checked the truck, though she was guessing the bomb might be a one-time deal now that she was on the run.

Well, not literally on the run. But in hiding.

Damn! This was too hot to sit on for two days.

She found a phone booth and placed another call to the captain, bracing herself to get chewed out. Only this time she got voice mail.

Savannah went for broke and came clean about everything she'd done since talking to him. She even threw in the information about her apartment being searched before she hung up. Then she headed for the cabin, her gut churning. Frustration and worry replacing the adrenaline she'd been riding on.

How was she going to help bring in the bad guys if she was holed up in the cabin? Sure, there were compensations— her agitation increased—*if* Kye was there. But if she'd wanted to play the part of the little woman who stayed at home while the men handled the dangerous stuff, then she would have *married* a cop instead of becoming one!

With a sigh of frustration she got off the highway, slowing to a respectable speed until she got on the private ranch lands, then she put the truck into four-wheel drive and let loose, leaving a trail of dust in her wake and regaining her sense of humor in the process. No, it didn't look like she was anxious to get back to a certain long-haired guy who sent her libido into overdrive.

And yet her blood thundered through her heart and head and cunt when she fishtailed to a stop in front of the cabin and Kye emerged. Tight expression. Tight jeans. A man in the grip of serious testosterone overload.

He was on her the second she slid out of the driver's seat. Pushing her against the side of the truck, one hand in her hair, the other on her breast in an unmistakable gesture of ownership. His lips and tongue taking hers in a storm of furious passion and domination.

Savannah didn't resist him, had no thought to fight him. It was a reaction to seeing the cop watching her apartment. To making the connection between drugs and the car bomb. To danger.

That's what she told herself. A fleeting thought that didn't matter anyway. Kye was a walking, talking, sexual fantasy and she wanted him like she'd never wanted another man.

The kiss was a plundering, savage show of strength ending only when he pulled his mouth from hers, both of them panting, struggling for breath. His eyes flashing green fire. "Where have you been?"

"To town. To call the captain. I left you a note."

He stripped her shirt and bra off without saying anything else, tossed them to the ground before once again pinning her to the truck. His mouth ravishing hers, his tongue thrusting aggressively.

She struggled to get her hands between them. Ripped his shirt open when she succeeded, sent buttons scattering to the dirt as heat coursed through her with the feel of his chest pressing against her own bare flesh, flattening her breasts under the weight of his body.

Savannah moaned and closed her eyes. Burning up from the inside out. Sure that if he didn't put his cock inside her soon she was going to implode.

She was so hot. So hungry. As though a single look from Kye, a single touch had set her breasts and pussy on fire.

"Please, Kye," she said when he let her breathe again.

"Take your pants off."

Her cunt clenched in reaction to his hard command. Liquid arousal rushed to her inner thighs, soaked her thong, making her glad to strip it away from swollen flesh and let the air strike her body.

Feminine satisfaction filled her at the feral expression on Kye's face. Lust and need. Harsh desire. His chest rising and

87

falling in short pants. His hands at the front of his pants, jerking the zipper down and freeing a swollen, leaking cock.

Savannah licked her lips. Her knees weakened with the sudden desire to go to them, to take him into her mouth. But before she could do it he took her arm, forced her a few steps away from the truck and then along the side to where the cab ended and the bed began.

He turned her, bent her over so her hands rested on the edge of the truck bed, her legs spread, a carnal version of cops and robbers. She couldn't resist. Savannah looked back over her shoulder at him. "Are you going to frisk me now?"

Kye answered with his body, closing the distance between them so his cock slid through the juncture of her thighs and over plump wet cunt lips, glided against her abdomen. "I'm going to do more than frisk you."

"Good," she said, and her response was a match to gasoline, the end of anything other than burning, feeling, screaming as Kye took her hard and fast, took her over and over again, biting her each time she climaxed until finally they were both leaning against the truck, its smooth, sun-warmed metal the only thing keeping them upright.

They remained against the truck, panting, momentarily sated, in harmony until Kye said, "You will not go anywhere without me again. You will not disappear as you did today. I won't tolerate it. I won't allow it."

Savannah's first impulse was to laugh. To tease him about being a caveman. Her second impulse was to get pissed. To put the hurt on him the same way she'd done numerous times when her older brothers tried the word *allow* on for size.

She wriggled out from between Kye and the truck. Her emotions ping-ponging between the two extremes until finally tilting toward anger as she remembered how worried she'd been about *his* disappearance.

"You better cool it with the *allow*, Batman," she said, scooping up her clothes. "And here's a little bulletin for you.

You disappeared before I did. Without even bothering to leave me a note. At least I had the decency to tell you what I was up to and that I was coming back. For all I knew, you'd hit the highway and thumbed your way to parts unknown after getting—" She broke off and strode toward the cabin door, knowing she'd better stop before she said something she'd regret.

Shock ripped through Kye. Outrage. Did she truly think he would leave after mating with her? Would leave without a word? Disappearing as though she was a conquest who meant nothing to him? Hadn't he repeatedly told her she belonged to him?

Only she didn't. She belonged to another by Council law.

Pain joined the outrage. Spiking into him, opening a gaping wound in his heart so that desperation poured in. He chased after Savannah. Raw emotion coalescing—focused on her insult to his honor—demanding he punish her for it.

"My absence this morning was necessary," Kye growled as soon as he stepped into the cabin. "I would never disappear from your life without knowing you were safe and cared for by others."

Savannah stopped in the bathroom doorway. Taking in his aggressive stance. The harsh lines of a face. The pain etched there.

She'd hurt him. And just like that her own anger faded, replaced by a shimmer of guilt. "I'm sorry for implying you're the kind of man who would hit the road after getting laid. But I was worried when there was no note, no way to find you, no way to know if you were hurt or in trouble and needing help."

Her concern poleaxed Kye. Cut right through the wild emotion and re-centered him. "I offer my apology as well. I thought you would sleep most of the day and I would be back before you woke up."

Savannah rolled her shoulders, her body relaxing as she offered him a smile. "Okay then, we're good. I'm going to take a quick shower." Her smile turned teasing and love surged into him. He was already moving toward her when she said, "For the record, Batman, the sex was fantastic, mind-blowing in fact, but it wasn't so overwhelming that I needed to spend most of the day in bed recovering."

Kye laughed. Humor, anticipation, lust mingling together, his earlier resolve to punish her returning, re-formed by her playfulness, her challenge.

Impulse guided Savannah's actions. Relief that they were back on solid ground. She dropped the clothing and bolted, getting only a short distance before Kye captured her and wrestled her to the bed, managed to get her face down and draped over his thighs.

She jerked, shouted in surprise when he delivered the first stinging slap to her buttocks. Arousal coated her inner thighs with the next one, her body turned on while her mind still struggled, processed.

Savannah moaned when Kye smoothed his hand over his ass cheeks, forged between her legs and dipped into her slit before spanking her again. Each strike driving thought and self-consciousness further away until she was lifting to meet his hand, hyper-aware of the firmness of his thighs, the hardness of his erection, the full, flushed cunt lips between her legs.

"Please," she whispered, arching upward, his hand delivering its blow before sliding between her legs. His fingers going once again to her channel. Pushing in, making her cunt clench as it tried to grip and pull them deeper.

"Please what?"

"Fuck me."

He fucked into her with his fingers. Then retreated. Teased over her swollen labia before pushing in again. "This way? Or with my cock?"

"Either. Whatever you want."

And with a roar the earlier desperation returned. What he wanted was her. Now. Forever.

Kye moved, putting her on her back and reaching to the nightstand for the *bouren* strip he'd worn earlier to keep his hair out of the way, using it to secure her wrists to the headboard.

He'd thought the wildness inside him had eased by sinking his mating fangs into her as she'd writhed underneath him in pleasure as he took her against the truck. But each coupling only increased the need he had for her. A primitive desire fueled by both the Vesti mating fever and the uncertainty of their future together.

He couldn't lose her. Not to death. Not to another male.

A scream of denial built inside him. Swelling in his chest so he covered Savannah's lips with his in order to prevent it from escaping. Kissed her until the taste of her, the feel of her underneath him became his only reality. Her mouth and tongue, her soft curves what he needed to gentle the emotion raging inside him, to slow the heart pounding erratically, to calm his thoughts so they became centered on pleasing her, on savoring her.

With a groan he slid down her body and latched on to her nipple, licking, biting, drawing comfort from her breasts even as his cock throbbed against his belly.

He suckled until she was arching beneath him, begging for him to free her hands so she could touch him. Until she was whimpering, tilting her pelvis, her arousal dampening his flesh as her clit stabbed him in a tiny, hard demand for attention.

Only then did he leave the succor of her breasts, kissing downward until he claimed the engorged knob, sucked it into his mouth, struck it, rubbed his tongue over the naked head until Savannah came in a violent, thrashing orgasm, his name on her lips, her scream freeing the one lodged in his chest.

Kye removed the *bouren* tie and returned to his earlier position, reveled in the feel of her arms around him as he slid his penis home. His lips soft on hers. His thrusting echoing the gentleness of his mouth. Slow now. Deep. Lasting. A rhythm meant to endure for a lifetime. His release a long surge of liquid heat that consumed them both and brought a temporary peace.

* * * * *

"I've got to check in with the captain this morning," Savannah said, rolling to her side and running her finger along the seam of Kye's lips, a fresh pool of lust forming in her belly, rippling through her womb and breasts at the sight of his sleep-tousled features.

He opened his eyes and sucked her finger into his mouth, biting down on its tip and sending a lash of heat to her nipples and clit so that she clamped her legs together in response.

Sensual promise flared in his eyes. Masculine confidence.

He rubbed his tongue over the end of her finger, making her shiver with memories of how that same tongue had swirled over her clit, teasing it, striking it until she'd come.

Yesterday had been a blur of sex. And the day before… From the moment she'd gotten back from her trip to town and he'd held her against the side of the truck, it had been one orgasm after another.

Amusement rushed through her when she thought about the clothing she'd gotten for Kye. How it was still bagged in the front seat of the truck because he appeared to be a born nudist.

He hadn't bothered getting dressed even when they were out of bed, or off the floor, or not on the couch, or… Well, even when they'd been outside looking at stars and identifying the different constellations, he'd stayed naked.

She grinned. Not that she objected. The man was gorgeous.

"What are you thinking?" Kye asked, his arm snaking over and pulling her against him. Laughter threatening to escape though he knew her mirth was most likely directed at him.

He'd never imagined how important it would be to have a mate with a sense of humor. Never considered it in his dealings with the opposite sex. He had merely enjoyed them, as they had enjoyed him. Their Ylan stones and the lack of the Vesti mating fever telling them it was a temporary liaison. And in truth, he had rarely risked burrowing into their hot, wet feminine sheaths.

There was no birth control on his world. Pregnancy almost always led to a permanent bonding because there was no guarantee for either the male or the female that another pairing would yield a child. Even before the Hotaling virus, the birth of children was a revered event. A blessing bestowed.

Kye buried his face in Savannah's hair, his arms tightening around her as visions of her swelling with their children filled him.

The Vesti were a physical race and he was no inexperienced male. The ritzca oil created and produced by the Araqiel clan-house aided in taking a woman's back entrance, heightening the need and lubricating the tight muscles so the pain and pleasure of penetration blended into unbelievable ecstasy for both the male and female.

Kye's cock throbbed with images of taking Savannah in that manner. Of preparing her for the binding ceremony where she would be claimed by both of her mates at the same time.

Love and fierce passion cascaded through him. Chased by the nearly overwhelming terror that had followed him from San Francisco.

How could he give her up if the male whose claim was sanctioned by Council law wanted another as a co-mate?

The pain and fear lingered until her wet tongue swirled over his nipple, making him gasp as his cock pulsed, smearing a measure of his semen on her abdomen as well as his.

He felt her smile against his chest, groaned when her teeth grasped his nipple, the link between it and his penis a burning hot wire of excruciating need.

"Savannah!"

She laughed, reducing him to helplessness and driving all thought from his mind by taking his shaft in her hand, pumping, brushing her thumb over the slick tip as her mouth and teeth and tongue worked his nipple.

The mix of pain and pleasure, sensation, swamped him, filled him until he shouted, shuddering and jerking as hot seed blasted through his cock, their bodies so tightly melded his release splashed across his stomach and struck the underside of her breasts. The intensity of what he felt for her very nearly reducing him to tears.

She had become his world.

With a final kiss to his chest, Savannah untangled herself from Kye and sat up. "I'm hitting the shower, Batman, alone and before this stuff dries or we'll never get out of here."

He laughed, making her heart soar, filling it with an emotion she was afraid was love. Not that she was opposed to love, but something was bothering him. Something she needed to get out in the open.

At times there was an almost desperate quality to their lovemaking. Not an *I haven't been laid in years so now I have to make up for lost time* kind of desperation, but a *this might be all the time we have together* kind of intensity. And yet…what was she supposed to make of that sense of desperation in the face of his claims and demands that she belonged to him?

Savannah sighed. Men. Put on this Earth to drive women crazy in one way or another.

She took her shower and then dressed, lingered over memories of the last few days, even as she accepted what had to be done next.

She'd let him shower first. She'd fix something to eat. Then while they were eating, she'd ask the tough questions. And she wouldn't stop asking them until she had answers.

Maybe she'd hate the answers. Maybe they'd hurt and disillusion her. But she'd rather hear the truth up front and figure out what to do about it than have this thing with Kye turn into a sad country song about loneliness and heartbreak.

Chapter Eight

ഇ

Draigon paused in the act of sitting down, the chimes sounding throughout the living quarters of his parents' home and announcing a visitor. *You are expecting someone?* he asked his father.

No. A tortured sigh escaped as his father looked at the Fett board they had only just finished setting up in preparation for spending most of the day pitted against each another.

It is better to be interrupted now than after the game starts, Draigon said, smiling, already knowing what his father's next words would be.

As long as our guest is not longwinded.

Draigon laughed. *If Mother were here, she would scold you for a lack of hospitality. Lucky for you, she and Zantara are at the market. I will see to our unexpected visitor and endeavor to hurry them along.* He left the table, using the Ylan stones in his wristbands to send a command so the solid-appearing crystal wall reabsorbed a portion of itself and formed an opening.

Greetings, Cousin, Jeqon said, watching surprised welcome give way to wariness, seeing the exact moment Draigon remembered he was a Council scientist, one assigned to Earth and the finding of human bond-mates. *May I enter?*

Of course. Draigon stepped back to allow Jeqon into the living quarters before extending his arms, grasping Jeqon's forearms so their bands touched in traditional greeting.

Draigon's father joined them at the doorway, also greeting Jeqon in the traditional manner, asking as he did so, *You have come on Council business? You have come with news of a match?*

Yes.

I will summon the others.

No, Uncle. I would speak with Draigon privately first.

Draigon's father stiffened. Courtesy demanded he say, *I will leave the two of you to your discussion then*, but when their eyes met, Draigon saw his father's desire to remain and learn about the human bond-mate, to openly discuss which of the Vesti might make a suitable co-mate. If any would know, it would be Jeqon.

Jeqon had many friends among the Vesti. And was now assigned to Earth, where he had gained a deeper understanding of the humans.

Those qualifications were enough for Draigon to value Jeqon's opinion in its own right. But for his father, it was also important that Jeqon was a member of the Lahatiel clan-house. That Jeqon's uncle, Raym, sat on the Council.

For a moment Draigon hesitated, very nearly asked his father to stay. But in the end he said nothing and his father left the dwelling.

Draigon led Jeqon to the table where the strategy game which was to have provided hours of entertainment now waited for his father and one of his brothers. He wondered at his cousin's hesitation. At the need to speak privately about a matter that affected all in the Baraqijal clan-house. *You have found a match for me?* Draigon prompted, uneasiness filling him at Jeqon's continued delay.

"Yes, her name is Savannah Holden," Jeqon said, changing to the human form of communication. Deciding it was better suited to both the topic and the care required in order to navigate through the minefield of this particular conversation.

He studied the game on the table between them, a strategy game somewhat similar to the chess game on Earth, though much more complicated with its expandable three-dimensional board and the pieces representing not only archetypes but natural hazards and enemy fortifications.

Fett was popular on Belizair and he knew the rudiments of how to play, but he was not drawn to it. Especially not with the intensity the bounty hunters seemed to be. If he was successful in pressing Kye's suit, in convincing Draigon to accept Kye as a co-mate, both men would have this game in common and Jeqon knew many a deep and lasting friendship had been forged over a Fett board.

He sighed inwardly and ran the tip of his finger over a sculpted game piece of golden Ylan stone. At the moment he felt the task in front of him would require all the strategy and finesse of a master Fett player. Savannah's friendship with Krista and Draigon's with Adan were a great advantage. But it would require careful handling if he hoped to get Draigon to look past his long-standing dislike of Lyan and accept Kye on his own merits.

Jeqon said a silent prayer to the Goddess and her consort, asking them to aid him. So much was at stake, not just for Kye and Savannah and Draigon, but for all those on Belizair.

Hadn't he experienced firsthand how dangerously close ancient prejudices and grudges were to rising to the surface? To returning their world to those long-ago days when Vesti and Amato warred with one another. Hadn't he been on the receiving end of hostile looks and angry outbursts from both his uncle Raym and his sister, Zantara, for his continued friendship with those of the Araqiel clan-house, the Vesti house that had unknowingly brought the Hotaling virus to Belizair?

If those on his world were to survive the threat of extinction, then the baggage of the past had to be lost. The distance between the two races closed forever. The first children would soon be born and Jeqon was proud to have played a part in finding a solution for the unmated males of Belizair.

"It is not common for Council scientists to involve themselves beyond matching a human female to a male on Belizair and notifying the male of his good fortune," Jeqon finally said, Draigon's stiffening at the words *good fortune* making Jeqon frown and question, "Was your DNA included in the database of those seeking a match by mistake?"

Draigon forced himself to relax. "I had thought there would be more time to get used to the idea of a human mate and a Vesti co-mate. To prepare. My brothers submitted their DNA when the first pregnancies were announced." He squared his shoulders. He was committed to this course and he would see it through. "Tell me about this Earth female, Savannah."

"I can show you a picture of her. I think you will be pleased to learn her hair is the deep red of a Sarien fire crystal."

Some of the tension eased from Draigon's chest. He and Jeqon had never been close, and yet he found it easier to accept a human mate knowing that his cousin was involved in the process and had taken the time to deliver the news himself, and if his earlier comment and his nervous handling of the game piece was an indication, perhaps to offer advice on a possible Vesti co-mate. "You have seen her?"

"No, the images I have are provided by another."

"Tell me of her first."

"Savannah is a policewoman."

Draigon settled more easily in the chair. A policewoman. It was a good start.

"She is friends with Adan and Lyan's bond-mate Krista. They should be arriving shortly. Perhaps you will even have a chance to meet Krista before they disappear into the housing set aside for them and are not seen again until she is pregnant. By all accounts Adan and Lyan are completely enamored of her even though she has led them on a wild, emotional chase."

Draigon's spirits lightened further at the mention of Adan's return. At the prospect of seeing Adan's happiness. "I will time my departure in order to meet them when they arrive in Winseka."

"You have prepared for the trip to Earth?"

"I have studied, not extensively as I did not expect to be matched so quickly. My knowledge is incomplete but it should serve me for the short time I will be there. I intend to stay only long enough to claim my mate and return to Belizair with her."

Jeqon nodded. "It would be best if Savannah was brought here quickly. She is in great danger. While she was with Krista an explosive device was detonated. It now appears your bondmate was the intended target. If Lyan and Adan's mate hadn't guessed at the danger and acted, both women would be dead. Lost to us."

Draigon stood with such force that several of the game pieces tumbled over. "Where can I find Savannah?"

Jeqon also stood, still holding the golden-colored game piece representing the messenger of The Goddess. "She is safe for the moment. Lyan and Adan were nearby when the danger to Savannah was first recognized. They assumed responsibility for their mate so the Vesti bounty hunter watching Krista could take possession of Savannah. If he had not been there to do so, then she would have been killed shortly thereafter. A sniper was lying in wait for her. He had no choice but to use the Ylan stones and destroy the human trying to kill her." Jeqon paused. "I have made a report to the Council. He broke our laws and risked exposing our presence in order to save her. But in light of the fact that Savannah is important to Krista and has now been found to have the Fallon gene sequence as well, the Council has decided not to sanction him."

"I owe him much," Draigon said, suspicion forming at the directness of Jeqon's gaze, at the underlying hint of where the conversation was heading.

"He would have saved her regardless of whether or not she carried the Fallon gene. She is Krista's friend and when he saw her, the Vesti mating fever struck him. When she nicknamed him bat-man, he believed she was his match. He is the one who came to me with a sample of her DNA."

Disbelief. Anger. Gratitude. All of them tumbled around inside Draigon as knowledge congealed into a dark mass in his chest and gut. "He has already touched her?"

"She reached for him and he thought it was his right. His duty to pleasure and protect her."

"Who is he?"

Jeqon set the game piece down next to another symbolizing a chaotic whirlpool capable of destroying even the most powerful figures if they stumbled into it. "Kye d'Vesti."

Denial roared through Draigon. The force of it so overwhelming that he almost turned his back on Jeqon and walked away from the offered bond-mate—from the human woman who had given herself to Lyan's cousin, who had already felt the sting of the Vesti mating fangs as she was mounted. But as Draigon's emotions swirled and clashed violently, his gaze landed on the Fett game. On the fallen pieces. Knocked over when he had first heard of the danger to Savannah.

For long moments Draigon struggled to gain control of himself, to restore order where chaos reigned. His comment of only a moment ago rising unspoken over the board. *I owe him much.*

Draigon steeled himself, standing straight under the weight of responsibility he carried on behalf of his clan-house. What choice did he have but to accept the male Savannah had already chosen? The male who had both found her and kept her safe.

"I will accept him as my co-mate. You will make note of it in the records?"

"Yes."

"Thank you. I will speak with my parents then go to Winseka."

Jeqon nodded and left.

101

Draigon lingered for a few moments, his thoughts a confusion of duty coupled with honor, blended with surprised anticipation—curiosity as he realized Jeqon had never provided an image of Savannah.

He picked up the scattered game pieces and placed them in their correct positions, then with one last look at the Fett board, Draigon reached out mentally to find his family members. To share the news of his match with them.

* * * * *

Kye grimaced as he joined Savannah in the kitchen. Between the look on her face and the stiff new Earth garments he'd put on, he knew their breakfast was going to be an uncomfortable ordeal. She made him think of those times when he had been summoned to the Council chambers so that Raym d'Amato could question him, could attempt to delve into his thoughts and motivations, no doubt intent on determining how similar they were to Lyan's.

If his future weren't so uncertain Kye would find amusement in how closely his feelings now matched his cousin's. How desperately he wanted to ignore Council law. To take what he wanted, what he needed. To ensure that Savannah remained his.

But the situation on Belizair was desperate. And his honor, the honor of his clan-house, demanded that he wait for his fate to unfold.

The irony of having his future with Savannah rest in the hands of Raym's nephew, Jeqon, was not lost on Kye. But Jeqon had always been his own man. His black hair and black-veined wings setting him apart in looks from the flame-haired members of his clan-house. His many friendships among the Vesti widening the distance.

Kye took the plate of food Savannah offered and carried it to the table. Sitting. Watching as she took up a position across from him. Waiting for what was to come. Her expression warning him that her mind was busy and she would no longer be distracted by sex.

Savannah studied Kye, not sure whether to be worried or pleased at how uncomfortable he looked. He knew what was coming. She could see it on his face. And yet... Now that the moment had arrived she found she wasn't in such a big hurry to ask the hard questions.

She reached for the jar of boysenberry jelly, taking time to slather it on her muffin, her stomach suddenly protesting the thought of food. "The clothes okay?" she asked, grimacing, wondering if reminding him that he was wearing stuff she'd purchased was a good way to start the conversation.

"I would rather be naked. But the clothing fits as it is supposed to."

Savannah laughed despite the knot in her stomach. "Yeah, well, you'd rather be naked and I'd rather *see* you naked. The only problem with that particular look is I'd have to arrest you as soon as we got to town." She paused, seeing an opportunity to start her questions. "I'm assuming if you were following Krista, then you must have abandoned your car near The Dive. We could get close enough for you to retrieve it when we go into Reno today."

Kye stilled. A jolt of excitement and nervousness spearing through his chest. Her mention of Krista providing an unexpected opportunity to see how she felt about sharing herself with two men.

He forced himself to mimic Savannah's casual actions, smearing jelly on his bread as he tried to plot the course of their conversation. "You are correct. I was driving a car. But I am not alone here. My car has already been reclaimed by those I work with."

Interest flickered across her features. "You work *for* someone? Or *with* someone?"

"In the past I have worked for clients outside of my...community. But presently I am working within it. That is how I came to be following Krista. To ensure her safety until my cousin and his partner could reclaim her." Kye grinned despite how important the conversation was to his future...to their future. "I am still amazed by the spectacle of them walking her to her car and kissing her, of them allowing her to leave in the first place after a night in their arms."

"You know about that?" Savannah's eyes widened. "So are Lyan and Adan a couple?"

Kye jerked as though he'd been hit, the muffin he'd just taken a bite of suddenly choking him. Savannah stood as his face reddened but he waved her away. His choking turning to laughter, then tears. "By the stars, no! Lyan and Adan are not lovers. The V—no. It is not our way." He wiped the moisture from his eyes and cheeks, scrambling to regain control of both himself and the conversation. "Krista told you she had been with both of them?"

Now he watched with interest as color moved through Savannah's face and she shifted in her chair, suddenly finding great interest in the food on her plate. "Sure, women talk the same as men do. Obviously." She glanced up at him and lifted an eyebrow. "You know, we have our fantasies too."

Kye's cock surged to life and pressed urgently against the uncomfortable Earth clothing. "I would like to hear more about these fantasies. About *your* fantasies."

Savannah was surprised smoke wasn't coming off her body. God! Her fantasy was sitting across the table. Now all she needed was to scrounge around in the truck for some of her ropes and leather straps. "I'm not sure you could handle my fantasies."

"Try me."

Oh yeah. *Tie me.* Savannah shook her head. "All I'm going to say is that ropes are involved, Batman. Any more and we'll never make it to town today."

Heat flared in Kye's eyes and Savannah clenched her legs together. Damn. If she didn't know where it would lead, her fingers would be on her clit and her nipples right now.

Kye closed his eyes briefly. The fork loaded with eggs halted midway between his plate and his mouth. She was killing him.

He dropped his hand to his lap, tempted to release his cock, but if he did so... They would indeed never make it to town.

Kye gripped his penis through the stiff fabric of his jeans. Cursing again the clothing he had been forced to wear since gaining an assignment on Earth.

It was a difficult feat but he forced his mind away from the painful erection and the erotic fantasies rushing through his thoughts, made himself concentrate on returning to their original conversation. Only this time he saw no reason for subtlety—which was just as well since subtlety was not a strong point of his clan-house. "Lyan and Adan will do all in their power to convince Krista to live with them as their bond-mate. Their shared wife."

"That's going to be a tough decision for her. She loves being a teacher. It's all she ever wanted to be." Savannah shook her head and took a sip of coffee before adding, "Even in San Francisco flaunting the fact she's part of a threesome could make it difficult to keep her job—impressionable young minds and all of that." She cocked her head and looked at him. "So they're serious about her?"

"There will never be another for them."

"That's serious."

Kye hesitated. Savannah had already proven herself to be intelligent and there were things he *could not* reveal to her, and yet he wanted to prepare her for his world. "Krista will be able to teach if she accepts Lyan and Adan's offer and returns home with them. The sight of her with her new...husbands...will be cause for celebration among us, not censure."

"Where's home?" Savannah asked, pouncing as he'd feared she would.

Kye shook his head, his chest tightening when her eyes narrowed with suspicion. "We live apart."

Her gaze dropped to his wristbands and the Ylan stones pulsed against his skin. "You're part of a cult."

A startled laugh escaped. Once her human ancestors had both worshipped and feared his! "No. But you have already commented on how difficult it would be for a woman to be part of a threesome. We live in a place where such a thing has come to be…expected. Even necessary."

Holy shit. Was he saying what she thought he was saying? "So guys usually pair up when they want to settle down with a woman?"

"Yes," he said, his face closing up. The sight of it causing pain to sear through Savannah's heart—not because she wasn't going to experience her favorite fantasy, but because the *this might be all the time we have together* desperation of his lovemaking finally made sense. He'd probably already agreed to be some guy's partner in claiming a woman and couldn't back out of it now.

Well, okay. She could deal with that. She hadn't asked for promises. Hadn't expected them. It had been fun while it lasted—but she *wouldn't* be bringing him back to the cabin with her after they got to town.

Outside of a little rough and rowdy sex she just wasn't into pain, especially emotional pain. And besides that, she needed to get busy trying to figure out what The Ferret knew. She wasn't sure exactly how she was going to swing the captain's cooperation yet, but once she'd argued her case— namely that *she* was obviously the one The Ferret wanted to talk to—then maybe the captain would relent. She couldn't remain in hiding for the rest of her life

Savannah rose from the table, taking her dirty dishes to the sink. Kye rose and followed her. His heart thundering in his chest from witnessing the play of emotions on her face.

He stopped behind her, trapped her against the counter, her back to his front as he braced himself for her reaction, her rejection. "Does the idea of sharing yourself with two men repulse you?"

The dishes clattered the last few inches to the sink. "Aren't you already taken?"

His hand went to her breast, cupping it through the clothing. "No."

"There's only one of you here."

Kye dared to nuzzle against the deep red of her hair. To smile against her neck though every Vesti instinct railed against the necessity of sharing a mate. "And I could keep you satisfied without the aid of another, but the choice isn't mine to make. Does the idea of sharing yourself with two men repulse you?"

"No," she said, burning his lips with the hotness of her blood as it moved through her neck and across her cheeks.

"Good." He gave her a sucking bite then retreated, caution urging him to take the conversation no further until he had spoken with Jeqon and knew his own fate. "I thought perhaps we could target shoot before leaving for town," he suggested.

Savannah's mind spun with questions. She wanted to ask if Kye had a third in mind to join them in bed. She wanted to believe he'd fallen as hard for her as she'd already fallen for him. As Krista had fallen for Lyan and Adan—and them for her. But for the time being Savannah was happy to gather up emptied aluminum soda cans and set them a short distance from the cabin to serve as targets. To concentrate instead on besting Kye or at least equaling his ability as they fired a rifle in friendly competition.

"Perhaps when we return from town we can experiment with some rope play," Kye teased a short time later, probably to distract her so her last shots would stray away from the target.

It didn't work. Though it was a close call. Savannah grinned and lowered the rifle. "We'll see, Batman. But just so you know what I'm thinking, I'm going to be the cowgirl and you're going to be the rough stock that needs to be roped, thrown down and tied up."

Kye laughed with easy masculine confidence. "Now that is a true fantasy. Even if I were to give you a handicap, there is no way you could do what you envision."

"Hold that thought," Savannah said, leaning the rifle against a tree and heading for the truck to get her lariat.

Chapter Nine

ఈ

Even braced for the sight of Lyan, Draigon could not suppress the flash of anger he felt when he saw the Vesti emerge from the portal building. What had started out as childhood animosity had intensified, solidified over time, and it did not help that Lyan's feelings mirrored his own, that Lyan bristled and glowered as soon as they were within speaking distance, causing Adan to jump in as he was often required to do, to say, "This is not the way to forge peace between our peoples."

As it always did, it took several seconds for Adan's words to penetrate, to break the staring contest that was habit when Draigon and Lyan encountered each other. But when it was done, Draigon turned his attention to Krista and felt his breath catch in his throat at her fragile beauty. She was delicate and exquisite. Soft and golden. Completely desirable.

He glanced at Adan. "I come to greet your new bond-mate and to tell her that soon her friend will join her on Belizair. The scientists have determined that the human female, Savannah, has the Fallon gene marker that matches mine."

"To harm one of the Vesti is to declare war on all of us, Draigon," Lyan said, drawing Draigon's gaze and causing fresh anger to rush through him, Lyan's words a confirmation that he knew his cousin had already mated with Savannah.

"There will be no war. In true Vesti fashion, your cousin took what did not belong to him, but my mate would be dead if he had not been there to interfere. For that reason and that reason alone, I will accept him as a co-mate."

Draigon once again forced his attention away from Lyan and back to Krista, this time leaning forward and pressing his lips to Krista's, a taunt to Lyan and yet a sharing with Adan. As Jeqon had said, Adan's happiness and possessiveness of his bond-mate was easy to see.

When the kiss ended Draigon turned and strode past them, toward the portal, his steps light and hurried. He had reconciled himself to taking a human mate though he had never been drawn to any female other than those of his race, and the thought of a female with no wings had been a leaden weight in his chest. But the instant he saw Krista he understood why some of the Fallon had been fascinated by the women on Earth, why he had not seen any of the other human females brought back to Winseka. Their mates had yet to let them out of bed!

Draigon's heart quickened and his cock grew hard in anticipation. Where before he had been resigned, now he was anxious to get to the task of securing his mate and bringing her home, breeding her so that his line would continue.

He entered the transport chamber, glad he had been granted permission to jump from the portal exit to where Kye and Savannah were, otherwise he would have been forced to endure endless Earth-hours using their primitive means of transportation.

Draigon grimaced. By all accounts, Earth was a backwater of a planet and he did not intend to remain there for long. He would secure his mate and return before the third sun rose and set on Belizair.

The stones in the chamber pulsed in a sequence of light and color and Draigon braced himself as the Ylan crystals in his wristbands pulled on the energy around them, preparing for the transmutation that preceded transport. The air becoming charged, and then before he could take a breath, he was on Earth.

He paused long enough to change into the clothing stored in a room adjacent to the transport chamber then he used the

Ylan stones to both hide his wings and to transport him to Kye's location. And for a moment Draigon could only stare in amazed disbelief at the sight before him.

I would stand and greet you properly but as you can see, I am tied up right now, Kye said, his amused voice jerking Draigon's attention from the sight of a bound Vesti warrior lying on the ground to the human standing over him.

As if sensing his presence, Savannah turned toward Draigon and lust poured into him even as the breath was forced from his chest. He moved forward with only one thought, to claim his mate.

Holy fuck! Where had he come from! Savannah wondered as she scrambled for the rifle leaning against a tree and jerked the rope at the same time so the knot hogtying Kye's wrists to his ankles like a calf in a rodeo event would pull free.

Whoever Mr. Red was, he was coming toward them fast. And though he wasn't armed, he looked deadly enough without a weapon. She grabbed the rifle just as he got to where Kye had rolled over and was now sitting, freeing himself from the rope.

"Stop right there," Savannah said, chambering a round and pointing the rifle at the center of the stranger's chest, watching as his gaze dropped to the weapon, his face reflecting surprise and then amusement. But he did as she commanded, not taking his eyes off her even when Kye rose to his feet.

"This is Draigon d'Amato," Kye said. "He means you no harm."

Savannah's eyes narrowed, not liking the way Kye's body radiated tension. Not liking the way he'd phrased his comment. She didn't lower the rifle.

"He might not mean *me* any harm, but what about you?"

Kye forced himself to relax, but by the stars, it was hard! When he had first seen Draigon he had assumed the Amato was now working for the Council scientists. He had assumed Draigon was to guard Savannah while he returned to San Francisco and spoke with Jeqon. But Draigon's reaction to the sight of Savannah, his telepathically delivered announcement that *he* was her mate by Council law had very nearly devastated Kye. Of all the Amato who could have been matched with Savannah...to have it be this one...a man long at odds with his cousin Lyan.

Surely our mate does not intend to discharge that primitive weapon into my chest, Draigon said, sending hope flooding into Kye, disbelief. His thoughts caught on a single word—*our* mate.

You have accepted me as your co-mate? he asked, saying to Savannah, "He means me no harm either. I was expecting a third to join us. Though I had not intended to be caught in the position Draigon found me in."

She lowered the rifle, suspicion still radiating from her, filling Kye with both pride and amusement. *Did Jeqon tell you she has been trained to serve as a policewoman among the humans? Be warned, she is intelligent and observant. Very little gets by her.* He paused, daring to ask the yet unanswered question again. *You have accepted me as your co-mate?*

Yes. The answer was a hostile growl but for the moment Kye was filled with relief and gratitude. Even happiness. Until Draigon said, *Leave us.*

The command was enough to bring the Vesti desire to hoard a mate roaring to life, burning through Kye's veins with the same heat of the mating fever. He stiffened. Torn between the primitive urge to fight Draigon for possession of Savannah and the knowledge that he *must* share her with the flame-haired Amato.

Kye took a deep breath and forced a calm he did not truly feel into his body. He concentrated on the lessons he had learned in dealing with the Council members who looked on him with hostility and suspicion. It would serve no purpose to antagonize Draigon, though Kye had no intention of being a lesser mate to Savannah. For the moment diplomacy rather than challenge was necessary. *I cannot leave. She must go to town in order to report to her captain. It would be safer for her if both of us were there to see to her protection.*

Draigon's face tightened. Every cell in his body announced his desire to be alone with Savannah. But finally he gave a slight nod and some of the tension drained from both of them.

Savannah watched the play of emotions over Kye's face and through his body. There was something going on between the two men—not sexually. But something. The air was practically vibrating around them.

The long hair and the bands on Draigon's wrists said he was from the same place as Kye. And between the conversation she'd had with Kye over breakfast and him saying, "I was expecting a third to join us," it would be logical to think...

Savannah grinned. Now that she didn't have to worry about defending herself and Kye, she could salivate over Draigon's hard-muscled body. Could even undress him mentally and imagine herself in bed with him.

Damn, close the paddock gate before the stud could escape!

Too bad it was time to head to town.

The thought triggered an obvious question now that she was over the surprise of Draigon showing up. How the hell had he gotten to the cabin without her noticing his arrival? Because now that she was looking, she wasn't seeing any form of transportation, not even a bicycle. And while it was possible to walk in, he wasn't covered in dust and sweat.

Savannah turned away and brought the rifle up, emptying the chamber by firing at one of the cans she and Kye had been using earlier for target practice. Satisfaction filling her as it tumbled and danced backward. "We'd better get going," she said, lowering the rifle and unloading the

113

remaining bullets as she walked past where Kye and Draigon were standing.

It took fifteen steps to come to the end of Draigon's trail. Or what she assumed was probably his track since she and Kye had trampled the area around the cabin with their target practice and spontaneous roping event. Amazing. The trail just disappeared the same way Kye's had done. How did they do that?

She swung around to face them, allowing her gaze to linger on the picture of Kye and Draigon standing together like a well-matched pair of stallions wearing identical expressions of wariness.

She focused on Draigon. "So you're a bounty hunter too?"

"Yes," Draigon said, and she smiled at the pride radiating off him.

"You and Kye are going to have to teach me that disappearing trick you've got going."

Draigon's face tensed and his body stiffened. An answering look and stiffness appeared in Kye. Savannah shook her head, *The Twilight Zone* theme song playing in her head. But she didn't have time to figure out what the hell was going on with them. "We'd better head out," she said again. "I've got to call the captain and if he gives me the thumbs-up, then I'm going to start asking around for The Ferret."

I will not allow this, Draigon said. Images of carrying her into the cabin, forcibly restraining her if necessary, flooding his mind. The savage need to have her look to him for pleasure and protection filling him. The intensity of his emotions foreign to him.

Draigon took a step forward, needing to close the distance between himself and Savannah, to take possession of her physically and lay down the rules that would apply to her now that he had arrived on the scene.

Careful, Kye said, placing a hand on Draigon's arm. *She does not yet know you. She does not yet understand your claim to her. And the word* allow *is best used with caution when it comes to* Savannah.

Draigon shook Kye's restraining hand off. Accepting what the Vesti said even as he resented the reminder that he was a stranger to Savannah while Kye already knew her intimately.

Doubt trickled into Savannah as she watched the odd interplay between Draigon and Kye. The wild emotions flickering in Draigon's eyes, the tightening of Kye's face.

She must have gotten it wrong. Unless the men where Kye came from paired up by pulling names out of a hat, she couldn't see these two getting together and living happily ever after with the same woman. Right now she was having a hard time picturing either one of them letting the other one in the bedroom.

Even without a single word being exchanged, she was starting to feel like a coveted bone caught between two phenomenally exquisite purebred dogs. And strangely enough, she didn't find it flattering.

Savannah grinned — but then her kink was two guys at once, not two guys fighting to the death over her. She turned and headed for the truck. She didn't have time to referee, choose between them or kick some ass right now. Which meant they were going to have to work their little turf-war out themselves.

Or not, Savannah concluded a little while later when Kye finally pulled the truck over and parked in front of a phone booth. It had been a long drive from the cabin, with her trapped on the truck's bench seat between two tense men.

Despite the general — and erroneous, as far as Savannah was concerned — assumption about redheads being hot-tempered, she prided herself on having a great sense of humor and being a pretty easygoing person. But in one short trip with Kye and Draigon she'd had enough of whatever was going on between them.

Yeah, they were both drop-dead, drench-your-panties gorgeous. Yeah, having two permanent guys was a favorite fantasy of hers. And if one of them was the strong, silent type, that was okay. God knew, she could come up with plenty of words on her own. But there still had to be a connection. And connections weren't formed without at least some conversation.

What had transpired in the cab of the truck didn't qualify as "conversation" in her mind. Every question about how they knew each other or where they were from, or their jobs and training as bounty hunters, brought an odd delay, almost as though they were trying to get their stories straight. And then when one of them finally answered, all she got was a bare minimum of information. She was willing to play twenty questions when it came to The Ferret because hopefully that was going to fall under the heading of job description, but damned if she was going to do it when it came to her sex life.

Savannah shook her head as she waited for Kye to get out of the truck so she could slide out. Her feet touched the ground and a little jolt traveled up her body and into her heart as her eyes met his. He looked all business, serious, and she didn't think it was just because of the call she was getting ready to make. "One question," she said, tilting her head slightly in the direction of Draigon who now stood next to what passed for a telephone booth. "Does he have anything to do with the conversation you and I were having earlier?"

"Yes."

She waited, but when it became obvious Kye wasn't going to say anything more, Savannah sighed. "Okay then. That was my one question. Now here's my one follow-up comment. It's not going to happen unless a major attitude adjustment happens with you two." That said, she did her best to shut both of them out of her thoughts so she could concentrate on what she was going to say to the captain.

Dismay rippled through Kye as Savannah moved to the phone booth, pointedly turning her back to both him and

116

Draigon. Symbolically shutting him out, her comment making anxiety curl in his stomach.

What conversation does she refer to? Draigon asked, positioning himself at Savannah's back.

Kye replayed what had transpired with Savannah during breakfast, the memory restoring some of his hope and making him grateful she was willing to accept two males. Not all those who had been matched with humans carrying the Fallon marker had returned to Belizair with a mate. Some had failed because the woman could not be persuaded to accept a second lover.

By the stars, he couldn't lose Savannah now. Not when happiness was within sight. Not when the seemingly impossible had occurred and Draigon had accepted him as a co-mate despite Draigon's long-standing dislike of Lyan. A dislike that was mutual though Kye was uncertain as to why his cousin and Draigon had always been at odds with one another.

Kye walked over to the phone booth. Noticing for the first time how stunning Savannah and Draigon looked together with their fiery hair and green eyes.

We must make peace, Kye said, resolutely shutting the door on the cultural heritage of his ancestors. Forcing even the fantasy of having Savannah to himself from his thoughts.

He had felt Savannah's growing impatience and irritation as she tried to engage Draigon and him in conversation. And while it was a major accomplishment she was willing to accept both a Vesti and Amato lover, he had learned enough about her over the last few days to realize now how foolish it had been to think she would easily be convinced to leave Earth. She had brothers and cousins, parents and grandparents, uncles and aunts. A job she enjoyed. Goals.

Kye grimaced. His service to the Council and the necessity of learning to compromise apparently would apply to the claiming of a mate as well. As long as she remained on

Earth, she needed to be protected. A challenge that was best met with two mates. And competing against Draigon would only succeed in driving Savannah away.

We must make peace, Kye repeated, opening his memories and thoughts to Draigon. Allowing him to see all he had learned about Savannah.

Draigon reeled under Kye's openness. The mix of Kye's emotions adding to the turmoil of his own as he learned more about the bond-mate who had already become a fever in his cock and a longing in his heart.

Savannah left him feeling off-balance, off-center, uncertain and unprepared. She turned his carefully ordered world and expectations into chaos.

He had thought she would welcome him with open arms. Instead she pointed a primitive weapon at him and regarded him with suspicion.

He had thought after seeing Adan's mate that his own would be soft and fragile, and yet she was as fierce and cunning as any warrior.

He had thought that because she was a law-keeper, they would interface naturally and conversation would come easily. But instead each answer had to be shortened, adjusted because he could not tell her of Belizair and the worlds he had served on.

And though he had never voiced the belief out loud, or acknowledged it to himself, at his core he had thought a human female, a being not blessed with wings by the Goddess, would be...sexually unappealing.

But the sight of Adan's mate and then his own mate Savannah had been like the blast of energy from a Ylan stone. Leaving him pulsing with need and yet filled with nervous uncertainty. Frustrated and angry. Aroused. Overwhelmed.

It was a blow to his pride to be wrong about so many things. And the sight of her with Kye, both what he had witnessed with his own eyes and what he had now seen through Kye's memories, only added to his feelings of desperation and uneasiness. His feelings of isolation and exclusion. She was *his* mate by Council law and yet he had been reduced to the role of an interloper!

Draigon stiffened. The wild mix of his emotions coalescing, focusing on a single target. Kye d'Vesti. The cousin of Lyan d'Vesti. *When we are done in town then I want you to leave us. You have had days with her. Now it is my turn.*

Anger rushed into Kye, stirring the possessive instincts of the Vesti and making it a challenge to stay the course of his good intentions and earlier resolve. *If Savannah will accept it, then I will leave her in your care,* he said, forcing his thoughts away from Draigon in favor of focusing on Savannah and the conversation she was having with her superior officer.

Chapter Ten

ॐ

"Holden, I ought to bust you right down to meter-maid. What part of *I'm ordering you back to wherever you're holed up, right now and stay there* wasn't crystal clear to you?"

"I—"

"Save it. It's too late. This is out of my hands now. You want your shot at the action? You got it. But you better watch your ass because if you go maverick the guys you'll be reporting to are going to shred any hope you have for a career in police work—and that's only if you don't end up behind bars for obstruction."

Savannah's heart beat triple-time in her chest. "What guys?"

"The ones you're going to be meeting as soon as we finish our little discussion. Vaccaro and Kelleher. FBI."

"Shit."

"Yeah, and you've landed right in it. Now you've got to do your best to get out of it without doing too much damage to yourself. Career-wise and heath-wise. Watch your ass, Holden. It'd put a serious dent in my supply of salsa and my poker fun if I had to deliver bad news to your family."

"What can you tell me?"

"Not a lot. After I got your message I did some checking to see if your apartment was on anyone's watch list. No takers. Then I did some asking around about the Easy Times Casino and what may or may not be going on there. Then I looked into your informant's rap sheet and made a couple of phone calls to New Jersey and found out Becky Jaworski had bailed out her boyfriend a couple of times—one Ricky Nowak,

120

otherwise known as The Ferret to you. Nice nickname. I better not find out you've got one for me."

Savannah grinned. "I don't. But only because I can remember your real name."

"Keep it that way. The link between Becky Jaworski Traynor and Nowak was a good catch, Holden. Especially as Traynor's wife now seems to be in the wind same as Nowak is."

"Missing as in someone has filed a missing person's report?"

"Not as far as I can tell. And don't ask me for more. That's as far as I got before having the Feds show up at my home to tell me that what you were doing on your *vacation* was their problem now and I shouldn't ask any more questions about Traynor, Nowak or the Easy Times."

A shiver of excitement danced along Savannah's skin. The Ferret was right, whatever he knew, it was big time. Big enough to involve the Feds. "So where do I meet Kelleher and Vaccaro?"

The captain told her, even gave her directions before saying, "If you don't get answers that satisfy you, call me. That's where I draw the line here. I don't want you operating in the dark. My people aren't going to be used as cannon fodder by the Feds." He hesitated then added, "Something's going on over in Vice, besides you stepping on toes and pissing people off. So watch your back there too."

Savannah's stomach went queasy. "Bad cops?"

"I don't know, Holden. It's just a gut feeling, but I want you playing with a full deck if you insist on playing."

"Thanks, Captain."

"I'm wasting my breath here, Holden, but if things get too hot and you want out, call. Got it?"

"Got it."

Savannah dropped the receiver into the cradle and looked up to find Kye and Draigon doing the weird twin-expression thing, both of them wearing identical frowns, both of them radiating tension.

A tendril of uneasiness uncurled in her chest as her gaze wandered downward, encountering the odd wristbands they wore. Kye's set with swirling purple stones, Draigon's set with dark red stones flecked with gold.

For the first time it occurred to her how easily they could abduct her and take her back to their home—wherever that was—and the thought ratcheted up the level of adrenaline already coursing through her at the prospect of being involved in a big case. She only had Kye's denial that they weren't part of a cult. She didn't have proof either way as to whether it was true or not.

Savannah rolled her shoulders then realized what she was doing—loosening up in case there was a fight. But it didn't stop her from stepping away from the half-shell of the phone booth in order to give herself room to maneuver. She hadn't grown up among brothers, cousins and ranch hands without learning to tell when trouble was brewing. One look at Kye and Draigon said trouble had arrived.

"You heard?" she asked, meeting Kye's eyes.

"Yes."

It was close to a growl and despite the tension in the air and the prospect of being in on a big investigation, Savannah's nipples went tight. "Good. So here's the deal. I'm not against you two coming to the meet with me. I'd rather not leave the truck unguarded. If the Feds ask, then I'll tell them I've got a couple of bounty hunters turned bodyguards at my back since I'm still officially on vacation. They're not going to like it, but they'll have to live with it since they wouldn't be asking for my help if they didn't need it." That was a given. But she didn't care *why* she was being asked, only that she was finally getting her chance.

"No," Draigon said.

It is a mistake to fight with her over this, Kye said.

You intend to allow her to put herself into danger?

There is no allowing or disallowing. She is a policewoman, a law-keeper here. How can you expect her to be other than what she is? What I do not intend to do is to make her so angry that she tries to send me away, Kye said before retreating to the truck.

Draigon turned his attention back to his now scowling mate. A sickness forming in his chest at the possibility Kye was right and that Savannah might truly become angry enough to spurn him.

"No, as in no, I don't like your plan?" Savannah asked, not bothering to hide the irritation that had been simmering since Draigon arrived on the scene. She'd been willing to cut him some slack since she could see how awkward it could be to suddenly arrive and try to turn a twosome into a threesome, but he was in for a rude awakening if he intended to turn macho on her—at least outside of the bedroom.

"Getting involved is too dangerous," Draigon said.

"News flash. I'm already involved. Besides the great sex, why do you think Kye and I are holed up in a cabin in the middle of nowhere?" She frowned. She'd had a fleeting thought earlier that the reason for Kye's disappearance the first morning they were at the cabin might have been to get in touch with Draigon. To explain the situation and call for backup, maybe even help Draigon set up camp nearby—which would have explained Draigon's sudden appearance on the scene with no visible means of transportation. But now…

Savannah shook her head. Dealing with them was beginning to make her feel like she'd actually stepped into *The Twilight Zone* and right now she just didn't have time for it. "Look, Draigon. Here's the situation. I am going to meet Kelleher and Vaccaro. You can stay here or you can come with me. Your choice but make it now." She decided to soften the challenge to his ego by adding, "This is my big chance and I'm not going to blow it because I let a gorgeous man go all caveman on me."

Warmth from the knowledge that she found him desirable flowed into Draigon despite his anger at her decision to place herself in danger. But there was no mistaking the determination in Savannah. No mistaking the truth in her words. She would leave him standing where he was, and without Kye's assistance there was no way he could force her back to the cabin. The only thing he could do was to go with her, to keep her safe until he could claim her and convince her to leave this primitive planet.

Between us we can see to her protection, Kye sent from the truck, as if reading Draigon's thoughts. *The Council rules are clear. Bond-mates must agree to return home with us of their own free will. She will not walk away from this in favor of a future we are forbidden from disclosing.*

It rankled, but Draigon knew Kye was right. *I do not like this.*

Nor do I. She does not yet have the protection of the Ylan stones and this planet is more primitive than many where the Amato and Vesti serve as law-keepers. But until Savannah has closure in this matter she will not consider what we will ask of her.

Draigon nodded slightly. To Savannah he said, "I will come with you. But do not expect to be without one of us guarding you at all times."

"I don't think it's going to be a hardship having you two as bodyguards," she said, her quick smile and amused laugh stirring the heat in Draigon's cock and making his chest expand with anticipation.

They returned to the truck with Savannah once again sitting between the two men. Once again feeling their tension, and yet the nature of it seemed to have changed, making her think Kye and Draigon were concentrating on the possible danger ahead rather than whatever else had been going on between them.

Maybe her earlier guess had been right after all. Maybe both men had just been feeling awkward. Kye because he'd had her to himself for the last few days. Draigon because he was the odd man out.

I could keep you satisfied without the aid of another, but the choice isn't mine to make, Kye had told her, and now that she thought about it, the words didn't sound like those of a man who wanted to form a threesome. Which would explain why Draigon's sudden appearance hadn't exactly been a welcome sight to Kye.

She grinned. Well, they had a minute before they got to the coffee shop for the meeting with the Feds. Too bad she was sitting in the middle and couldn't watch both men's expressions at the same time. Then again, she could compensate.

Savannah turned her head slightly so she could watch Draigon's face as she placed a hand on Kye's thigh. Tenderness flashed through her when she saw a flicker of longing, uncertainty in Draigon's eyes before his spine stiffened and his face became unreadable. "So have either of you ever shared a woman before?"

Kye's thigh jerked under her palm, "No. It is not the way of —"

"I have done so with one of my brothers," Draigon interrupted, sending a flash of jealousy through Savannah when his gaze grew heated with the memory of it.

She looked away and exhaled a long release of breath. Damn, that backfired on her a little bit. Yeah, the rational part of her mind knew she shouldn't be bothered by Draigon's little trip down memory lane, but...

Savannah shook her head, clearing it. She needed to get a grip. Their reactions had proven her theory. The rest would come — she snickered — the rest would cum. But as the meeting place came into view, she pushed thoughts of her love life away in favor of detective work.

The coffee shop was old-fashioned. A stand-alone building with large plate glass windows looking out into a small parking lot.

A long Formica-covered counter separated the customer area from the work area. Bar stools lined up in front of it like soldiers, the heavy metal poles topped with round vinyl seats, all of them empty, waiting for customers to arrive and take up their positions.

Kye parked the truck directly in front of the window. Close enough for Savannah to spot the man she'd seen outside her apartment sitting with the one who'd been at the bus stop a short distance from the residential hotel. "Those are our guys," she said, watching as the strawberry-blond lifted his hand to his brow—a signal she thought at first—but then he left it there, cupped, like someone shielding themselves from a glare even though the sun wasn't streaming directly into the coffee shop window.

Kye and Draigon opened their doors and got out, Savannah followed, but not before she saw the dark-haired man who'd been watching her apartment frown and shield his eyes also. Weird. Then again, she was starting to think this was just going to be a day full of *Twilight Zone* moments.

"There's no reason for us not to join you at the table," Kye said. "We are all professionals and clearly they have seen you with us." To Draigon he said, *I have been on this planet for one of their Earth years and only twice have I heard of humans demonstrating such a reaction as these two men are displaying— shading their eyes and squinting as though they cannot trust what their eyes are telling them. Both times the reactions were from women carrying the Fallon sequence. Women with some ability to pierce the veil of protection the Ylan stones provide and see us in our true form.*

Draigon's thoughts went immediately to his cousin and the sorrow and anger that now hovered around her, a heavy burden Zantara was unable to shake off. *Have the scientists found males on this planet who carry the Fallon genes?*

Not yet. But most of their efforts have been directed at locating human women.

We must gain DNA samples from these men.

Those are my thoughts as well.

Savannah hesitated for only a second before reversing her earlier decision. Kye was right. The three of them were obviously together and she had no intention of withholding information from Kye and Draigon if knowing it would help keep them all safer.

"Okay, but you two are *with me*, not the other way around," she said, entering the coffee shop first to prove her point.

The strawberry-blond was Kelleher. The man who'd been outside her apartment was Vaccaro. And if the narrowed, squinting glances they kept giving Kye and Draigon were any indication, neither of them was pleased to have her bounty hunters turned bodyguards at the table with them. Well, she couldn't help how they felt about it. It was a done deal as far as she was concerned.

Savannah introduced Kye and Draigon and stated her intention to keep them fully informed. Kelleher and Vaccaro exchanged a glance and she had the weird suspicion they were expecting as much — then she remembered the captain knew about Kye. He'd probably passed the information along to them. "What's going on at the Easy Times Casino? Laundering drug money?" she asked as she sat.

Kelleher's eyes met hers before moving downward to a manila folder on the table in front of him. He opened it and extracted a photograph. A gray-haired man with flabby skin and an erection that was probably Viagra induced — though it was possible the girl's lips hovering a breath away from it had been the inspiration. "Recognize her?"

Savannah's gut sickened at the sight of the underage prostitute. The young girl's eyes closed with the tightness of someone trying to block out what was happening to them.

The picture deepened Savannah's desire to get involved and on either side of her, Draigon and Kye vibrated with anger. She glanced at them, her heart flooding with warmth at the looks on their faces. The desire to right a wrong so clearly demonstrated in the photograph.

"I recognize her," Savannah said. "Her name's Holland."

"This involves the two policemen we encountered in your informant's apartment?" Kye asked, making the connection between the captain's gut feeling about something wrong in Vice and the underage girl Savannah had told him about.

"Creech and Mastrin," she said, revisiting the moments when she got the girls and the pervert john back to the police station, viewing them through a different lens this time. Had there been a flicker of recognition in Holland's eyes when the vice cops showed up? Fear?

Maybe. Savannah couldn't be sure. "Does this involve Vice?" she asked Kelleher.

"Vaccaro will hit on that in a moment."

A second photograph landed on the first, redirecting Savannah's attention. In this one Holland was stretched out next to the man. An older girl straddled his waist, his age-spotted hands fondling her breasts as she fucked him. "What about this girl?" Kelleher asked.

"No."

"The kid's half-sister, Ivy." There was no hiding the disgust in Kelleher's voice. "Both of them have been in foster care for most of their lives. Ivy's been out since she was seventeen. Holland's been running away since she was ten. Always ends up wherever her sister is. The last time she ran, Social Services finally threw in the towel and granted Ivy custody. There's an eight-year age difference between them."

A third picture landed on the other two. Before Kelleher asked, Savannah said, "She's one of the girls I hauled in the other day. Camryn. It looked like she was pimping Holland and another minor. I'm sure you know more about it now than

I do. I was pretty much shut out once the *Wrath of Vice* fell on me."

Kelleher laughed and for an instant it was easy for Savannah to forget he was FBI. He had great eyes and a smile that probably had women melting out of their clothing when he turned on the charm.

She nearly laughed out loud herself when both Kye and Draigon repositioned themselves on either side of her, crowding in on her as though they could pick up on the tenor of her thoughts. It was a welcome distraction from the pictures, though she only allowed her thoughts to drift for a moment before getting back to the business at hand. "So this is about blackmail?" she asked, knowing Vaccaro and Kelleher wouldn't be showing her the photographs if this was only about prostituting underage girls.

Surprise flickered in Kelleher's eyes. A glimmer of respect surfaced in Vaccaro's.

"He's the mayor of a small town near the Mexican border. Also co-owns a trucking company. Either of those may or may not be relevant," Kelleher said. "Usually plays in Vegas. Blackjack and roulette. Doesn't make a secret of his once-a-month trips there. He's a moderate gambler, sets limits and sticks to them. To the hometown crowd, he's a happily married man who dotes on his granddaughter, a kid who just happens to be thirteen, same as the underage girl you hauled in."

Savannah pushed the photo of Camryn aside, revealing the picture of the mayor with Holland and her sister. This time she studied the mayor's face. He looked like a willing participant though she'd bet her paycheck he hadn't known there was a camera focused on his activities.

Kelleher pulled a copy of a Social Services sheet from the folder and placed it on the table. Holland's picture appeared in black and white, along with a birth date and a partial history. "This was sent with the blackmail shots. But there's no way to determine who made the original copy. The girl's file has been through a lot of hands and there were no prints to pull from the sheet that came with the pictures."

Savannah rearranged her assumptions with these new facts. She'd thought the girls were laundering drug money, not involved in blackmail. But obviously they were—though it was always possible they didn't know about the camera. "Since Holland and her sister are here and not in Vegas, and you guys are here and not in Vegas, I assume the mayor changed his usual pattern and came to Reno to play."

Kelleher gave another mouthwatering smile. "Got it in one. He arrived compliments of the Easy Times Casino marketing program. Found the girls thanks to a helpful floor worker, who now can't be found to answer questions." The smile dimmed. "And neither can the girls. We're interested in the sisters plus Camryn."

"What about the other underage girl I hauled in?"

"Back on the street. Stayed one night in the shelter then ran. We've talked to her, but she claims not to know where the others went."

Thirteen going on a hundred. Hardened. Savannah had been a cop too long to believe everyone could be helped. She looked down at the blackmail pictures. "So where were these taken? The Easy Times?"

Chapter Eleven

§

"No," Kelleher said. "An apartment around the corner. The camera setup was gone but we caught a break. The place wasn't rented out and hadn't been since the girls used it, so we got in without a warrant. Ivy paid cash and used a fake ID, but the manager picked her out when we gave her a choice of pictures."

"Any prints?" Savannah asked.

This time it was Vaccaro who laughed. A husky sound to go with his dark good looks. "Yeah, two different sets. An out-of-state police chief and an oil company executive with a military record, which is why there were prints on file for both of them."

Savannah grinned. "Let me guess, they both got complimentary stays at the Easy Times Casino and didn't think twice about it since just about every casino in Vegas and Reno has a marketing plan offering comp packages."

"You're right," Kelleher said. "But if they're being blackmailed, they're not talking."

Savannah's attention moved to the folder. It looked like there were additional 5x7 glossies in it. "So who's behind the blackmail? The girls?"

Kelleher emptied the rest of his coffee cup then pulled out another photograph. "We're not sure. This is Becky Jaworski Traynor. As of a few days ago, missing, either voluntarily or involuntarily. It's not widely known, but she runs an escort service with a clientele that's exclusive to the men who stay and gamble at her husband's casino. We're fairly certain she knows about the underage girls, though it's not clear whether or not they're officially on her payroll. When her girls are on the clock they usually go back to the hotel room with the men they're escorting around Reno. As far as the blackmail goes…" he shrugged and pushed the file over to Vaccaro, "we don't know what she knows."

The dark-haired agent set the photo of Becky Traynor aside and spread two new ones out in front of Savannah, both of well-dressed men exiting the Easy Times Casino. He followed those up with three *Wanted* posters. "Just so you know what you're getting involved in."

Vaccaro tapped one of the glossy photos. "Errol Abrego, Psycho I." His fingers moved to the next one. "Jose Abrego, Psycho II." With a glance he indicated the three *Wanted* posters. "The Cousins. The Guzman brothers—though at this point in time we're not sure which side of the border they're on. They're all bad news and should be considered armed and extremely dangerous. Especially The Cousins. They're wanted for a wide range of crimes, including murder."

"They're drug dealers?" Savannah asked.

"More like enforcers and lieutenants."

The captain's comment about this somehow involving Vice stirred in Savannah's thoughts. "Is Vice working this?"

Vaccaro and Kelleher shared a look. "No," Vaccaro said. "They're out of the loop."

"Why?"

Another glance between the two Feds then Vaccaro shrugged. "The couple of times an informant has lived long enough to get something to us about the Abrego brothers, Psycho I and II have been tipped off somehow."

The earlier queasiness returned. "You think someone in Vice did it?"

"Could be coincidence," Vaccaro said, his tone telling Savannah he didn't believe it. "And right now, we've got another angle to pursue." He glanced down at the photographs. "The Abregos are regulars at Traynor's casino. Come in a couple times a day, convert cash to chips, gamble a little while then put the rest of their chips in the vault where at some point they disappear." Vaccaro placed a final photograph on the table. "Carlos Dominguez. Lives in Mexico City and is suspected of running an operation to smuggle drugs and people across the border. So far we don't have anything on him. Plays it smart and keeps plenty of insulation between his legitimate businesses and his criminal interests. Comes to Reno once a month."

"And stays at the Easy Times?" Savannah asked.

"No. But he gambles there and always wins big. The money gets wired to an offshore account. All nice and squeaky clean. He's also married to a woman Steven Traynor went to college with. So there's a connection there." Vaccaro scooped the photographs into a pile then placed the last item from the folder on top of them.

Savannah recognized it immediately. Ricky Nowak aka The Ferret's rap sheet. Which brought them full circle as to why she was being pulled in. Not to investigate — Vaccaro and Kelleher seemed to have most of the pieces or knew what they were missing — but then she wasn't surprised by that. "So you want me to show my face, ask around and see if Ricky surfaces."

"Exactly," Vaccaro said. "You've already stumbled on the link between him and Becky Traynor. The car bomb and the search of his place say to us that he knows something. We're guessing that in addition to whatever he was trying to pass on to you, he probably knows where she is too. We need them found. Preferably alive and talking."

"What about the rest of the investigation?" Savannah asked, waving a hand over the photographs, knowing what the response was going to be but wanting a shot at the action anyway.

Kelleher and Vaccaro shared a look. Kelleher said, "You'll get glowing praise in your personnel file for assisting. Maybe enough of it to tip the scales and get you into detective work. But basically your part in this is to make contact with Ricky

Nowak and either bring him in to talk to us or, second choice, find out what he knows and pass it on. The only reason we've shared the bigger picture with you is because of your captain." Kelleher's eyes narrowed. "Apparently he has ties to your family. He insisted you know going in what you might be up against."

Kelleher began gathering the photos and putting them back in the manila folder. Savannah put her hand on the Social Services sheet with Holland's picture on it. "You've got another copy of this, right?"

"Yeah, you can take it. You can take the picture of the friend as well. For obvious reasons I can't give you the ones with the mayor in them."

Savannah pulled the photograph of Camryn to her side of the table and Kelleher added, "Same thing goes for the girls. You find them, you call us. We need to figure out what they know."

Vaccaro leaned forward, directing his comments to Draigon and Kye. "Any word about this investigation gets out and your wings get clipped nice and short by the Bureau. Trust me, you don't need that kind of grief."

The slightest tensing of the muscled thighs against her own was the only indication Draigon and Kye gave of being bothered by Vaccaro's comment.

"Savannah's safety is our only concern," Draigon said, his voice smooth and confident and sending a bolt of warmth straight to Savannah's heart. "If we find you are withholding information or purposely placing her in jeopardy by making her a target then we will seek retribution."

"I think we all understand each other, Draigon," Savannah said, putting her hand on his forearm and squeezing, frowning at seeing identical squints on Vaccaro and Kelleher's faces again.

"I will add my warning to Draigon's," Kye said, his face serious, his body posture threatening. "We don't get mad, we get even."

Kelleher shook his head and abruptly got to his feet. "We'll be in touch," he said, pulling out a wallet and tossing several bills on the table next to his empty coffee cup, then taking out a business card and writing on the back before handing it to Savannah. "Call the cell number right away if Nowak makes contact or if you find the girls."

Vaccaro also stood, still squinting. He dropped some cash on the table and handed Savannah a card with a number already scribbled at the bottom. "Same instructions as Kelleher's. Call me even if you've called him. Only call me at least once a day to check in, more often if you hear anything useful."

She pocketed the cards as the two left, then turned to Kye. "We don't get mad, we get even? Not exactly the kind of words you want to throw at Feds."

Kye grinned. "I have grown fond of the saying. Perhaps it will become the motto of our house."

A waitress stopped next to the table before Savannah could completely wrap her mind around the *our house* bit.

"Can I get you something?" the waitress asked, putting the cash Vaccaro and Kelleher had left to cover their coffee on her tray.

Kye removed a fifty-dollar bill from his pocket as she reached for the dirty dishes. "I would like to take these two cups with me, in separate take-out containers, please.

The waitress stared for a long second. Then blinked. Processing the request and the fifty dollars being offered to her. "Be right back," she said.

Savannah held her laughter until the waitress had disappeared into the kitchen. "Now she's seen it all. Exactly what do you think you're going to find on Kelleher and

Vaccaro's coffee cups? Evidence of drug use? Fingerprints that tell us they're the bad guys impersonating the good guys?"

"I want to make sure I know who I am dealing with," Kye said, leaning over, lightly nipping the place where he'd marked her neck.

Draigon's forearm tensed against her palm, making Savannah's heart swell and her thoughts return to her earlier conclusion about him feeling like the odd man out. She squeezed his arm again and leaned into him when Kye straightened away from her. She brushed her lips against Draigon's cheek, inhaling the masculine scent of him and becoming aroused in the process. "It might be hell on my career, but that was sweet of you to threaten a couple of Feds on my behalf," she said then laughed, giving him another light kiss.

Heat moved through Draigon. Flowing from the place where her lips had touched his skin and traveling downward, piercing his heart on the way to his cock.

For an instant he was paralyzed, held in place by her first display of affection. Her teasing. The emotions raging inside him a stark contrast to the frozen stillness of his body. Only breaking free when there was no way to contain them.

He turned his head, his mouth meeting hers in a searing kiss that was only the beginning of all they would share.

Savannah melted against him, opened her mouth under the pressure of his. Draigon's need obliterating the awareness of anything but him.

His body vibrated with unspoken words and feelings so intense it seemed like a silent primal scream from the soul, and she responded to it. The hand resting on his forearm traveling to his chest, capturing the fierce, fast rush of his heart against her palm. The fingers of her other hand going to his hair, freeing it of the tie holding it in place, then spreading the luxurious strands of golden-red across his back and shoulders.

Savannah groaned and moved closer, undone by more than just the bold dueling of his tongue with hers. Undone by the depth of his desire and her own answering rush of need.

In the periphery of her consciousness she registered the waitress's return. But the press of firm masculine lips to hers, the slide of his tongue against hers, the feel of Draigon's hand on her side, burning through her thin top and tormenting her with its nearness to her breast, were too wonderful to pull away from.

Only the need for breath ended the kiss. And even then it was followed by a quick press of lips. A silent promise for later.

Savannah's laugh was husky, her nipples visible points when she sat back in her seat, her eyes dancing with mischief as some of the heat faded. "I should have known. The brooding, silent ones are always powder kegs just waiting for a spark to ignite them."

Draigon's eyebrows drew together in confusion and dismay. Did she think him brooding? Did she think he was shy and needing of assistance when it came to coupling and mating?

He pulled her to him, this time holding her so that her luscious breasts were flattened against his chest, her nipples hard against him, their presence sending a current of lust straight to his cock as his mouth captured hers, as his tongue pillaged and dominated, communicated his desire and also his ability to pleasure her.

They were both panting when they separated, and yet satisfaction roared through Draigon at her flushed features, at her stunned silence. He was beginning to think his bond-mate was rarely left speechless and it pleased him that he had managed it.

This time when she smiled and laughed, her happiness poured into him, though her comment about waiting until they got home before stirring up a hornet's nest made no sense to Draigon until Kye's thoughts touched his with a picture. Kye's voice also holding amusement when he said, *The people on this planet have an amazing number of interesting sayings, Savannah more than most.* And as if to prove his point, Kye focused his attention on Savannah. "Shall we hit the road?"

"Yeah, let's hit it before the Wingman and I get arrested for having sex in public."

The nickname jolted Draigon. Did the name she was bestowing mean she saw hints of his true form? "Wingman?"

Savannah's eyebrows drew together at the tone of his voice. Hope and confusion, a questioning, as though the nickname was important to him. And for an instant she wondered why she'd called him that—then again, nicknames had always just come to her out of the blue. Her subconscious picking up on something maybe. She'd never stopped to analyze it.

She was terrible with given names, so she usually just went with the flow. But Wingman? Where had that come from? She wasn't a pilot and at the first glimpse of a war movie, she was history. Then again, Draigon's kiss had sent her soaring.

"Flyboy works too," she said, teasing him, watching as his aristocratic nose tightened and he returned to brooding silence, making her laugh and relent. "Wingman it is then. Let's get out of here and see if we can hunt down The Ferret or the girls."

They rose, Kye scooping up the two takeout containers, each labeled to reflect who had drunk from the coffee cups they contained. He had little doubt that the Council scientists would find traces of the Fallon in Kelleher and Vaccaro. It made the thought of leaving Draigon and Savannah alone after they'd finished their business in town acceptable, even palatable. To be able to offer hope to the women of Belizair...

* * * * *

Primitive. And ugly. Even more so than some of the establishments found in the Kotaka Gaming Sector, Draigon thought as he followed in Savannah's wake, moving through yet another crowded, garish casino. Both he and Kye remaining in the background, guarding, protecting and yet never allowing too much distance between Savannah and them.

Draigon maneuvered around a bank of slot machines, glad Savannah was away from the streets and alleyways, pawn shops and rundown tenements where she had spent a large part of the day cornering oily, shiftless men and women whose behavior advertised that their compliance and cooperation could be had for a small price and with no questions asked.

He had known Earth was a backwater planet, though the view from the cabin had surprised him with its beauty. But now, surrounded, bombarded by noise, crowded, contained in a building which did not welcome either fresh air or sunshine, Draigon could not wait to finish this business of claiming Savannah and return to Belizair, though it was a task he no longer believed would be accomplished easily or quickly. Savannah was as driven as any bounty hunter and yet rather than put him off, he found he was pleased by her fire and determination.

Jeqon had told him that Adan was completely enamored by his human bond-mate even though Krista had led him on a wild, emotional chase. Draigon already felt the same about Savannah.

A day spent watching her work, seeing her skill and strength, her intelligence and integrity, as well as admiring her curves, the movement of her body, her voice—all of it left him enthralled. Hot and hard and anxious to mount her, to sheathe his cock in her tight wet channel and claim her body, to spill his seed as he brought her to orgasm.

He sifted his stance, surreptitiously tugging at his pants, concluding as he did so that human cocks must be smaller

139

than those of his race. He had been on Earth for less than a day and he already hated the clothing he was forced to wear. The tightness of it over his erection was a constant source of irritation. An irritation that blossomed into a silent snarl when Savannah altered her course and joined a man at the casino bar.

Who is he? Draigon sent to Kye, anger filling Draigon when the human male smiled at Savannah in way that clearly showed his intention to seduce her.

I do not know, Kye growled, both of them moving closer. Kye positioning himself in front of a slot machine and feeding tokens into it. Draigon entering the bar and taking a seat in a booth, only to be immediately joined by a large-breasted woman who smelled of sex and heavy perfume. Who tried to crowd him against the wall, her hand making an aggressive foray into his lap as Kye's shout of laughter sounded in his mind.

Savannah was dying to turn around and watch Draigon disentangle himself from his conquest, but she had to content herself with watching him in the mirror behind the bar. "Tell me something, Holden," her companion said, noticing her attention, though her choked laugh had clued him in to the scene in the first place. "Is long hair on a guy really that much of a turn-on? She didn't even look at me when I sat down."

"Could be because she thought *vice cop* when she saw you," Savannah said, meeting Fowler's eyes in the mirror. "What are you doing in here anyway?"

"I could ask the same about you. Seems like every place I've gone today I've heard you were there asking about Ricky Nowak and a couple of those girls you hauled in the other day. What gives? I thought you were on vacation. I also thought you were trying to stay below the radar screen until things die down in Vice. Like I said before, you want to work Vice, I'll put in a word for you. Hell, I could even offer to help show you the ropes."

His voiced dropped with the last sentence, making it sound intimate, and Savannah's nipples tightened despite the fact she wasn't interested in him, not now anyway. Fowler's eyes flickered to her chest in a subtle move and he smiled, a GQ flash of teeth that might have turned her into a puddle at his feet if her sex drive wasn't already keyed to Kye—and after the kiss in the coffee shop, to Draigon.

She forced her attention back to Draigon's attempts to free himself from the blonde, noticing his scowl and harsh expression seemed to be cooling the woman's interest. Poor guy, he looked like he might explode and she got the impression some of it had to do with her being with Fowler.

Savannah grinned. Yeah. The silent ones were always the ones to watch.

"Hey, Holden, you're not doing anything for my ego," Fowler said, drawing her attention back to him. "Besides, I thought I heard one of the guys in the department say you had a dark-haired pretty-boy with you over at Nowak's apartment. A bounty hunter who acted like a boyfriend."

"You can name names. I take it Creech and Mastrin are still gunning for me?" She wondered if the names Abrego, Guzman or Carlos Dominguez would ring any bells with them then shut the thought off. There was no proof there was a leak in Vice.

Fowler shrugged. "You know how they are. So what gives? How come you're looking for Ricky Nowak?"

Savannah toyed with a stack of cocktail napkins on the bar. She was pretty sure Fowler had already heard it from Creech and Mastrin, so she didn't see any harm in repeating it. "Ricky set up a meet with me, then he was a no-show."

"A meet at The Dive? The same place Nowak's car blew up?"

"That's the place."

Fowler gave a low whistle and shook his head. "You need a keeper, Holden." His eyes met hers again, smoldering with intensity this time. "Let me give you some advice. Not cop to cop. But friend to friend. Because I hope that's what you consider me. You should take your vacation time and leave Reno for a while. My gut's telling me that whatever Nowak knows is going to get him killed, and the killers are going to clean house when they take him out."

"Just your gut?" Savannah asked, figuring Vice's golden boy probably knew more than he was saying and if he could pump her for information, she could return the favor.

"Just my gut. Whatever Mastrin and Creech have going, I don't know the details. Only that they caught you at Ricky Nowak's place after it had been trashed and they're working a case involving some underage girls, one of which you've taken an interest in." He shook his head. "You've been a cop long enough to know better than to get emotionally involved. I'm assuming that's why you're asking around after the girls."

The picture of Holland's face, her eyes tightly closed in the photograph, joined the images Savannah had from the day she'd hauled the girls and the pervert down to the station. "I don't think it's too late for one of them."

"I'm going to kick myself for encouraging you. Which one?"

"The thirteen-year-old. Holland." Savannah pulled the folded page from the Social Services' file out of her pocket and showed it to Fowler.

"I'll keep an eye out for her." He checked his watch. "I've got some time before I'm meeting a snitch. You want to grab something to eat?"

Savannah's stomach growled at the mention of food. "No, thanks, I'm going to pick up some takeout from Bert's."

Fowler laughed. "One meal from that place and I have to go to the gym for a couple of hours." He rose from the stool and placed his hand on her shoulder. "I mean it, Holden, take a vacation. Get out of town and think about putting in for Vice when you get back." The GQ smile flashed, his eyelids dropped. "You're a beautiful woman and I don't want to see you get hurt in whatever Nowak's got going."

"Thanks," she said and watched him walk away as she replayed the conversation, revisited the smiles, the serious eye contact, the touches—and had to laugh. Men. Some of them were just programmed to compete, though with his looks she wouldn't have pegged Fowler for the type. Then again, maybe the blonde ignoring him and going for Draigon had tweaked his ego. Maybe the knowledge she went for long-haired guys had made her a challenge.

A week ago she might have felt the heat between them, but right now she had enough on her plate. Her gaze went to Draigon who was alone but still looked wound up, then to Kye who had emerged from somewhere and didn't look happy about her encounter with Fowler. Oh yeah, she had enough testosterone on her plate if their expressions were anything to go by.

Chapter Twelve

ဢ

Savannah left the bar and headed for Bert's, a hole-in-the-wall bar and grill within walking distance of the glitz but a world away in ambiance. It was a cheap place favored by prostitutes and down-on-their-luck chronic gamblers.

If she was just looking for information, she would have hit it first, but she'd saved it for last on the off chance word would travel fast and The Ferret might show up or get a message to her. They'd met at Bert's a couple of times, accidentally. Joked about it a few more times—how it was one of the things that told him she was okay for a cop, because she would detour to Bert's just to buy the fried chicken there.

It was a good place and a good way to end the working day—not that she had a lot to show for it, but she figured she'd stirred up enough shit. Now she had to give it time to land and hope someone would step forward and come clean—metaphorically speaking.

It bothered her that she hadn't found a trace of Holland, her sister Ivy, or the friend, Camryn. Then again, maybe they were on their way back to Vegas.

Savannah's eyebrows drew together as she replayed the conversation with Kelleher to make sure she'd gotten it right. Yeah, he'd said the three girls had come up from Vegas about six months ago. She wondered why—not that Reno wasn't full of action, but it wasn't Vegas.

Damn, she should have asked Fowler if he would give her a contact name in the Vegas PD. He'd only been the golden boy of Vice in Reno for a little under a year. Before that he'd been in Vegas. She made a mental note to hunt him down if she didn't get any leads on the girls soon.

Savannah walked into Bert's and found the place empty except for a stubble-jawed man behind the counter. Bert himself.

"The usual?" Bert asked, straightening the grease-spattered white apron covering a T-shirt that wasn't in much better shape.

"Better triple it." Savannah's stomach growled and her mouth watered. All of a sudden it seemed like way too much time had passed since she fixed breakfast for Kye.

Bert nodded and turned, poking and prodding, selecting pieces that were precooked and throwing them on the grill for some extra heat before dropping them into a large take-out container.

"You hear anything interesting lately?" Savannah asked.

Bert grunted. "Lot of people are suddenly looking for Ricky Nowak. Including you."

"You got names, besides mine?"

"Some cop names, but you'd know about that."

"Vice cops?"

"Maybe."

"Creech and Mastrin?"

"I'm not naming names."

"Anybody else?"

"Some other names, foreign, but I make a point of forgetting them as soon as I hear them."

"Abrego?" Savannah asked, thinking about the men who served as lieutenants for Carlos Dominguez, the two brothers Vaccaro had dubbed Psycho I and Psycho II.

Bert shrugged. "Like I said, I don't remember them. I don't want to remember them. Remembering can be bad for your health and I got a business to run, a family to worry about."

"You hear from Ricky Nowak lately?"

"No." Bert closed up the carton of chicken and placed it in a bag. "You want biscuits and coleslaw?"

"Sure."

He got out another carton and started scooping coleslaw into it.

"You remember that tip you gave me, about the underage working girls?" Savannah asked, straightening when she saw his hands shake. Not much. But enough for intuition to kick in. "Ricky tell you about them?"

Bert didn't answer either question. "You going to want drinks with this?"

"Maybe. One of the underage girls is missing. So are her sister and her sister's friend." Savannah pulled out the folded Social Services sheet and a now dog-eared photograph of Camryn. "You recognize them?"

Bert's shoulders slumped in defeat. "Look, all I know is what Ricky asked me to pass on to you. Okay? I don't know anything else. I don't want to know anything else. Now do you want drinks with this stuff?"

Savannah grinned, thinking the puzzle pieces were starting to look like they could all be found in one box. A box named Ricky *The Ferret* Nowak. "Sure, three of them. Diet Coke for me, hold up on the other two for a second." She went to the door and stepped outside, spotted Kye leaning against the corner in the alley next to Bert's. "Might as well eat in here," she told him, thinking it was possible Ricky might show up, and besides being really hungry, if they sat toward the back, no one could see them from the street, which made it safe enough and a hell of a lot less cramped than waiting and eating in the cab of her truck on the way back to the cabin.

Kye joined her before she paid for the food and insisted on doing it. Draigon came in a moment later and they claimed a table. Savannah had to hand it to them, they'd stayed close, guarding her as they'd promised, but they'd given her enough room so none of the people she'd questioned seemed aware Draigon and Kye were with her.

"I did not like seeing that man in the bar touching you," Draigon said. "He desires you."

Savannah looked up though she continued to remove the food containers from the bag and place them on the table. "I'm not sure about the desire part, but Fowler is my one friend in Vice." She laughed, unable to stop herself. "And I'm surprised you could see anything with the blonde plastered on you. I thought she was going to have a screaming orgasm just rubbing against you."

Draigon stiffened and she felt guilty for teasing him. Poor guy. He really needed to lighten up. She reached into the carton containing the chicken, her gaze shifting to meet Kye's. "Breast or drumstick?"

Kye didn't disappoint her. He smiled, a lecherous parody of masculine appreciation as his attention went to the front of her shirt and the outline of her nipples, hardened now that her mind was veering away from the case and moving toward all the things that might happen when she got back to the cabin with her self-appointed bodyguards. "Breast," he said, putting so much emphasis on the word Savannah's cunt clenched.

She handed him a piece of chicken, then asked Draigon, "What about you?"

His eyes were on the front of her shirt, too, his face tense, his focus so extreme her nipples tightened further into hard, painful knots. "I will take a breast as well." His gaze lifted. "The woman who accosted me was a nuisance I tried to handle without drawing attention to myself. Had you been in danger, she would not have deterred me from protecting you."

Savannah reached over and touched his hand, brushed her fingertips across the wristband with its oddly swirling gold-flecked red stones and intricate etchings of something that looked like — she squinted — a phoenix? It made her smile. He was such a contradiction. She met his eyes. "I was just

147

teasing you. I know you would have been right there if I needed help."

She pulled her hand back and placed the chicken on his plate, then selected a drumstick for herself, filling them in on what little she'd learned asking about The Ferret and showing the pictures of the girls. Ending by saying, "I'm game to call it a day now since I made a point of saying I'd be back around tomorrow. Who knows where The Ferret is holed up and how long it'll take for him to surface. He will. That's what my gut tells me and it makes sense considering he's the one who sent me the chips—" She shrugged. "I've done what I can do for today."

Savannah polished off a second drumstick and took a wing as Kye and Draigon were reaching for another breast, but where Kye dug into his food immediately, Draigon seemed unable to look away from the piece she was working on. "What?" she finally said, wondering at the expression on his face, a mix of curiosity and horror as she licked her fingers clean. "Haven't you ever seen anyone eat the wing before?"

Draigon shuddered slightly despite the delicious taste of the food. Like most on Belizair, he ate little meat when he was home. But when he was on other worlds, his diet more often included it—and yet he rarely chose to eat creatures with wings. Until she pulled the wing out of the bucket, he had not known what manner of beast they were eating.

"What is this food called?" he asked, realizing by Savannah's startled expression that he should have put his pride aside and asked Kye directly.

"Chicken," Kye said, straight-faced, though his voice carried a hint of amusement at Draigon's expense.

With the word came an image. Not from Kye, but from Draigon's memory, from the material he had studied before leaving Belizair. A study he was coming to think had been far too brief, one limited by time and covering only the most rudimentary information.

Draigon shifted uneasily in the chair. Torn between the desire to take another bite of the chicken breast still in his hand or to set it aside. Aware that Kye and Savannah were both studying him intently.

"Haven't you ever eaten chicken before?" Savannah asked.

"No."

Her eyebrows lifted. Her expression showed her curiosity. But before she could question him further, Kye redirected her thoughts, saying, "Where we are from, some have an...allergy...to eating anything winged and feathered."

Immediately Savannah's face flooded with worry, filling Draigon's chest with incredible warmth. "Are you feeling okay?" she asked.

"I am fine. The food is fine." He took another bite of chicken to prove the truth of his words.

Savannah's attention remained on him for long moments and her concern burned a path straight to his heart. When she finally reached for another piece, a leg this time, Draigon relaxed, glad his moments of ignorance could be set aside and forgotten.

"Bert makes the best chicken in Reno. Except for my grandmother's of course. Nobody does fried better than Grams." A smile played over Savannah's lips and Draigon found he could now read her intent to tease. "When this investigation is done, I'll swing by the ranch and have Grams cook up some Prairie Oysters for you guys. They're a real treat and Grams has a recipe that's been passed down for generations." Savannah paused a heartbeat, long enough for Kye and Draigon's thoughts to merge as they tried to interpret how oysters could be found on the prairie. Then apparently satisfied by whatever she read in their expressions, Savannah said, "Of course, it might mean you guys will need to stick around for awhile. Until it's time to castrate the bulls. Though I guess if Grams is only cooking for a few people I could probably get permission to go ahead and round up some of the stock and cut them ahead of time. If you're interested in playing cowboy, you could even help."

It wasn't necessary for Draigon to touch his thoughts to Kye's in order to feel the other man's horror. Both of them stiffened in their seats, their legs closing automatically, as though protecting their own testicles.

Primitive, Draigon said. *Like the Ewellians who eat the hearts from certain water beasts in order to gain courage.* To Savannah he said, "I have no need to eat the testicles of bulls in order to become aroused or gain stamina. You will not find me lacking when I claim you for a bond-mate."

Savannah blinked, surprise bursting through her followed by laughter so hard she had to wipe tears from her eyes. God, if she didn't know better she'd think Draigon was from another planet. He must not get around very much. Even his speech was so…Old World. Formal.

"Eating bull testicles probably did start out as a superstition," she conceded when she could stop laughing. "But that was a long time ago. Now they're considered a delicacy by some and a tradition by others. And really, they're good. Especially the way Grams cooks them. Sliced nice and thin, coated in wine and hot sauce and rolled up in cornmeal and flour, then…"

She grinned, deciding from Kye and Draigon's alarmed, slightly queasy expressions that she'd had enough fun—for now. Also deciding to leave Draigon's comment about claiming her alone, even though her body was humming with interest.

Savannah surveyed the empty food containers on the table. "Guess we might as well head back to the cabin. Our work here appears to be done."

The men stood and helped her dispose of the trash. Then after a brief consultation, they decided to continue as they had been doing since leaving the truck in a secure parking garage. They separated so Savannah would appear to be alone.

Draigon and Kye left together. Savannah hovered near the front door, waiting for them to get far enough away to split up.

"You got a number Ricky can reach you at?" Bert asked, looking up from a magazine he was reading behind the cash register.

Savannah hesitated. Considered her options. She didn't want to believe there were bad Reno cops involved, but finding out The Ferret was linked to both the money laundering and the blackmail scheme was making her a little paranoid.

She had to wonder about the hang-ups on her voice mail at the station. Had to think some of those calls were from Ricky, maybe too afraid to leave a message because he wasn't sure who was checking them — which would explain why he'd sent the casino chips but no note. Hell, for all she knew, he hadn't counted on his prints being lifted and run. She frowned, feeling the paranoia form a tight ball in her stomach as she remembered the captain's comment the day she'd been in his office. *Just to be on the safe side, use a pay phone. And don't use the same one twice.* She'd taken his order at face value, considered it a reasonable precaution. But now she wondered if he'd already gotten wind of something. And maybe knew more than he was letting on. Maybe it was more than a gut feel that had caused him to say, *Something's going on over in Vice, besides you stepping on toes and pissing people off. So watch your back there too.*

Cell phones were traceable but tracing them left a trail. If Mastrin and Creech — She stopped herself. They were innocent until proven guilty. Yeah. She didn't like them. Bad chemistry. A bad start. Whatever. They'd just rubbed each other the wrong way from the very start.

Creech because she'd pulled him over and ticketed him for speeding before she found out he was Vice. Not that she would have let him go. He was doing forty in a twenty-five-mile-per-hour zone.

Mastrin because she'd broken up a bar fight he was in and hauled him to the station in the backseat of her patrol car along with the guy he'd been fighting, only to find out Mastrin was undercover. But hell, that actually worked to his benefit, made him look legit. And *she* should have gotten a pat on the back—or an apology—for the trash talk she'd had to put up with from him.

"Well?" Bert prompted.

Shit. It was a risk. But she could spend days trolling dives and casinos and wandering the street waiting for The Ferret to feel brave enough to approach her. She gave Bert a phone number. "That's my cell. If Ricky contacts you, pass it on. Otherwise forget you have it. Okay?"

"It's already starting to slip my mind."

Savannah nodded and left the building. She didn't expect trouble but she still checked out the street, noted the people on it then walked with purpose and awareness toward the part of town where they'd stashed the truck.

Four blocks later and she was in an area with seedy bars boasting lap dances, cheap drinks and a blind eye toward whatever was happening at the tables. Savannah slowed, tempted to linger, to stop and flash the pictures of Holland and Camryn for a second time in one day, to ask around again about The Ferret, but before the idea took hold, a car with dealer plates jerked to a stop next to her. Two men spilling out even as she was already going for her gun. Recognition instant though their *Wanted* pictures had been grainy.

They were on Savannah before she could bring the gun up.

The first one slapping her across the face with enough force to tumble her backward to the concrete.

The second Guzman brother kicking her forearm so the gun skittered away.

"Yo bitch, you've got your nose in business where it doesn't belong," a third, the driver, said, leg going back, ready to deliver a kick to her head.

But before he could say more, before any of them could do more, Kye and Draigon were there, coming out of nowhere, their fury scorching and vibrating the air. The sound of violence filling it as Savannah rolled over and scrambled for her gun.

Do not kill him! You will be detained, Kye shouted in Draigon's mind, stilling him as he very nearly used his superior strength to break the neck of the man who'd dared to strike Savannah.

With a growl, Draigon wrenched the attacker's arms behind his back, using the *bouren* tie from his hair for the purpose it had been created — to restrain law-breakers. Took a gun and a knife from his sullen prisoner, then moved to the driver, still unconscious from the blows both he and Kye had delivered.

Draigon removed the unconscious man's weapons then shifted his attention to Savannah, fury roaring though him at the reddened mark on her face, relief mixing with pride as he took in her steady, confident stance, her gun trained on the man Kye had subdued.

"Thanks for the save," she said, retrieving a plastic flexi cuff from her pocket and tossing it to Kye.

"Do you have another restraint?" he asked, glancing to where Draigon hovered over the downed driver.

Savannah shook her head then spoke into her cell phone.

The man Draigon stood over stirred, moaned, and Draigon found himself wishing the assailant would regain consciousness and take up the fight again. Even with the danger past, Draigon still wanted to kill these men. And the savagery of his emotions made him uneasy. The quickness in which he had broken Council law, used the Ylan stones to close the distance between himself and Savannah, unsettled him.

Draigon took a deep breath. It was done. And should word get back to the Council, he would stand before them in their judgment chamber and defend his actions.

Just as Lyan d'Vesti has done numerous times.

The thought was unwelcome, disquieting, and Draigon pushed it aside in favor of focusing his attention on their prisoners.

Savannah retrieved Vaccaro's business card. The local cops would probably wonder how the FBI had gotten on the scene so quickly—then again, he might just wait for the Guzman brothers to get to the station. Their *wanted* status gave him jurisdiction and a way to question them.

"You give your report yet?" Vaccaro asked when she finished updating him.

"No." She heard sirens. "I've got about thirty seconds before I have to say anything."

"Okay. Keep your explanations short and simple. You don't know who they are. You don't know why they attacked you. And don't mention either my name or Kelleher's."

Savannah rolled her eyes at the unnecessary warning. "And in exchange for my silence you'll share whatever you learn from The Cousins, right?"

Vaccaro made a sound. Choked laugh or strangled groan. Without seeing his face, Savannah couldn't be sure which. "I'll be in touch," he said and hung up.

Savannah put the phone away, grinning at Kye and Draigon. Still amazed and awed at how quickly they had gotten to her and subdued all three men.

"You guys can guard my body any time, anywhere," she said, her nipples and cunt tightening when their eyes flared, conveying just how intimately and thoroughly they intended to possess and guard her body.

Patrol cars began arriving on the scene and she braced herself for the endless questions and answers. "Let the fun begin."

Time slowed to an almost unbearable crawl for Draigon and he quickly came to appreciate Kye's intervention. Had he killed the human... He breathed a sigh of relief when Savannah finally said, "Let's hit it." The saying making sense to Draigon for the first time. Between the assault on his bond-mate, the repetition of going over the events and the tight Earth clothing, he did indeed feel like hitting something!

Kye pulled Savannah into his arms and covered her mouth with his as soon as they returned to the truck. The fierceness of his grip and the savageness of his kiss communicated his feelings about the attack. He could not lose her!

He shuddered, reluctant to pull away. And yet he knew that he must.

I will take the DNA samples to the scientists in San Francisco, he said to Draigon.

To Savannah he said, "Draigon will remain with you. I have errands to run, including getting us a new vehicle for these trips to town."

Their eyes met. Heat moving between them.

"You'll be back tonight?" Savannah asked, her cunt lips swelling, moistening at the thought of being alone with Draigon. Her clit stiffening at the thought of Kye joining them later.

"Yes," Kye said, his voice a husky promise.

Chapter Thirteen

სი

Determination filled Draigon. Bolstered by the attack, by his own conviction Earth was a primitive, dangerous planet. Reinforced by the unrelenting stiffness of his cock and the terror of losing Savannah.

When they arrived at the cabin, he would use his body to prove she both belonged to him and needed him, to convince her to return home with him. He would pound into her until she agreed to a binding ceremony, until she accepted the wristband he had crafted for her.

Draigon tightened his grip on her hand until she sounded a protest, his heart raging when she said, "You're too wound up, Wingman. You need to relax, blow off some steam, let it go. I'm not sure you're cut out for bodyguarding duty."

His foot shifted to the brake, bringing them to an abrupt halt on the dirt road leading to the cabin. "I cannot tolerate your being in danger," he said, and immediately knew it was the wrong thing to say at this point in their courtship.

Savannah's eyes flashed then narrowed with temper, her body stiffened as she tried to pull her hand from his. "I'm a cop, Draigon. Danger comes with the territory. Same as it comes with being a bounty hunter. I hope you're not going to tell me what's okay for a man isn't okay for a woman."

A muscle spasmed in his cheek. By all that was holy to the Amato, he wanted to lay down the law, to tell her she was too important to risk, that on Belizair she would be safe, free to explore and make friends among the other human women while they awaited the birth of children, to...

A fresh fear rippled through his stomach. Some of his earlier confidence giving way to doubt with the realization at how difficult the task ahead truly was. She would never be content with such a life. Even on such short acquaintance he could see her body vibrated with energy while her mind raced, looking for puzzles to solve and observing the world around her, all in readiness to right any wrong she might find.

Draigon pushed the thoughts away and forced a deep breath into his lungs. He needed to concentrate on the immediate task at hand. One his cock was well prepared to handle.

A small measure of peace returned to him as he recalled Jeqon's words and reminded himself that even Adan—and Lyan, a man not troubled by boundaries—had struggled to claim their bond-mate.

Draigon brought her hand to his lips and pressed a kiss to it. "I do not wish to argue with you, Savannah. This is the first opportunity we have had to be alone as you and Kye have been alone."

Her body softened, the anger leaving her face to be replaced by the teasing smile Draigon was coming to both love and dread. His heart raced in his chest when she closed the distance between them. "Still waters run deep," she said, making him want to laugh and yet protest at the same time. But he could only groan when her finger brushed across his bottom lip as she whispered, "I don't want to argue with you either."

Savannah's tongue traced the seam of his lips and Draigon was lost, assaulted by emotion and desire. His thoughts dissolving under wave after wave of need. Not just the needs of the body for release, but the hunger of the heart, the craving of the soul. For a future. A home that was more than walls of crystal.

"Savannah," he said when the kiss ended, realizing as he did so that his hand had gone to her breast, was even now cupping it, pressing the hardened nipple against his palm.

She laughed, a sound that had his cock pulsing and jerking, his eyes lowering to her chest, his breath coming in shallow, rapid pants as she freed her hand from his and began unbuttoning the front of her shirt, slowly revealing curves and lightly tanned flesh. Making it impossible for him to look away.

Savannah couldn't help herself. It was like taking a dare and climbing onto a bronc or a bull. Like standing on the bare back of a horse and urging it into a canter. There was something about Draigon that made her want to be reckless, as though her own recklessness would free the man from the control and restraint he imposed on himself.

She grinned. Or maybe it was just the heated look on his face. The hooded desire, with just a touch of longing, like a boy standing in front of a store window and wanting what was displayed there.

Not that she would ever consider him a child. He was all man. Hard and fierce. Strong. Utterly and completely masculine.

She opened the front clasp of her bra and the flimsy material pulled back, one side falling away from her breast to expose a nipple already puckered, aching for the feel of Draigon's lips.

Her cunt spasmed and clenched at the way his nostrils flared and his eyes darkened with lust. She moaned when he lifted his hand just enough so the other bra cup could fall free, so flesh could touch flesh, a calloused palm first and then fingers, grasping, rolling, squeezing and tugging, exploring as he watched, his attention completely focused on her, on learning what she liked, how to please her. His face showing his satisfaction when she whimpered and arched into his touch, when suddenly it wasn't enough and her hand dropped to her lap, unbuttoning her jeans and jerking the zipper down so her fingers could slip inside.

"By the Goddess, you undo me," he said, his expression so hungry Savannah tangled her fingers in his hair and tugged, whispered, "Put your mouth on me."

He complied with a groan, going willingly to her breast, his mouth and tongue rough, wet, teasing over the taut nipple and feverish flesh when she wanted firm sucks and nearly painful bites. She pushed against him, writhed, tried to make him clamp down, but he resisted until she began begging, his name filling the cab of the truck, turning into moans when he suckled as though he would pull every ounce of pleasure from her body, as though he would pull her very soul into his own.

She leaned back against the passenger door, taking him with her, moaning as his hand pushed hers aside, as he fought the awkward angle and the tightness of her jeans so his palm could slide along her pubic down, his fingers reaching wet arousal and flushed, swollen cunt lips.

"Draigon," she whimpered, widening her legs, shifting, tilting her pelvis so his slick fingers could enter her, could torment her as she imagined what it would be like when his cock filled her. "Harder," she begged. "More." And he groaned, repositioned himself, putting more of his weight on her as his mouth covered hers and his fingers pumped into her, his palm striking her clit and sending pleasure through her with a jolt that nearly tumbled them both to the floor.

It took a moment for the haze of desire to lift, for Savannah's sense of humor to rush in as she realized the truck was tilting at an odd angle. And then tenderness flooded her at the embarrassment staining Draigon's cheeks for having forgotten to set the brake or put the engine in park.

He sat up stiffly. His damaged pride a wound that made her ache.

She scrambled to his side, pressing her lips to his cheek, her hand to his chest. Stroking him. "You can rock my world anytime," she said, blurting out the first thing that came to mind, immediately grimacing as she looked at the boulder now kissing the bumper of the Chevy, preventing it from traveling further down the hill.

Her words landed. Leaving Draigon stunned. And then the laughter came. Forced out of him from deep within and expanding until tears flowed down his cheeks.

Never had he found such amusement in one of his own errors, in his own carelessness and lack of control. But Savannah's easy humor took the sting of his failure away and replaced it with a memory that would no doubt be used against him in the future—and yet even the prospect of being teased about this event filled him with happiness rather than dread. Connection instead of alienation. Savannah's laughter adding to his own joy.

When the laughter ended Savannah brushed her lips against his. "I like you like this. All loosened up with a sense of humor and some macho he-man thrown in just to keep me on my toes."

Draigon closed the nearly invisible distance between their lips, his tongue stroking into her mouth, caressing, a tender communication more poignant than words, a coming together that left them lost in their own world for long moments.

Her lips were swollen when he pulled away, her eyes half-closed, her face reflecting hunger and yet peace as well, comfort. With him. With the intimacy they would soon share. He kissed her once again, this time hard and quick, and then he turned his attention to maneuvering the primitive vehicle back on to the road.

Savannah was torn between getting down and dirty or getting naked and clean as Draigon slammed to a halt in front of the cabin. She climbed out of the truck but before she took a step he was there, standing in front of her in all his masculine glory.

She gave him the once-over, her gaze lingering on the impressive erection pressing against the front of his jeans, and she couldn't suppress a snicker. Couldn't resist saying, "What do you think, you *up* for the hot tub?"

He wasn't as quick as Kye in *getting it*. There was a fleeting frown—confirming what Savannah had concluded earlier, that Draigon must not get away from his insular community very often—then a glimmer of masculine understanding. A heated look as he took her hand and placed it over his erection. "Whenever you are near I am always *up* for whatever will please you," he said, his voice deep and husky and flooding her panties with arousal.

She laughed and rubbed her palm up and down his jeans-covered cock, reveling in the way his face immediately tightened with desire, his focus on her so complete he made her feel as though she was the only woman in the world for him. "Let's do it," she said and this time his response was immediate, confident, an echo of her own words. "Yes, let's do it."

They left a trail of clothing around the side of the cabin as Savannah led him to the hot tub her brothers and cousins had built, the water heating automatically with the aid of energy derived from solar panels, the tub actually "sunken" since the guys had built a small deck around its rim. *So all we have to do once the babes are primed is to roll them out and climb on top,* one of her cousins told her the first time she'd seen what they'd done to the line shack.

Not that she was any better. She'd filled the tub with water this morning in preparation for a little action with Kye after they got back from town.

Her gaze slid down Draigon's rock-hard body, finding it every bit as arousing as Kye's. Her smile growing more sultry when his cock bobbed in greeting. She couldn't say she was sorry it was just the two of them—for now, for this first time together.

Draigon stood still under Savannah's scrutiny. His gaze traveling over her naked form. By the Goddess, her beauty nearly blinded him. Had he once thought humans were less? Unblessed because they didn't have wings?

There was nothing fragile about his mate, and yet her lack of wings engendered such feelings of protectiveness in him that he couldn't bear the thought of leaving her side. No wonder the Fallon had often walked on Earth! No wonder some of them had stayed!

And while he still held the view that Earth was primitive, the thought of lingering in the hot tub—an experience not indulged in on his home world because it was difficult, if not impossible, for most to transmute their wings on Belizair—of covering his body with Savannah's, of bathing his cock in the hot depths of her cunt even as the rest of him was encased in heated water, had his penis straining, leaking, urging him to seek her welcoming sheath.

She closed the distance between them and wound her arms around his neck. His hands went to her waist, pulling her against him so flesh touched only flesh for the first time.

"If you keep looking at me like that, I'm going to go up in flames," she said, brushing her lips against his, leaving him breathless from the sheer pleasure of holding and being held by her.

"Perhaps we had better get into the water then." But he was loath to let her go even though he wanted to explore her body more thoroughly. Wanted to be in a place he could more easily couple with her.

In the truck Draigon had thought to take her immediately. To take her hard and fast. To escape the fury of his emotions by burying himself in her body. But as they slid into the hot tub and moved into each other's arms again, the world around them slowed and urged them to slow as well, to savor this first joining. To make it more than a hurried mating.

He groaned as his lips took hers, as their tongues rubbed against each other, his earlier resolve to explore her body weakening with the feel of her slick folds against his throbbing cock, of her breasts against his chest.

Draigon lifted his mouth from hers, his heart soaring with joy at the way her green eyes sparkled with so many things. Happiness. Acceptance. Anticipation. Desire.

"You have already become my world," he told her, fearing it was too soon for such a confession but unable to stop himself from giving it to her.

Surprise rippled through Savannah along with a touch of recognition, déjà vu, the conversation in the bar with Krista flooding in. Krista's question and her answer to it.

Do you still believe love can happen a few heartbeats after lust at first sight?

Yeah. I think it's possible to recognize someone you can spend your life with at the same time your hormones are in overdrive and you want to jump his body.

Oh yeah. She thought it was possible even if she wasn't ready to admit to Draigon or Kye that they'd become the embodiment of her every fantasy and she couldn't even contemplate doing without them.

Savannah speared her fingers through Draigon's hair and pulled his mouth back to hers. Telling him with a kiss, with the press of her body to his, what she wasn't yet willing to tell him in words.

Draigon allowed more of his weight to settle on Savannah, his heart thundering in his chest, the wild beat of it pulsing through his cock as his tongue delved into the wet heat of her mouth. Her unspoken message singing through him. Filling him with hope.

She enthralled him. Made him feel so many different emotions that they often overwhelmed him. Left him uncertain, unbalanced, sometimes feeling as untried as an inexperienced youth, sometimes feeling like an uncivilized barbarian.

Savannah was meant for him. As surely as if the Goddess had looked beyond Belizair and found the one who would complete him, the one who would give him what no other could. Children, yes. But they had become a joyous consequence of forming a mate-bond with Savannah and no longer the primary reason for doing so.

He shivered when her hands caressed his shoulders. Moaned when her foot caressed the back of his leg, the movement tilting her pelvis so his cock rubbed against her stiffened clitoris.

"I want you inside me," she whispered when the kiss ended, her words driving a sun-hot shaft of need from his heart to his penis.

Draigon shifted position, found the submerged bench and leaned back, pulling Savannah on top of him. His earlier fantasy of bathing his cock in the hot depths of her cunt as the rest of him was encased in heated water rushed in and only masculine pride enabled him to command rather than to beg. "Take all of me then."

She laughed, her husky laugh his only warning as she did what he'd ordered, took his penis in her hand and guided it to her entrance, slowly impaling herself on its rigid length, fucking herself on him an inch at a time, her fist limiting the depth of his penetration until he was growling, bucking, wild with need for her. Until he took control, forcing her arms around his neck as his fingers dug into her buttocks and held her into position. His mouth fusing with hers. His tongue thrusting against hers as he claimed his bond-mate, as he swallowed her screams of release and filled her with his seed, his hopes for the future. The lava-hot rush of semen only opening the floodgates to the passion he felt for her.

They lounged in the hot tub afterward, caressing, teasing, lips separating only for breath or muted conversation. Each moment forever etched into Draigon's memory.

He wanted to ask her to bond with him, to accept the band he'd crafted for her and allow him to put it around her wrist. He wanted to ask her to go home with him. But he knew it was too soon even though he was already completely lost in her.

Reluctantly he left her mouth, trailed kisses to her ear, her neck, downward, the bliss of the heated water suddenly a barrier, an impediment to what he wanted, what he needed. To taste her. To explore her. To claim her completely.

With a low growl he scooped her up and placed her on the sun-bleached cushions covering the deck, his mind rebelling at the thought other men might have been here with her, might have experienced this with her. Kye he could accept, less reluctantly now that he had seen the truth of Kye's earlier assessment, the need for two males to keep Savannah safe while she remained on Earth. But the thought of anyone else — Draigon latched on to Savannah's nipple, biting, sucking, laving. Aggressive now. Wanting to mark her. Wanting to imprint himself so thoroughly on her that she would never remember another male here with her like this.

Savannah arched into Draigon, her legs opening, splaying wantonly. Her cunt lips already flushed, parted, coated with arousal.

The memory of her cousin's words making her laugh. Oh yeah she was primed. And she wanted Draigon to roll on top of her.

She groaned in protest when his lips left her breast, when he slid lower, putting distance between his penis and her pussy.

She tangled her fingers in his hair, prepared to drag Draigon upward — until his mouth found her slit. His tongue dancing over her swollen flesh, delving into her and making her cunt clench in a desperate attempt to hold him, to pull him deeper.

His hands held her in position, prevented any possibility of escape, but she was a willing prisoner. The jerks of her hips punctuated by gasps as she tried to fuck herself on his tongue just as she'd done with his cock.

He growled and took control, used his weight and strength to hold her motionless as his tongue and lips assaulted her, alternating between thrusts and licks to her slit, to her clit. Until she was panting, writhing, screaming in release.

Satisfaction roared through Draigon as he covered Savannah's body with his own. As he pushed his cock into her, the sensation so intense he wanted to remain still, to savor it forever. He longed to be on Belizair where he could show her his true form, where he could spread his wings above them as he made love to her. But when she wrapped her limbs around him and smiled, eyes full of feminine satisfaction and desire, he gave himself up to the moment. To the need. His body pumping into hers in a dance as ancient as time, in a rhythm that had no borders, that transcended universes. Her sighs joining his groans. Her orgasm summoning his own.

Chapter Fourteen

ഇ

Concern flickered across Jeqon's face when Kye entered the scientific chambers. "There is trouble with Draigon?"

"Other than the fact he is probably coupling with Savannah at this very moment?" Kye said then grimaced, raising a hand to halt any comment by his friend. "It is not the Vesti way. But…truly, I have accepted that Savannah will belong to both Draigon and me. And if we are to remain on Earth for any period of time, it will take two men to keep her safe. I am indebted to you for arguing my case so convincingly. Had I known beforehand that Draigon was her mate by Council law, I would have held no hope at all he would accept me as a co-mate. So all goes well. Perhaps even better than expected. She accepts the idea of two mates."

"So what brings you here?"

"Hope for our women," Kye said, closing the distance between them and setting the take-out containers he'd been cradling in his arm on the table. Choosing to save time and explanation by mentally replaying the events at the coffee shop, Kelleher and Vaccaro's shielding of their eyes, their strange glances, Vaccaro's amusing threat to Draigon, to clip his wings nice and short.

Jeqon laughed, his eyes dancing. *The Baraqijal are more serious than most of the Amato. I cannot imagine Draigon was amused by the threat, especially from a human male.*

True, Draigon has not yet come to enjoy Earth and those who live here as you and I have. Speaking of others, has there been news of Lyan and Adan's progress with Krista?

They returned to Belizair today. Jeqon's eyebrows drew together. *Draigon intended to wait for their arrival. To meet Krista and tell her that Savannah would soon be joining her in Winseka. Did he not do so?*

We have not spoken of it. Kye frowned briefly then grinned, remembering Draigon's unexpected arrival on the scene just as Savannah had been demonstrating her skill with the rope. *Savannah has kept us both occupied. If it had occurred to him, I believe he would have eased his way by speaking of Krista. I think he was dumbstruck by our bond-mate.*

The grin slid into a somber expression. "I am not sure how easily we will get Savannah to agree to come home with us. She has a large family on Earth, one she is close to. I cannot see the Council, or even the others who have returned to Belizair with their human mates, being in favor of allowing those essential to our survival as a people to travel back and forth. And once there are children involved..."

Jeqon's expression grew somber. "As I have heard it said here, *Where there is a will, there is a way.* It is early yet." He turned his attention to the containers, opening the first one and retrieving it, touching Kye's mind again in order to verify that Kelleher was the strawberry-blond. *He would appeal to our women,* Jeqon said, *with wings he would look Amato.*

"I cannot think of an instance when the Fallon sequence has been found in a human male."

"There have been none, though we have tested only randomly. So far most of the women we have identified have been like Krista, only children or those who lost touch with their siblings at an early age. As far as I know, none have male relatives of interest to us."

Kye watched as Jeqon finished sampling the DNA from the mug and applied a liquid substance to it before placing it into a machine. He was anxious for the results, but he had long ago learned to refrain from asking the Council scientists for technical details. To do so was to invite a headache. "You will want to test Savannah's brothers and cousins?"

"Yes." Jeqon reached for the second carry-out container. "Perhaps there is some way you can use the task of gaining samples to your benefit when it comes to Savannah."

Kye nodded, seeing no point in denying the obvious. Other bounty hunters could be assigned, but it would make the most sense for Draigon and him to do it. And if some of Savannah's family also carried the Fallon sequence...

For the first time, he truly appreciated the good that might come of Draigon being Savannah's mate under Council law. Of Adan being Lyan's co-mate in the claiming of Savannah's friend. Both Adan's clan-house and Draigon's were old, well-respected, with many allies.

Kye left Jeqon to his work, knowing from experience it got done more quickly without distractions. He went to the large, glassed living room and stood in front of the windows, watching the sailboats and fishing boats on the bay.

There were similar bodies of water on Belizair, but neither the Vesti nor the Amato were drawn to them, not in the same way humans were. But then on Belizair, wings made many of the water sports and activities found on Earth either impossible or unpleasant. And though some along the coast caught fish as a means of livelihood, it was an expensive delicacy and not a mainstay of either the Vesti or Amato diet.

Kye tried to imagine what Savannah's reaction to his world would be, and once again felt uneasy. Before Draigon's arrival they had spent much of the morning slaughtering a wide variety of cans and paper targets with her primitive Earth weapons. And as they had done so, Savannah had spoken of her family, regaling him with tales and exploits involving cattle.

It still amazed and appalled him. This idea of using valuable resources to raise living creatures only to turn them into a food substance that fed fewer people than would have been fed if the resources had been directed otherwise. He had known it was the human way. But none of the Fallon mates he had seen to had been involved in such activities.

And yet…he had acquired a taste for the Colonel's fried chicken. And when he had followed Krista around the country, the biscuits with sausage and gravy she frequently ate had finally tempted him into trying them.

By the stars, his mouth was watering just thinking about them.

Jeqon's reflection appeared in the window, distracting Kye from thoughts of food. He turned, asking, wishing to hear the answer so clearly written on Jeqon's face. *They are descendants of the Fallon?*

Yes! Both of them, just as you predicted.

"You will tell the Council?"

"They will be informed shortly. The other scientists are duplicating my work now. When their conclusions have been reached and found to match mine, then we will take the results to Belizair and discuss how to proceed." Jeqon's face grew serious, pensive. "But we will have to tread cautiously. There is no guarantee this discovery will make a difference for our women. You will speak of this only to Draigon?"

Kye nodded. "To raise our women's hopes only to crush them would be unbearable for all of us."

"I will make sure the Council knows who is responsible for this discovery."

"Thank you."

"You will stay here for the night?" Jeqon said, his body turning, his attention beginning to drift to the activity taking place in the laboratory.

"No. I will go to the transport chamber in the Sierras and claim one of the automobiles along with additional clothing for Draigon and myself. Then I will return to Reno and see what I can do to assist with this investigation Savannah has drawn us into."

Jeqon laughed, his attention completely on Kye again. "Be careful and try not to do anything to remind the Council you are Lyan's cousin."

* * * * *

"Guess I should have put a key under one of the cushions or left the back door unlocked," Savannah said as they made their way around the side of the cabin, stooping to gather discarded clothing as they went.

Draigon chuckled, the sound of it causing her to pause and look back over her shoulder, her eyes widening at the sight of his cock, already full again.

"I'm impressed," she said, licking her lips and making his cock jerk with the image of seeing his bond-mate's mouth on the very part of him she was admiring.

She snickered, no doubt well aware of his thoughts, her eyes sparkling with both amusement and carnal intention as she redirected her attention, bending over to pick up her bra, the movement drawing his gaze to where long, sleekly muscled legs met at the junction of her thighs, to a vulva swollen, partly opened in a seductive bid for another kiss, for another fucking with his tongue.

Draigon groaned and took himself in hand as fire raced through his shaft and his balls tightened, heavy once again and full of seed. His gaze moving up from feminine lower lips to creamy buttocks and the cleft between them.

Lust roared through him with thoughts of spreading those luscious cheeks and taking her anally. A common form of lovemaking on Belizair but one not as widely practiced on Earth if the material he had studied in preparation for claiming a bond-mate was to be believed.

Jealousy moved in just as it had when he had claimed Savannah on the cushions next to the hot tub. Possessiveness as he wondered if a human male had already known her in that way. If Kye had.

Draigon's grip tightened on his penis. His other hand balled into a fist on the gathered clothing. The palm of his hand encountering the tiny tube Jeqon had given him before leaving Winseka.

For an instant, it felt as if time itself stopped, as if even his heart stopped. The hot blur of intention colliding with the means to have what he wanted.

Draigon released his cock in order to dig the tube of ritzca oil from the pocket of his jeans. Then dropped the hated Earth clothing back to the ground. Closing the distance between himself and Savannah as she remained bent over, reaching for her lacy underwear.

His arm snaked around her waist, the hand going unerringly to her mound, his fingers finding what his eyes had already shown him. Wet, swollen, female flesh.

"Oh god," she said, shuddering, thrilling him, widening her legs so her clit stabbed his palm, so he could bury the tips of his fingers into her tight sheath.

"No," he commanded when she would have straightened and stood. His penis throbbing when she obeyed. A fine layer of sweat joining the water from the hot tub in coating his skin. Savannah's passion nearly burning him alive.

He leaned over, kissed the back of her neck and across her shoulders, his cock raging, urging him to take her when his lips trailed over the place Kye had marked her.

Draigon bushed his knuckles down her spine. The tube held in his fist absorbing heat though it wasn't necessary.

The ritzca oil would warm the moment it touched skin. Its properties releasing with the contact, lubricating Savannah's back entrance even as it made her more aware of each nerve ending and heightened the need for sexual release.

He tightened his arm around her waist and buried his fingers deeper into her cunt in order to keep her from moving away. Then he opened the fist skimming along her backbone enough to free two fingers and yet retain possession of the tube, brushed his fingertips across the cleft of her ass before pushing between her cheeks and circling the puckered skin surrounding her anus.

She jerked against him but didn't fight, didn't protest. And he dared to say what was on his mind. "I will have you here next."

Savannah whimpered in response, her cunt clenching and unclenching on the fingers embedded in it. Her arousal flooding his cupped hand as lust whipped through them both.

Her hand covered his, pressing his palm against her clit. "Bed," she said, the word little more than a pant though it was a shout in Draigon's mind.

He released her but only long enough to get into the cabin. To tumble her onto the bed, onto her back, his hand once again going to her mound, cupping her, though this time his fingers delved into her slit only long enough to gather her wetness before moving to her anus. Her splayed legs and aroused expression stirring a beast he didn't recognize in himself.

"You have done this before?" he growled. Jealousy and possessiveness raging through him. Threatening to steal his pleasure.

Savannah's eyes widened slightly. Understanding flickering in them. Surprise.

"Once. But it wasn't good for me." A smile teased over her face, finding a small purchase place in his chest, widening it when she said, "I think you can make it better."

In a flash the wild surge of emotions shifted form, becoming masculine confidence and arrogant challenge. He dared any memory to remain after he had finished with her.

Draigon opened the tube and pulled his hand away from her body, coated his fingers with the ritzca oil, his cock throbbing, already anticipating what would happen as he worked his way into her back entrance, as first his cockhead and then his shaft became saturated with the oil. As sensation intensified for both of them, pain and pleasure blending in moments of exquisite need and agony.

By the Goddess. He might well die on Earth from making love to his bond-mate!

Savannah's chest filled with tender emotion as she watched the expressions flit across Draigon's face. He was a fascinating contradiction. A puzzle she could spend a lifetime trying to sort out. A sexual addiction she had no interest in being cured of.

She wound her arms around his neck and pulled him back to her, welcomed his kiss even as she tried to keep from tightening when his fingers stroked over her anus. Unexpected heat flared through the dark orifice.

She arched, swallowing his groan of triumph and pleasure. Her body rioting, her heart rate spiking, racing, her legs widening, allowing him more access so he could prepare her as every nerve ending seemed to come alive. To demand that he fill her.

Within seconds she was pleading, welcoming the invasion of his cock, straining to take more of him, crying out as he worked himself in, stretched her, filled her, his face a mask of stark masculine need, his breathing as ragged and sharp as her own.

He stilled when he was all the way in, his gaze locking with hers in unmistakable ownership, his words an echo of Kye's. "Admit you belong to me."

"I belong to you," Savannah said, needing what he had to offer so badly she couldn't find it in her to tease, only to demand. To beg. "Now fuck me. Please."

And he did, sliding in and out of her nearly virgin hole until she was screaming, coming. Her fingernails scraping along his back and pulling him over the edge with her.

* * * * *

Kye parked on the bottom level of the garage across from The Ferret's apartment building. He didn't truly expect to find proof regarding the identity of the sniper he'd killed that first day. But until this moment, he hadn't been free to return and investigate though the image of the sniper's primitive weapon and the ease in which Savannah could have died were a horror he would not soon forget.

He used the open stairway to reach the upper floor of the garage, moving cautiously, soundlessly, muted lighting illuminating both stairwell and garage, eliminating the mask of darkness the night sky would have otherwise imposed. There were cars of every description housed in the building and he could only shake his head in amazement at how much space was required to keep them protected from the sun and readily available for their owners' use.

If those on Belizair used such vehicles their world would soon become as polluted as parts of Earth had become. Their natural resources would disappear under the onslaught of a technology that left environmental carnage in its wake. That caused its people to lose touch with the natural world around them, to cease caring for it as a steward should do.

The god of the Vesti was a wandering god, their beliefs simple compared to the Amato. And yet one belief was shared by both races. They were to care for Belizair. To do nothing to harm it. And in return, Belizair protected those who lived on it. Making them impervious to attack from outside forces. Or at least it had been so before the Hotalings virus.

Much of a bounty hunter's work came from guarding Vesti and Amato workers and interests on other worlds. Where products such as the Vesti ritzca oil and the silky material used to fashion garments were produced and created.

There was no ugly sprawl of manufacturing plants or warehouses, office complexes or giant shopping malls on Belizair. Their planet was a paradise. Maintained in simplicity, in balance with the natural world around them. Its inhabitants leaving for stretches of time to work or explore, but never permanently unless death took them. And even then, most believed their spirits returned to Belizair.

Kye eased from the stairwell, alert for the presence of others and the danger they might represent. But all that greeted him was the sound of scraps of paper rustling, of drink cups rolling, stirred by a breeze. The subtle crackling and popping of a cooling engine. The smell of oil and concrete. Rubber and gasoline.

He moved to the short wall, glanced at The Ferret's apartment building, seeing in his mind's eye the spot where Savannah's truck had been parked, walking along the wall until he reached the spot where the sniper had been. There was no trace of him, or of his weapon. But Kye hadn't expected there to be. Not here. Not in this spot. The Ylan stones would have left nothing visible.

Kye looked around him, saw things as the sniper would have seen them. Forced his thoughts to become those of a sniper.

From the garage The Ferret's apartment wasn't visible. But Savannah's truck had been. And even now, well into darkness, the street between the parking garage and apartment building was busy, unlike the nearly abandoned streets near The Dive.

It would have been risky to park along the curb, to wait for an opportunity to shoot and then to merge into traffic without being seen. Yet from the garage...especially if the would-be killer had intended to wait for Savannah to get into the truck, especially if a silencer was attached to his weapon...

The killer could easily have placed the weapon in the trunk of a car and escaped, perhaps even on foot, in the confusion that would follow when those below realized a murder had been committed. Or more likely, two murders.

He doubted the killer would have left him alive. Not when he couldn't be sure of what Savannah might have told him.

Kye turned and focused on the cars close to where he was standing. A smile forming when he saw the van immediately in front of him.

Its height would have easily blocked the sniper from view and given him time to conceal a weapon if necessary. With a few steps, the rifle could have been pushed under a seat.

Kye moved closer, looked through the tinted windows of the van. Finding what he was looking for. Perhaps. A rifle case, though he couldn't be sure.

A small laugh escaped as Kye remembered Jeqon's warning. *Be careful and try not to do anything to remind the Council you are Lyan's cousin.*

Not for the first time since meeting Savannah, Kye admitted that perhaps he was more like his cousin than he had once believed. If he could be absolutely sure the van belonged to the sniper, if he thought he would gain important information, he would not hesitate to tear the vehicle apart—even knowing he was leaving his own fingerprints in doing so.

But even if he dared to break into the vehicle, he had no access to the fingerprint records the humans favored for identification purposes. Nor did he have the supplies necessary to retrieve prints from the van.

He had only a hunch. Only the quick image of the man he had killed. His face partially obscured by the weapon, though Kye believed the man was one of the Abrego brothers.

Kye elected to memorize the license plate. The make and model of the van.

He would give the information to Vaccaro or Kelleher directly, or have Savannah feed it to them. He would have to come up with a story to interest them in the vehicle since there was no body, no gun, no clear evidence of a sniper.

Kye retraced his steps to the stairwell. Torn. Tempted to return to the van. Afraid it would disappear—though he had no proof it had anything to do with the man he had killed. He tried to push his misgivings away in favor of the logic on which he was basing his actions. And yet by the time he had gotten to the lower level of the garage and the Council car, now outfitted with those tools he had found useful while serving the scientists as a bounty hunter, his resolve had faded in favor of an Earth motto that might well have been created by his cousin. *It is easier to gain forgiveness than it is to get permission.*

He retrieved a small thin wire from the car and returned to the van, satisfaction, righteous justification rushing through him when he retrieved the slick, black vinyl case from underneath the van's seat and opened it, the velvety outline inside proving it had housed a weapon.

Kye took a few moments to search the rest of the vehicle. But other than the registration papers bearing some unknown corporation's name, the van was spotless. He tucked the registration in his pocket and locked the doors behind him before once again retracing his steps, only to stiffen when he encountered the two Vice cops hovering near where his own transportation was parked.

Creech, red-faced despite the cooling evening, leaned against a nearby car. Mastrin, the one who had called Kye a rent-a-cop, waited at the base of the stairs, jacket open, his hand on his firearm. "Well, well, well, if it isn't Holden's pretty boy."

Chapter Fifteen

ဆ

Savannah lay on her side facing Draigon, admiring the hard planes of his face, the aristocratic nose, the full masculine lips and the flow of hair that rippled across the pillows. God, he was gorgeous. Every bit as gorgeous as Kye. Every bit as addictive.

Her fingers made lazy circles on his chest, moving closer to a hardened male nipple then retreating, her smile widening when he grumbled and grabbed her hand, covering his nipple with it, the brilliant green of his eyes visible from beneath lowered eyelashes.

She tugged at her hand and he released it when she leaned in, pressing her mouth to his, tracing the seam of his lips with her tongue, coaxing him into opening for her. Into welcoming the kiss, the lazy exploration of tongue against tongue while her hand traveled lower, pausing to explore the taut muscles of his abdomen before moving on.

He was already semi-hard, but his cock pulsed in greeting when her hand arrived, filled with blood when she curled her fingers around warm flesh, stroked. Up and down. Up and down until his hips were lifting off the bed, his tongue rubbing aggressively against hers, building toward a demand that she cede control to him and let him cover her body with his, a demand she wouldn't be able to refuse—if she allowed it to go that far. With a husky laugh she ended the kiss. "Oh no, I've got something else planned."

Savannah rose to her knees and said, "Slide this way." Anticipation rushing through her when he allowed her to position his body so she could kneel above him, could offer

179

her breast as she tormented his nipple with her tongue and lips.

She moaned when his mouth took her offering, her nipple tender from all the attention it had received. The feel of Draigon's tongue and mouth making it seem as though a heated wire ran from her breast to her cunt. His suckling riding the thin edge between pain and pleasure. Each pull on her nipple making the muscles in her channel clench and release, each brush of his tongue making her clit pulse — all of it burning her from the inside out, coating her skin with a light sheen of sweat so that when he groaned and urged her lower, she didn't resist.

Draigon shuddered as Savannah's lips teased their way toward his shaft. He had never thought to die of pleasure, but his bond-mate was killing him with her attention.

He jerked when her soft mouth finally touched the head of his cock, cried out against the wet lips of her cunt when her tongue circled the tip of his penis, his own tongue thrusting into her slit then going to her clit, mimicking her strokes to his cock head, sucking the engorged knob when she took him into her mouth and did the same to him.

Lust was a roar removing all thought, a rush that left no room for anything but sensation, for fierce desire that demanded everything. He drowned in her scented arousal, burned in her arms, gave himself completely up to Savannah even as he reveled in the way she gave herself so freely to passion, to him.

* * * * *

Kye forced his body to relax in the presence of the two Vice cops. He didn't trust them. Didn't like them. And yet he could not afford to antagonize them.

They could kill him with their primitive weapons if he allowed them such an opportunity. Or they could delay his return to Savannah with a trip to the police station if he let them goad him into saying or doing something they could charge him with. Kye decided to ignore them, to try to get to the car without confrontation.

Mastrin and Creech closed ranks, blocking his path. "Where's your girlfriend?" the heavily jowled Creech asked.

Kye shrugged and lied. "I do not know where she is at the moment."

Creech sneered. "Maybe she's holed up in a hotel room somewhere and the other pretty-boy we heard she'd hooked up with is holed up in her."

Kye stiffened, his entire body screaming with outrage, with the desire to rip the policeman in front of him into pieces for speaking of Savannah in such an insulting manner. Only his training, his time serving the Council, stayed him from yielding to emotion. The sight of both Mastrin and Creech tensing, as though hoping he would attack and give them reason to arrest or kill him, providing additional reason for Kye to refrain from violence. But it didn't cool the anger coursing through him.

Mastrin took up where his partner had left off. Smiling, an oily expression that didn't reach his eyes. "Every redhead I've ever been with has been a hellion in the sack. But I've never had to call in reinforcements."

Kye considered his options. He would not turn his back on either of the men, and he suspected they would continue to block his path if he tried to move around them. He did not want to kill them, nor did he think threats to report their conduct would work to his advantage. That left only conversation and the passage of time as weapons.

"If you have finished amusing yourselves at my expense, perhaps you will tell me why you are here," Kye said as the sound of a car entering the parking garage traveled to where they were standing.

Creech shifted his stance, looking over his shoulder to where beams of light were striking the wall. Mastrin said,

"Good question. And we could ask the same of you." The policeman's eyes dropped to the case in Kye's hand, his eyes narrowing. "What's inside?"

"Nothing. It is empty."

Mastrin's body tightened, his stance becoming more aggressive. "Then you won't mind opening it and letting us see for ourselves."

"You have a warrant?" Kye asked, grateful he had prepared well for his work on Earth.

"We can take you downtown," Creech threatened.

"If you choose to do so, I cannot stop you."

Frustration flashed across Creech's face. He and Mastrin exchanged glances, a silent message passing between them before Creech said, "Look, we've gotten off on the wrong foot here. We don't have a problem with you. But we do have one with your girlfriend. She's messing up an investigation we've got going. Even today, when she's supposed to be on vacation, suddenly every time we turn around, she's been there, asking questions, making people nervous. We just want her to lay off before she screws things up completely and gets caught in the crossfire. 'Cause right now we don't know how far what we're investigating goes. We don't know how desperate the perps are going to get, and whether or not they'll shoot first and ask questions later. You see what I'm getting at? Tell her we'll overlook the outing today and won't make a big deal of it if she'll just remember she's supposed to be on vacation."

Mastrin nodded and added, "Look, she's hot. If she wasn't such a pain in the ass, I'd consider asking her out myself. So why not make this a win-win for all of us. Maybe you can keep her in bed for couple of days, keep her safe and enjoy doing it. I mean, geez, a guy could spend an entire day just admiring her tits—" He broke off when Kye tensed. "Okay, okay. Hey, no hard feelings." His gaze dropped to the case against Kye's leg. "That have anything to do with Ricky Nowak's place getting trashed?"

"No," Kye said, his tone matching the two men's, as though there were indeed no hard feelings. "Savannah spoke the truth. The apartment was ransacked when we arrived and we touched nothing."

Creech exhaled, a loud huff of air. "Okay then, we're done here."

* * * * *

Savannah woke, immediately alert though she couldn't remember dozing off after showering and returning to bed. An engine rumbled in the distance, the sound of it carrying on thin night air, speeding the beat of her heart. But when she started to scramble for clothing and her gun, Draigon laughed, momentarily tightening his arm and holding her back to his chest. "It is only Kye," he said, his voice so certain she didn't question him, and yet, how could he be so sure?

"I didn't hear a phone ring." In fact now that she thought about it, she hadn't seen either Kye or Draigon use a cell phone and her own was recharging on the kitchen counter.

Draigon closed his eyes briefly, burying his face in Savannah's neck, nuzzling her soft skin, kissing her, cursing himself for forgetting how smart she was even as he tried to distract her from her line of thinking. Relief pouring into him when she laughed, when she turned in his arms and arched, exposing the length of her neck, her breasts, bare, tempting, so lush that they never failed to draw Draigon's attention to them.

He kissed his way down her throat, not bothering to tease her with a slow approach but going directly to a well-loved nipple, latching on and suckling, feasting, swallowing her whimpers of pleasure, finding them as filling as their children would one day find her milk.

He hadn't intended to take her. To have Kye walk in on them while they were intimate, and yet something primitive filled Draigon, demanding he stake his claim in the way of beasts, not men.

With a growl he rose above her, used his strength to hold her so his mouth could remain at her breast even as he impaled her with a quick hard thrust, fucked in and out of her in a way that had her sobbing in pleasure.

He knew the moment Kye entered the cabin. Could feel the Vesti's wild mix of emotion along with his own. And it fed the need to dominate Savannah, to claim her until she was screaming in orgasm and fiery seed was burning through his cock, his release so violent he collapsed on the bed next to her, weak beyond all imagining. Too weak even to think, to protest, to do anything but watch as Kye's body covered Savannah's, as the Vesti's cock shoved into the place his own had just been.

Savannah wrapped her legs around Kye's waist, her body signaling that it needed him as desperately as she'd needed Draigon only a moment ago. "You guys have turned me into a nympho," she said with a laugh, and the red haze left Kye's mind. Reason returning, acceptance. The primitive roar of his ancestors dulling with the feel of her sheath, with her husky words. He had not liked seeing Draigon covering Savannah, fucking her. But it was impossible to stay angry in her presence. To think of anything but mating with her.

By the stars, even though she'd been taken repeatedly, her cunt was a fist around his cock, milking him of all that he had to offer. "Savannah," he whispered, holding her more tightly as he plunged in and out of her, his mouth going to hers, hungrily swallowing her sighs and moans, the intensity of both emotion and physical sensation leaving no room for gentleness, no time to linger. There was only a wild, rough rush to completeness. To ecstasy. To being one with her. A release that left him shaky, his muscles lax, his heart thundering in his head.

Kye shivered when she ran her fingernails down his back and over his buttocks, grunted when she nipped at his chin, laughed when she murmured, "You'd better get off me,

Batman. As much as I'd like to make a meal out of you, I need something a little more wholesome." She punctuated the statement by nibbling at his mouth. "And unless the great sex is making me hallucinate, I smell Chinese food. Did you bring some back with you?"

He rolled over, taking her with him so she sprawled out along the length of his body. "Yes." This time it was his turn to make her shiver as he scraped his nails along her back and over her buttocks. "I wanted to make sure you were well fed for the night ahead," Kye said, his cock stirring. A desire foreign to his nature invading his thoughts along with images of taking her again in front of Draigon. Of demonstrating his claim to her in front of another male. And on the heel of that need came thoughts of cooperation. Of taking her together in a true sharing.

Kye kissed her, hugging her to him before resting his hands lightly on her sides. "You'll have to get up on your own. I have no ability to push you away from me."

Savannah laughed and dipped her head, brushing her lips against his before rolling to the side and sitting on the edge of the bed. "I'm going to grab a shower first."

She showered quickly, donning a black g-string and one of the shirts she'd gotten for Kye, a green that matched his eyes, and hers, and now Draigon's as well. For some reason the thought of them all having that trait in common made her smile. She grinned. Hell, who was she kidding? *They* made her smile. And it was more than great sex, more than just having her favorite fantasy play out in the bedroom, and against the side of the truck, and on the kitchen table, and... Savannah snickered. The list could go on forever with Kye and Draigon serving as inspiration.

Savannah left the bathroom and found Kye and Draigon had already set the table. She paused at the kitchen counter only long enough to use the cell in order to check her voice mail at the station for messages. Her gaze going to a rifle case and auto registration, assuming they belonged to Kye and wondering at the name on the paperwork, Wray Investments, before concentrating on weeding through the few messages in the hopes The Ferret had called. He hadn't. Savannah set the phone back on the counter and joined Kye and Draigon at the table. They loaded their plates, silent for the first few minutes as they ate.

She ought to feel completely wiped out by all the sex, along with traipsing around Reno asking about The Ferret and the girls, plus the fight with the Guzman brothers—not that she'd seen a hell of a lot of action in it. But instead of being exhausted, Savannah felt an absolute, soul-satisfying contentedness that radiated outward and seemed to soak into every cell. As corny as it sounded, as crazy as it sounded, now that Kye and Draigon were on the scene she felt as though she'd found her place in the scheme of the things. Which wasn't a logical conclusion given she was hiding out in a cabin and wasn't much closer to getting back to her regularly scheduled rounds as a cop.

A small worry crept in at the thought of her job. About the reality waiting for her after this mess was behind her. Her conversation with Krista coming back to haunt her.

So what's holding you back? Are you afraid it'd get back to your principal and you'd get canned on a morals clause?

Yeah, something like that.

Savannah studied Kye for a moment then shifted her gaze to Draigon. They weren't just here for the party. They were here for the long haul. She felt it. She believed it. Everything they'd said and done backed it up. This wasn't casual for them. They were playing for keeps.

Kye's willingness to share her when it wasn't something he'd done before was part of the proof. Draigon's serious nature, the rigid exterior he allowed her to peel away, exposing his vulnerability, was another piece of evidence. She'd bet her favorite horse that Draigon didn't let many people see the man she'd seen in the truck when their make-out session had ended abruptly, the man who'd laughed at himself until tears streaked down his face.

Savannah sighed and looked down. Picked up an egg roll and swirled it in hot mustard. If they suggested living together, how long would it take before it became obvious to everyone that they weren't just roommates? And what would that mean to her chances of not only making detective but staying a cop?

Fair or unfair, cops were held to a higher standard. The department might not fire her over living with two guys who were also her lovers, but that didn't mean she wouldn't be encouraged to quit. There were plenty of jobs on the force she had no interest in doing. Jobs that would make turning in her badge a distinct possibility.

She sighed, remembering a conversation she'd had with some of her female cousins about how much they'd be willing to give up for a good man — *the* perfect man — *if* such a creature existed. Savannah took a bite of the egg roll, once again studying Kye and Draigon. How much would she be willing to give up in order to be with both of them?

Kye reached over and smoothed the skin between her eyebrows. "What are you thinking about? What worries you?"

Savannah tried to shrug the future aside. "Just thinking about Krista." Which was somewhat true. Thoughts of Krista had led her to thinking about the potential career problems that lay ahead because of Draigon and Kye.

Kye smiled and it instantly lightened Savannah's mood. "There is no need to worry about your friend. She is safe and well cared for. Draigon can attest to this fact. He witnessed Krista's arrival as he was leaving to come here."

"Krista's arrival where?" Savannah asked, her attention shifting to Draigon and catching Kye's wince out of the corner of her eye.

Draigon touched the smooth skin on the back of Savannah's hand, moving upward, wrapping his fingers around her wrist, wishing it was the band he had created for the binding ceremony touching her instead of his own flesh. "Our home...city, Savannah. A place Kye and I hope to take you. A place where your friend has already found happiness with Adan, who has been a friend of mine since childhood, and with Lyan who is Kye's cousin."

"Happy and soon to be pregnant, given my cousin's nature and Adan's," Kye said. "She will be lucky if they allow her to put on clothing or leave the living quarters."

"Barefoot, bare-assed and pregnant. Whose fantasy would that be?" Savannah said, her tone undecipherable to Draigon.

"You do not want children?" he dared to ask, steeling himself for her answer, knowing even as he did so that regardless of what she said, he would find it impossible to give her up now.

Wariness skittered along Savannah's spine. Whoa. How had things gotten so serious all of a sudden? Draigon looked like he didn't plan on breathing until she answered his question and Kye was doing a great imitation of a statue.

Shit. Savannah retraced the conversation in her thoughts and didn't know whether to be thrilled or worried. Yeah, these guys were definitely thinking long-term and serious. Picket-fences and children kind of serious.

She rolled her shoulders and told them the truth. "Sure, I want kids. In the future. In the *distant* future. As in, maybe once I've made detective." And then in a non-subtle attempt to change the subject, she asked Kye, "So did the mugs confirm Kelleher and Vaccaro are who they say they are?"

"The scientists are still investigating," Kye answered, grimacing when he saw her frown, when he read her intention to question him further. By the stars, she was a challenge! He decided to distract her, to replace her curiosity with a wrath he was sure to be the target of. "When I returned to Reno, I retrieved a case from a garage across from The Ferret's apartment building. It was fashioned for a sniper's weapon and I believe it might belong to one of the Abrego brothers. Perhaps Kelleher or Vaccaro would be interested in it."

Savannah's eyes widened then narrowed in suspicion. Her gaze going to the case and registration papers she'd noticed earlier then returning to Kye. "You went to The Ferret's apartment building?"

"No. Only to the garage." Kye shifted in his chair, hating that he couldn't tell Savannah the entire truth, that he had spotted the sniper and reduced him to particles days ago and now only sought to verify it was one of drug lord's lieutenants so he could determine which of their enemies was no longer a concern.

"And while you were checking out the garage, you just happened to stumble on a case that might have contained a sniper's rifle?"

Kye winced at the skepticism in Savannah's voice and decided that if he was to bear the brunt of her anger, he would rather have it over with quickly. "It was inside a van positioned in a spot which would conceal a sniper from view and yet allow someone to watch the front entrance of The Ferret's building. I have the automobile's registration papers as well."

Savannah closed her eyes briefly. She didn't know whether to laugh, cry or go ballistic. "Let me get this straight, you broke into a van and removed items from it? You're admitting to a cop that you broke the law?"

"I would not put you in such an awkward position," Kye said. "I am merely telling you of the items so you can decide whether or not to pass them on to Kelleher and Vaccaro for processing."

Savannah took a deep breath, reminding herself Kye was a bounty hunter and bounty hunters were notorious for playing by a different set of rules. Rules that could land them in jail just as easily as they could land a criminal behind bars.

Shit, a minute ago the thought of living with both of them openly had seemed like a potential career-killer. And now this! Wouldn't that be fun, having a boyfriend she was constantly posting bail for! The thought made her laugh, her sense of humor intruding despite how serious the underlying situation was.

"I'm forgiven?" Kye asked, his voice hopeful as he shifted closer. His lips incredibly persuasive when he trailed kisses from her ear to her mouth. "Keeping you safe is all that matters to me, Savannah."

"To us," Draigon said, also moving closer, unbuttoning her shirt and cupping her breast, toying with her nipple and sending heat straight to her clit. His hand following the trail of need, his fingers burrowing into her panties, dipping into her arousal before retreating to stroke and manipulate her swollen knob.

For a brief instant Savannah thought about claiming "foul", about pointing out that two against one wasn't playing fair, but as golden waves of pleasure rolled through her she gave herself up to their hands, their mouths. Didn't resist when they took her back to bed.

Chapter Sixteen

ဆ

They stretched Savannah out on the bed, working in concert, Draigon holding one wrist pinned to the mattress above her head while Kye held the other. Their lips slowly caressing her shoulders, then downward, reaching her breasts at the same time.

Savannah's womb fluttered with the feel of tongues and soft mouths. She cried out when they both began sucking, their movements timed so well it was hard to believe they hadn't done this together before, rehearsed until they'd perfected their technique, until words weren't necessary between them in order to coordinate their assault on a woman's body.

On her body.

She couldn't stand the thought of them with anyone else.

"Please," Savannah begged, spreading her legs, arching, starting to thrash as her clit throbbed in time to their sucks, as her channel spasmed, her cunt lips already swollen, opened. Needy.

And they responded, still in concert, their free hands roaming over her belly, lingering, petting the smooth skin and taut muscles before trailing over her hip and downward, exploring her inner thigh as though measuring her arousal by the wetness they found there. Forcing her to beg again, her *please* little more than a panting whisper.

Savannah's body jerked when their hands slid upward, closed her eyes against the intense pleasure as Kye's fingers circled and stroked her clit while Draigon's explored her slit, teasing over her flushed and swollen labia, dipping into her channel then retreating, fucking her with shallow thrusts so that her cunt became a desperate, hungry mouth, clenching and unclenching as it tried to capture his fingers.

Her panted pleas for release became sobs as they took her to the edge time and time again only to pull back. To start all over until she was hyper-aware of every inch of her body, of each place they'd been, and especially the places where they still touched. Their hands on her wrists, their legs thrown over hers, pinning her in place. Their lips on her breasts. Their free hands between her legs. Their cocks slick and hard and smooth against her thighs.

Draigon's mouth left her nipple and even the feel of air against her wet, love-tortured areola had her crying out. He kissed upward until his face hovered above hers. Their eyes meeting. His glittering, intense. Determined. "Accept the band I have crafted for you," he said, his fingers fucking into her, reminding her that he held the key to her release.

She arched, whimpered, would have promised anything to be allowed to come. There was no possibility, no thought of answering anything but yes.

His mouth took hers then and she could taste his happiness, his joy as his tongue slid against hers, as emotion poured into her, filling her, filling them both and making it seem as though it was only the two of them. Trapped together in a timeless golden-encased moment.

When the kiss ended, Draigon shifted and Kye was there. Eyes dark with need. Nostrils flared. Face taut. "Accept my band as well," he said, barely allowing her *yes* to escape before his lips were covering hers, his tongue plundering her mouth. His kiss savage at first, then gentling so she could feel his happiness, his satisfaction, his joy, all of it swamping her, a wave rushing through her and then receding, taking her with it. Leaving her burning, needing.

They released her wrists and ankles and Savannah took advantage of it when the kiss ended. Rolling, straddling Kye's legs. Her hand going to his cock, her first thoughts to impale herself on it, but then Draigon's fingers were between her thighs, coaxing her backward and onto her forearms and knees as Kye repositioned himself, his hands grasping the headboard, his penis now only inches from her face.

Heat roared through Kye, the desperate need for release. He had hated the thought of sharing Savannah with another, was still not quite comfortable with the idea of feeling Draigon's cock rubbing against his own in the tightness of their bond-mate's body, but he had never experienced such powerful need, such raw desire as he'd experienced when he and Draigon had worked together, suddenly of one mind, to make some progress in the claiming of Savannah.

Kye jerked when Savannah's tongue darted out, licking over the head of his penis and sending fiery bolts of pleasure through his shaft. Whispered "Please" when her hold on him tightened, when she took him into her mouth and began sucking, reducing him to the same helplessness in which they'd held her. His balls pulling tight, his cock throbbing, pulsing, screaming for release.

Savannah savored Kye's pleading. Feminine power and satisfaction filling her, only to be reduced to whimpering need as Draigon's fingers found her clit, gliding over it in time to her sucks on Kye's cock, teasing her until *she* was the one straining, quivering, allowing Kye his release and then crying out in pleasure when Draigon finally filled the empty needy place in her. His thrusts fast and hard, his testicles slapping against her flesh as her erect knob stabbed into his hand, shooting bolt after bolt of ecstasy through her until she came in a rush, her channel clutching him, milking him even as she tumbled into exhausted satisfaction.

Savannah woke in heaven, or close to it, with Kye pressed against her back and Draigon at her front, lying on his back with her arm across his chest and her leg between his. *God did it get any better than this?* She grinned. Hell no.

Reality was much better than fantasy, even if reality did come with complications—like sliding Kye's *suspected* breaking-and-entering past Vaccaro and Kelleher. Savannah grimaced. *Suspected.* Right. Then again, Vaccaro and Kelleher were after bigger fish so she had a feeling they weren't going to ask a lot of questions.

It took her a moment to notice the band on her wrist, to check her other wrist and determine it also had a bracelet on it. To remember how they'd tortured her by not letting her climax until she agreed to what they wanted.

Every time she looked at the bands she was going to think about Kye and Draigon's brand of persuasion. And as soon as she had the opportunity, she was going to bring out the ropes and reciprocate. She'd tie them to the bed one at a time and find every erogenous zone, then exploit it until they agreed to what she wanted—answers. About their home. Their people. Their culture. And especially why there were two men for every woman.

Oh yeah, they'd tell her everything she wanted to know and she'd reward them just like they'd rewarded her. With pleasure so intense it would knock them out.

She rose onto an elbow so she could study Draigon as he slept. He was a surprise. Her opposite and Kye's in a lot of ways. And yet she enjoyed him. Immensely. And not just because of the fantastic sex. He was the perfect fit for her and Kye. The straight-man on their comedy team. Adding depth and texture and richness with his presence.

She stroked his chest, loved how warm his skin felt against her own, smiled when he stirred and opened his eyes, revealing a wealth of unguarded emotion as his cock echoed his pleasure at waking to find her attention focused on him. Savannah leaned down, brushed his lips with hers, laughing softly when his cock pulsed against her thigh. "Someone's happy," she teased, moaning when Draigon's fingers tangled in her hair, holding her so he could spear his tongue into her mouth in a kiss that left no doubt what his intentions were.

"You are well?" he asked, the gleam of masculine satisfaction and pride telling her he would savor riding her into oblivion for a long time to come.

"Well and plotting my revenge."

"I am not afraid."

"You should be. Very, very afraid." But before she could elaborate, her cell phone began ringing.

Savannah scrambled out of bed, waking Kye in the process. Both men following her into the kitchen. Distracting her for an instant with their nakedness and their twin frowns — until she answered the phone.

"You still willing to meet?"

She gave Kye and Draigon a thumbs-up at the sound of The Ferret's voice. "Where?"

"How long will it take you to get on Three-forty-one heading toward Virginia City?"

"An hour, maybe a little longer."

"How soon can you leave?"

"As soon as I get dressed."

"Okay. Get on Three-forty-one. I'll call you later and tell you where to meet. Don't go past Virginia City if you don't hear from me." He paused. "Come alone. No other cops. I see another cop and you won't see me."

Maybe before the Guzman brothers had jumped her she would have agreed. Not now. "I won't bring another cop, but I had to get a couple of bodyguards since you set up the first meet."

"They with you now?"

Savannah looked up, finding Kye and Draigon standing right in front of her. Tension radiating off them. Their muscles tight, showing off warrior bodies though their expressions clearly said she wouldn't be going anywhere if it was up to them. "I'm looking at them."

"The guys you were eating with at Bert's?"

"Yeah. They come with me or I don't come at all," Savannah said, her sense of humor intruding as soon as the words were out of her mouth. Oh yeah, she was pretty sure Kye and Draigon had ruined her for any other man. Now she'd be lucky if she could make *herself* come.

"Okay. Bring them," The Ferret said and the line went dead.

Savannah delayed long enough to tell Kye and Draigon the plan then set the phone down so she could retrieve one of the FBI agents' cards.

She wears our bands, Draigon said, his gaze following Savannah's movements. *We should put a stop to this foolishness now.*

Is that wishful thinking? You have spent time alone with her. Do you truly believe it is possible to prevent her from doing this? Kye shook his head. *If you want to pick this moment to battle with Savannah, that is your choice. But I have to ask, has she given the bands more than a passing glance? Have you spoken to her about their significance?*

No.

Nor have I. They are pieces of jewelry to her. Nothing more. We knew this meeting was a possibility. And we will keep her safe. The sooner she is finished with this business, the sooner we can convince her to leave with us.

Draigon's frown intensified as Savannah walked toward them, Vaccaro's card in hand. He remembered the flash of Savannah's anger in the truck when he told her he could not tolerate her being in danger. Her heated reply found him easily. *I'm a cop, Draigon. Danger comes with the territory. Same as it comes with being a bounty hunter. I hope you're not going to tell me what's okay for a man isn't okay for a woman.*

He hated to admit it, but Kye was right. There would be no winning this fight with her. She was intent on her course of action and anything they did to prevent her from following it would undo the progress they had made with her. With a silent nod Draigon agreed with Kye's assessment and shifted his attention to Savannah's conversation with the FBI agent.

"I just set up a meet with Ricky," Savannah said, not surprised when Vaccaro answered on the first ring. "He's agreed to my bodyguards but says he'll disappear if he sees anyone else."

"Where?"

"Don't know yet. He's going to call me in an hour."

"On your cell?"

"Yes."

"Hold on. Kelleher's right here."

She could hear a muted conversation. Strategy rather than argument. Vaccaro came back on the line. "Okay. Whatever Nowak's offering, tell him you can promise him immunity and immediate protection if he's willing to talk to us. If he goes for it, call with a location and Kelleher and I'll come in and take over."

Savannah wrinkled her nose. *Right.* His easy agreement made her think they were going to use her cell phone to track her—if they weren't already doing that. Otherwise Vaccaro would never have let her call the shots. Rolling over was *not* the FBI way of doing things.

"One other thing," she said, glancing at the rifle case and wanting to get Kye's misadventure in the garage behind them. "You ever heard of Wray Investments?"

"Why?" This time Vaccaro's voice was all FBI.

"There was a van registered to Wray Investments in the garage across from Nowak's place. Inside the van was a case, now in my possession. The rifle is missing, but the layout of the interior says sniper to me." Not that she'd seen the inside of it for herself, but she trusted Kye's assessment.

"And how did you come by this, Holden?"

"So you know something about Wray?"

A sigh. "I'm beginning to see how you got your reputation for being a pain in the ass."

Savannah grinned despite her underlying worry for Kye. "Yeah, well, that's just a vicious rumor. Let me guess, Wray Investments is one of Carlos Dominguez's suspected front corporations." Another sigh on the other end. She pressed the issue. "We're wasting time here, Vaccaro. I'm supposed to be leaving to meet Nowak. Yes or no. Wray Investments is connected to Dominguez."

Vaccaro choked back a laugh. "Yes. Don't bother telling me the van was unlocked and the door was wide open, I'm just going to assume it was. You happen to get a license plate number?"

"Even better. I've got the registration papers." Savannah looked at them and read the license number off to him.

"Probably Errol Abrego. We've seen him in a van with those plates before."

"Which one is he, Psycho I or Psycho II?" She needed the tags Vaccaro had applied to the pictures in order to call up the facial images.

"Psycho I. There was no sight of him in the garage?" Now Vaccaro's voice was puzzled.

"None." Savannah hesitated. "Mastrin and Creech from Vice showed up as my...source was leaving."

"I'll pass the information on to Kelleher. You heading out now to meet Nowak?"

"Yes."

"Bring the papers and the case."

"Sure," she said to dead air.

Savannah closed the phone and looked at Kye. "Well, that went better than expected. Ready for the fun to start?"

Kye closed the distance between them and pulled her into his arms. "Ready for this to be over with so we can take you home with us."

"To meet the family?"

His gaze met Draigon's. "To keep."

Savannah hugged him and disengaged, ignoring the undertone she heard in his voice and shying away from thoughts of just how she was going to introduce Kye and Draigon to her family. "Let's hit it," she said after they'd dressed, using a dishtowel to keep from leaving her prints on the rifle case or the registration—not that she was convinced Vaccaro was going to process them. But then again, given Kye's involvement, she'd just as soon the stuff disappeared.

They took the SUV Kye had shown up with. Hoping they could arrive at the rendezvous unnoticed since they were the only three people who knew about the car. Probably. She wouldn't put it past Vaccaro and Kelleher to stake out the cabin though she hadn't seen any sign of a tail either leaving the ranch or when they got close to Virginia City.

Savannah checked her gun, frowning as she thought about Kye and Draigon being unarmed. It was an inconsistency, something she should have clued in to from the start. Then again, they weren't really bodyguards by profession, they were bounty hunters. Maybe the kind of jobs they took didn't require them to carry concealed—which was actually kind of a relief to her. Savannah's stomach churned thinking about what it would be like to love someone whose job put him in the line of fire every day.

She grimaced. Yeah, kind of like loving a cop. She put the gun back in her holster and picked up the cell phone to check the charge level and signal strength for the hundredth time. She nearly dropped it when it rang.

"Where are you?" The Ferret asked.

She told him.

"Okay. Do a U-turn. Pull in at the Gold Country Truck Stop. Go into the restaurant and wait." She passed the instructions on to Kye and a little while later they were pulling in.

199

The truck stop was busy but not crowded. There were maybe twenty big rigs lined up in three rows on the cracked asphalt parking lot to the right of the pumps. Savannah had seen it when it was worse. When bad weather going into California had drivers holed up and waiting, not wanting to get trapped in snow or delayed by chain-reaction wrecks.

They decided to go in together since The Ferret was expecting bodyguards. He surprised her. She figured she'd have to wait for him to show, if he showed at all. But he was sitting in the back, tucked behind a potted tree, the shine on its leaves screaming plastic.

Draigon stopped close to the door. "We will stay here."

Kye halted next to him. "He might speak more freely if he knows we are watching the parking lot."

"Thanks," Savannah said and kept going.

"I recognize the dark-haired one from outside The Dive," The Ferret said when she joined him.

"It would have been nice if you'd warned me your car was going to explode. If my friend hadn't pulled me back into the alley, I wouldn't be sitting here right now."

"You gotta believe me. I never saw it coming. I mean, not a car bomb. I would've warned you if I'd known."

The Ferret glanced around nervously, the profile of his narrow, sharp features reminding Savannah why she'd given him the nickname.

"Look," he said, "the day I called you to set up the meet I came home and found my place had been trashed. Then I go to The Dive and you're bringing someone else into it. What am I supposed the think? It made me nervous. All of a sudden a new face appears when every time I turn around someone from Vice is sniffing around, asking about me."

The Ferret pulled a pack of cigarettes from his shirt pocket, tapped the bottom on the heel of his hand so a couple of cigarettes popped into view. He pushed them down with his thumb, then immediately tapped the pack again, popping the cigarettes up like they were bread in a toaster. Pushed them down as he said, "I've got this friend. She's got information. Big-time information. Only there are complications. The kind that can put a person in the morgue."

"You're talking about Becky Jaworski, now Becky Traynor."

He took a cigarette out and put the pack back in his shirt pocket. "You figured that out."

"You sent the nickel and dime chips to the station. You wanted me to check out the Easy Times Casino, stir things up there, maybe find out Becky was missing and lots of people are asking around, looking for her even though her husband hasn't filed a missing persons report." Savannah cocked her head. "What I can't figure out is why you had Bert give me the tip about the underage girls Becky was running as part of her escort service. Don't tell me she suddenly got a conscience and decided they needed to be hauled off to foster homes."

"Becky didn't go to the playground and lure those girls into the life. They were already in the business." He looked uncomfortable and Savannah wondered if he'd told Becky that he'd passed on a tip about the girls.

"She knew they weren't legal," Savannah said.

"Yeah, well who can prove that?"

"The one, Holland, is thirteen. And now she's missing. Bert tell you that?"

"I thought you hauled them in."

"I did. Apparently nothing stuck. The one I'm most interested in helping is Holland. She's probably with her sister Ivy and another girl named Camryn. You know where they might be?"

"No." The Ferret rolled the cigarette into his palm and closed his fingers around it. "Look, I'm not saying it's okay to bang a thirteen-year-old, but that's not the big picture here.

The big picture is what Steven Traynor has going with a guy named Carlos Dominguez."

"Laundering Dominguez's profits from smuggling and blackmail?"

"What blackmail?"

"You saying you don't know anything about luring men to the Easy Times then hooking them up with the girls and taking the kind of vacation snapshots not meant for wives and children to see?"

"If that was going on, that was all Traynor. The girls were his idea, but he put the operation in Becky's name, let her run it. She signed a pre-nup, that's the only way he'd marry her. No alimony if they split. But she could keep whatever she made on the escort service while they were married."

"Sounds like a perfect motive for running a blackmail scheme along with the girls."

The Ferret shook his head. "Look, Becky didn't need the extra money. She wasn't planning on things ending with Traynor and he wasn't cheap when it came to buying her whatever she wanted. He's a guy who likes to have celebrities and bigwigs come to the casino. He likes to be seen and having a wife decked out in the finest is part of the show. But Becky knows the value of putting some cash aside in case things don't turn out the way they should. So she ran the escort service and liked doing it. She liked being a part of things."

"So what went wrong?"

Chapter Seventeen

ഔ

"Traynor couldn't keep it in his pants, that's what went wrong." The Ferret opened his hand and dropped the wilted cigarette to the table. "Becky's hitting thirty this year. You know how that is, right? Not personally, I mean, but you know what I'm talking about? Right? Thirty might as well be put out to pasture in Vegas, like banging your grandmother. It's not so bad in Reno..." He glanced toward the door and fidgeted with the salt and pepper shakers.

"She caught him cheating," Savannah said.

"Yeah. She didn't really think he was getting it somewhere else—I mean, Becky's a looker, and not to be telling tales, but she and I were an item once, and she knows how to keep a guy happy. Only she's approaching the big three-oh, so she had him followed. Found out he was sampling the merchandise. Using one of the girls she was running."

"One of the underage girls?"

"No. Camryn." His gaze met Savannah's. "You hauled her in. You got a take on her."

Oh yeah, Savannah had a take on her—and a huge dislike for Camryn's part in peddled underage girls. Big mouth, big attitude. *I got the world by the cock and I'm getting off on it*, was only a start to how Camryn could be summed up. And even without knowing Becky Jaworski, Savannah could put herself in Becky's mind. Imagine what Becky had been feeling. Finding out her husband was cheating. Not with a stranger, but with a girl who probably smirked and gloated, all those looks suddenly hitting their target and playing on Becky's fears, her ego. Her anger.

"Let me guess, rather than confronting Traynor, Becky started collecting information about his money laundering activities. Maybe thinking to negotiate a nice divorce settlement. Only he wouldn't cooperate."

"Wouldn't or couldn't. The guy he's been dealing with doesn't like loose ends or loose cannons. A couple of close calls and Becky came to me. That's why we're sitting here. She wants to deal." The Ferret sighed. A loud exhale that deflated him slightly. "She's got stuff on Traynor, but he's got stuff on her too."

"Running the underage girls?"

"Maybe more than that. I don't know."

Savannah was guessing the blackmail scheme was *the more* Traynor had on his wife. Especially if he was screwing Camryn and Camryn was in on it. But she believed Ricky when he said he didn't know anything about it.

The Ferret worried the collar of his shirt. "Traynor's the kind of guy who's got connections. Law-abiding ones and not so law-abiding ones. She didn't know who to trust. Which is why she called me and I called you. To start the ball rolling for a deal. She wants immunity from prosecution. She wants protection. And she wants to walk away with everything she's earned from the escort service. In exchange she'll hand over what she's got on Traynor and his dealings with Carlos Dominguez."

Savannah nearly smiled at the way The Ferret had brought the conversation to where she wanted it. "I'd say a deal is possible. Very possible. The FBI has been watching Traynor's casino for a while. They already figured the connection to Dominguez and they're anxious to nail them. Anxious enough that when your car blew up and word got around I was looking for you they actually went to my captain and called me in. They're willing to offer *you* protection and immunity right now. You take it and I'm betting you can get the same for Becky. That's the best I can do for you, Ricky."

204

The Ferret pulled at his shirt collar again, this time leaving sweat on the material. "You trust whoever you've been talking to?"

"Vaccaro and Kelleher. Yeah, I trust them to deliver on their promises. I told Vaccaro about the meet right after you called me." She pulled out the cell phone, deciding to gamble, to prove she could be trusted in order to close the deal. "But this is the weak link. It can be tracked by satellite. So I wouldn't put it past Vaccaro and Kelleher to be close by. If you want to clear out, I'll stay put long enough to give you a head start. Your choice. But if it were me, I'd take them up on their offer so I could get on with my life."

The Ferret picked up the cigarette, closing his fingers around it and finally asking, "You mind?"

Savannah grimaced. "Yeah. But go ahead if you have to."

The answer seemed to calm him. He shook his head and put the cigarette back in his shirt pocket. "That's why I called you to begin with. You play things straight. You're an honest cop." He retrieved the cigarette and put it in his mouth, letting it hang from the corner so it bounced up and down when he said, "I'll talk to the guys you've been talking to."

Savannah flicked open the cellular. "Now?"

"Yeah." The cigarette went back in his pocket. "Becky's not cut out for cheap motel rooms and staying out of sight."

Savannah didn't give him time to change his mind. She put in a call to Vaccaro. "Ricky's willing to come in and bring Becky Traynor in."

"What's your location?"

"You really need me to tell you?"

Silence. A bark of laughter. "We're down the road. I'm in a black Lincoln Town Car. Kelleher's in a dark blue one."

She closed the phone. "They'll be here in a minute. You sure you can't tell me where the three girls are?"

"What gives with the girls? Becky's got plenty on Traynor. More than enough."

Savannah rolled her shoulders. She wasn't going to remind him about the blackmail scheme. "Mainly I'm interested in the kid. Holland. She got to me."

The Ferret started to reach for the cigarette again but dropped his hand and rearranged the salt and pepper shakers then put them back in their original positions. "I'll ask Becky when I see her. She mentioned a place she kept. For clients who wanted to kick back, party, fuck, whatever. Maybe the girls are holed up there." He fidgeted for a few minutes. Wiped his hands on his pants, pulled the cigarette back out of his pocket. "Look, I got to get something from my car."

"Okay. The guys and I'll go out with you." Savannah stood, wondering what she'd do if he lost his nerve and tried to bolt.

"I've got to have a smoke."

"Fine. I'll give you space." She decided to gamble again. "Or I'll wait here. Like I said a minute ago, Ricky. This is your choice."

He rubbed his palms over his thighs, leaving a light trail of sweat. "No. No. That's okay." He paused as if a thought had just occurred to him. "How come you had a bodyguard with you at The Dive?"

"I didn't. He's a new addition to my life. He was actually following the woman you saw me meeting. She's a friend. He's related to her boyfriend. But to make a long story short, the boyfriend is on the scene now and Kye's at loose ends, so he's guarding me." *Among other things—like seeing to my sexual health.* Though Savannah tried to keep that thought off her face and out of her voice.

The Ferret nodded, apparently satisfied, and headed for the door.

Savannah saw the window of opportunity for getting answers closing. Once the Feds had him, she'd be lucky to find out anything. "You hear anything about someone in Vice passing on information to Dominguez or his lieutenants or Traynor?"

Ricky shook his head as they got to where Kye and Draigon had positioned themselves. "Everything okay out there?" Savannah asked.

"The trucks block a portion of the entrance," Kye warned as The Ferret reached the front door.

Movement caught Savannah's eye. A dark blue Town Car coming in. "That's Kelleher."

Savannah followed the Ferret out the door, his hurried steps making her hurry, making her nerves jangle despite the fact he was soon going to be someone else's problem.

She should have felt relieved. Instead she felt tense. Like a runner in a relay race who just had to stay ahead of the pack for a few more minutes, until the baton could be passed, and then she could collapse on the sidelines.

A big rig engine sprung to life. Then another. Then a third. Spitting clouds of diesel exhaust. A convoy ready to set off. Their sound masking any other for a moment.

The Ferret lit the cigarette. Stopped. Tensed. Aware of the Town Car approaching.

"That's one of the guys I was telling you about," Savannah said. Holding her breath. Waiting to see if Ricky was going to make a run for it.

He didn't.

She exhaled. Felt some of the tension leave as Kelleher pulled to a stop and got out of the car, leaving the engine running.

A black car came out from behind the trucks. Moving fast.

Vaccaro, Savannah thought, but her hand was already going to her gun. Her body reacting before her mind.

A second look. Shades of déjà vu. The black car from outside The Dive though only her subconscious had noted it.

She was firing even as the driver's arm emerged from the car with a gun. A shot going off even as she pulled the trigger and sent a second bullet toward the car.

The Ferret screamed. Pain and fear echoing in the air as Savannah unloaded everything she had and the car kept coming. Stopping only when it hit Kelleher's vehicle.

Two down, one to go, Savannah thought, mind cold, heart thundering in her ears, recognizing one of the Abrego brothers. Psycho II. The top part of his skull a mass of bone and blood against the dark grey car interior. She couldn't remember his first name.

"Jose Abrego," Kelleher said, bringing her back to the present, into an awareness of masculine sobs. She turned. Feeling like she was in slow motion. Suddenly afraid of what she was going to find.

Her heart nearly stopped when she saw the blood on Kye. On Draigon.

Then reality snapped into place. The moment moving into real time.

The Ferret was hit. Bleeding. But even to her untrained eye, he wasn't critical.

A crowd was starting to gather. Curiosity overtaking common sense and fear.

Then Vaccaro was there. Flashing his FBI badge and calling it in.

She knelt down next to Ricky and he grabbed her hand like it was his lifeline. "Hang on. We'll get you out of here."

"How the fuck...did they find me?" he asked, gasping out fresh sobs when Kye shifted his weight, applying more pressure to the wound on Ricky's shoulder. The blood oozing from underneath Kye's hand.

"Good question. One I intend to ask too," Savannah said. Feeling guilty. Pissed.

She'd assumed if her cell was being tracked by Kelleher and Vaccaro then they'd be watching to see if anyone else had a trace on it. Maybe not.

The rest of the day passed in a blur of statements. A trip back to Reno and the captain's office. A surrendering of her gun. An offer of counseling. Pats on the back. Questions. There was no way to hide the connection between her and Vaccaro and Kelleher this time, though the details of what they were involved in were kept under wraps.

"We'll debrief you as soon as we get Nowak squared away and Becky Traynor in protective custody," Vaccaro said before they parted company.

"You're on administrative leave now," Kelleher said. "Take a vacation for real. Get out of town. We'll investigate how Jose Abrego found Nowak."

"What about the girls? What about the blackmail pictures?" Savannah asked, riding the thin edge between anger and tears and hating every second of it.

Kelleher put a hand on her shoulder. "You've done your part. Now you're benched. That's standard operating procedure."

"Because I killed a guy who shouldn't have been there in the first place."

Kelleher speared his fingers through his hair on a sigh. "I'm sorry. I don't know what to tell you other than Vaccaro and I will look into it. The word's probably already out that Traynor's wife is coming in and we have Nowak. If Becky Traynor really has something on Dominguez and her husband, then we'll get the ball rolling to pick up Traynor and start extradition proceedings on Dominguez. Your part's done. There's no reason for anyone to come gunning for you now."

"What about the other brother?" She remembered the case and the registration papers still in the trunk of Kye's SUV.

Kelleher's eyebrows drew together. "We think he's back in Mexico. There's no sign of him. Just the abandoned van in the garage across from Nowak's place. You still got that stuff?"

"It's in the SUV."

"I'll track down your bodyguards before I leave and get it from them." He shrugged. "I don't think anyone's coming after you, but maybe you should keep the bodyguards with you for a little longer."

"I plan to."

"Good."

Savannah took a deep breath. He was probably right. It was probably safe—even if it didn't feel finished to her. Maybe because of the kid. Holland. She couldn't even explain it to herself why she cared so much—other than what she'd told Krista at The Dive. Holland still seemed vulnerable. Reachable.

"Will you give me a call if the girls surface?"

Kelleher shook his head. "Stay clear of this from now on. Got it? We'll debrief you ASAP." He put his hand on her shoulder again. "Thanks for the save. You've got good instincts and a fast draw. Any slower and we might all have gone down. I'll be in touch."

Savannah watched him go. Her emotions rollercoastering all over the place. She scrubbed at her eyes with the heels of her hands, suddenly wanting to be with Kye and Draigon more than anything else.

She stopped at her locker, intending to toss her cell phone in—then thought better of it. She was being paranoid. Hell, for all she knew Psycho II had followed The Ferret to the truck stop in the hopes Ricky would lead him to Becky Traynor. That made more sense than someone following her. She'd been watching for a tail, then Kye and Draigon had been monitoring the parking lot. It had all happened so quickly, a crazy attack instead of a sniper's bullet, and only when Kelleher had shown up and it became obvious The Ferret was going into custody.

Savannah rubbed the back of her neck and closed the locker without ditching the phone. She was out of the loop now — unless The Ferret called with the address where Becky's clients went to *kick back, party, fuck, whatever*. Then again, there was no reason why Becky wouldn't give the information directly to Kelleher and Vaccaro.

Kye and Draigon were waiting for her in the reception area. Their expressions grim and worried. Tense.

"Let's go," Savannah said, wanting to make it to the car before she melted against them, because as soon as she saw them she realized that what she wanted more than anything else, what she needed more than anything else was to be in bed with them. To feel their heated flesh against her own as the numbness started fading and the reality began setting in. The soul-deep realization she'd managed to keep at bay by answering questions and rehashing the event.

She'd killed a man.

She'd killed a man who deserved to be killed. Who'd asked to be killed. Who would have killed her in a heartbeat.

She didn't feel guilty. So it wasn't conscience.

She'd done what she had to do. What needed to be done. Known it was a possibility from the moment she first decided to become a cop. But now the images were bombarding her. An endless loop she couldn't seem to shut off. The words *I killed a man today* repeating themselves in her thoughts over and over again until they started to unnerve her.

And that was a pisser. A shocker.

A ripping away at the fabric of self-confidence.

She answered in monosyllables as Kye drove. They did the same. Their longest conversation occurring when Kye pulled into a hotel parking garage instead of returning to the cabin.

"This is probably a good idea," Savannah said. "Kelleher thinks Jose Abrego's brother is back in Mexico since he hasn't been seen and you found the van in the garage. Still, we're probably safer here. Harder for a sniper to pick us off." She squeezed their hands. "I should have left the cell phone in my locker. The Ferret calling with a lead on the girls is a long shot. He could tell Kelleher. Or Becky could. I had no right to…"

"Hush," Draigon said, leaning over and pressing a kiss to her mouth. Forcing her to be quiet.

"I believe we are safe from both of the Abregos," Kye said, his voice so confident that Savannah turned and looked at him, wondered for a brief instant if Kye had found the brother Vaccaro labeled Psycho I in the parking garage and had done something to him. But then she shook her head, clearing the thought. Her heart rate spiking and racing, her stomach clamping painfully at the reminder that he was unarmed.

They checked in and went to their room.

"I think I'd like a shower," Savannah said, hating it that her voice sounded shaky. That she just wanted to close her eyes, but every time she did, she relived the shootout. Started the internal dialog all over again. Only now there were additional questions. What if Kye had been killed? Or Draigon? Why had she allowed them to come with her when they didn't even have guns to defend themselves with?

They followed her into the bathroom, their behavior coaxing a laugh out of her, then a sigh as they began undressing her. She wanted to protest, to point out that she'd been bathing herself for a lot of years now, but she couldn't. She couldn't stand the thought of them being out of her sight yet. And their caring was a balm to her soul.

"You're upset," Kye said, kneeling in front of her, removing her shoes and socks then tugging her jeans and panties down while Draigon peeled off her shirt and bra.

"I'm having a harder time with this than I expected," Savannah admitted.

Draigon cupped her breasts, kissing along her shoulder, her neck, his body hot and hard against her back. "Forgive me.

I failed you. It was my duty to protect you, but it was you who protected me instead."

Kye stood and pressed against her front. "Forgive me as well. I was thinking only of the moment when The Ferret would be in Kelleher's hands and I could speak to you about a permanent bond. The burden of this death should not fall on you."

Savannah wrapped her arms around his waist and closed her eyes, savoring being held between two fiercely masculine bodies. Their combined presence making her feel as though she was in a living, breathing cocoon. Their warmth easing some of the tightness inside her. "There's nothing to forgive. I'm a cop and I was doing my job. I'll get through this."

"The taking of a life should not be a casual occurrence," Draigon said, smoothing her hair out of the way and nuzzling her ear. "Rightly or wrongly done it should leave its mark on you. The first time is the hardest, the most painful. The one that lingers the longest in your thoughts no matter whether the death was in self-defense or in accordance with the law."

Savannah turned her head slightly, shivering when the move centered her ear over his mouth and he explored the shell with his tongue. "You've had to kill someone."

"Yes."

Kye brushed her check with the back of his hand. "As have I. We will help you deal with this and in the future you will never have to know this kind of pain again."

"You can't guarantee that. Even if I quit being a cop, which I have no intention of doing, it could still happen again. I could still end up killing someone." She gave a shaky laugh. "Thousands of hours of playing shoot-em-up games with my brothers plus growing up on a ranch where killing livestock is… I thought I was prepared for this."

"You did what needed to be done," Draigon said, making her moan when his tongue explored her ear canal as one hand fondled her breast and the other stroked over her belly on its way to cup her mound.

"If something had happened to either one you…"

"Nothing did," Kye said and she whimpered when his mouth assaulted her other ear, his fingers spearing into her hair as his free hand also cupped a breast, tweaking and rolling the nipple, reminding her of the hours they'd spent suckling her, loving her.

"You guys make it hard to think," she whispered.

"Then don't think about anything but us," Draigon said. "Let us care for you as is our right, our duty."

It sounded old-fashioned. Strangely formal.

And yet it fit *him*. It fit *them*.

"For now," she murmured.

"For always," Draigon said, his hand leaving her cunt as Kye knelt once again and buried his face in the down of her pubic hair, licked along her slit then circled her clit. Striking it. Sucking it. Filling it with blood and sensation until the hood pulled back to expose the tiny, pleasure-vulnerable head.

She arched and shuddered. Unable to think of anything other than the white-hot shards of sensation pulsing through her clit, the feel of Draigon's tongue exploring her ear, his palm rubbing against her tender nipple as her womb fluttered.

"You already wear our bands," Draigon whispered, leaving her ear canal and sucking her earlobe into his mouth, holding it there, tugging gently, biting, before releasing it. "Agree to a permanent bond."

His fingers tightened on her nipple, tugged in the same rhythm as Kye sucked on her clit. Making her remember the perfect synchronicity of their movements when they pleasured her until she agreed to wear the bands — bands she'd since noted matched the ones they wore except for the lack of stones. Her right wristband engraved with the creatures found on Kye's band. Her left identical to the one on Draigon's wrist.

214

"You're not playing fair," she was able to say this time and Kye laughed against her cunt, dipped his head and plunged his tongue into her channel in a long French kiss before lifting his face and saying, "Isn't there a saying, *All's fair in love and war?*"

"You're forgetting my favorite saying," she managed between waves of delirious pleasure. "I don't get mad, I get even."

Kye chuckled. A husky sound of masculine confidence as he licked over the tiny head of her clitoris. "We can take anything you can dish out, beloved, and will come back for second servings." He sucked the swollen knob into his mouth, taking her to the point of orgasm before releasing her. "Agree to spend your life joined with us, Savannah. Agree to a binding ceremony," he said, punctuating his demand by spearing his tongue into her channel.

She closed her eyes against the pleasure. Knowing in a matter of minutes she'd be willing to promise them anything if they'd only allow her to come. Thinking again of the conversation she'd had with Krista days earlier. Understanding completely why Krista had fallen for Adan and Lyan if they were anything like Draigon and Kye.

"Open your eyes," Draigon whispered. "Look in the mirror and see your bond-mates pleasuring you as is their right, their duty."

Savannah did as he commanded and heat rushed through her body at the image captured in the full mirror. Kye kneeling in front of her, his face buried between her thighs as her fingers speared into his hair, holding him to her. Draigon behind her. His face chiseled perfection. His expression one of love, lust, determination.

He nuzzled her cheek with his, cupped her breasts and rubbed his thumbs over the ultrasensitive nipples so she arched, moaned, saw the flash of exquisite need in her own face. Whimpered when Kye renewed his assault on her clit, his lips surrounding it, sucking as his tongue danced over it until she was panting, pumping into his mouth, desperate for release.

Draigon's fingers captured her areolas then, his face becoming a taut mask of masculine intention. His attack on her nipples in perfect sync to Kye's assault on her cunt and clit. "Agree to go through a binding ceremony with us."

"Yes," Savannah said, crying out as they relented, as orgasm shimmered through her.

Chapter Eighteen

ඝා

They'd done it to her again, Savannah thought, used her body to get what they wanted. But how could she be mad at them? Especially when waking up with two gorgeous sex gods on either side of her was *exactly* her idea of heaven.

She eased to a sitting position. Glanced at the clock on the bedside stand and wasn't surprised to discover they'd slept through both breakfast and lunch.

Every part of her tingled as she took in the bronzed bodies, the hard muscles, the long hair spilling across the pillows and across their chests and shoulders. Damn, who'd have ever guessed men with long hair could be such a turn-on for her?

But they definitely were. Though it was a bit of a problem that they knew exactly how much she craved them. How much power they had over her. She was totally and completely hooked. Couldn't imagine sleeping solo now. But maybe it worked both ways. They were both pressed against her as though they couldn't stand to be apart from her even in sleep.

Savannah sighed and studied the bracelets they'd put on her wrists the first time they used her body against her. She'd known on some level that the things were more than just pieces of jewelry. But after last night...

Her womb fluttered. She was starting to think the bands might be their version of engagement rings.

You already wear our bands. Agree to a permanent bond.

Agree to spend your life joined with us, Savannah. Agree to a binding ceremony.

Was there any other interpretation possible?

Savannah didn't think so.

It made her a little nervous, but she wasn't freaking out—yet. Then again, she'd pretty much always lived by the seat of her pants. On gut instinct.

She loved Kye and Draigon. She thought she had a future with them. She *wanted* a future with them. And like she'd told Krista, she *did* believe in love at first sight. Or at least the possibility of recognizing a soul mate—or two—at the same time she was in the throes of lust.

A laugh escaped as she thought of all the wedding chapels in Las Vegas. Obviously she wasn't the only one who believed in love at first sight.

She absently played with strands of their hair, reliving the night, the almost non-stop sex starting in the shower after she'd agreed to a bond with them and then moving to the bed. They'd taken her on her hands and knees, anally, coaxed her into riding them, switched off who was lying on top and fucking her—brought her to orgasm so many times that there had been no room for anything else but physical sensation.

A small smile played over her lips. They'd done it for themselves, no doubt to reinforce their claim on her, and while she doubted either Draigon or Kye would admit it—to compete with each other. But mainly they'd done it for her—to keep her from thinking about killing a man.

And it had worked.

The repetitive loop of images and questions had stopped. Even now, revisiting what had happened, she felt...calm, accepting. It was a righteous kill. Unasked for, but unavoidable.

And she could live with it. She was okay with it.

Savannah slipped out of bed. Stretched. Only barely suppressing a groan when her body began cataloguing exactly how well they'd loved her the previous night.

Another laugh escaped. She might have to become a nudist. Because right now, the thought of clothes was pure torture.

Still, she couldn't resist snagging one of their shirts as she made her way to the kitchenette, buttoning only a couple of the buttons before making a pot of coffee and pouring herself a cup, then moving to the window. Thinking.

She was on administrative leave. Officially. Definitely. On the bench, as Kelleher had said. Sidelined. Out of the loop and off the investigation.

Which meant she should do what? Go on vacation— maybe even a honeymoon?

Savannah closed her eyes and leaned against the sun-warmed windowpane. The obvious thing, the thing she probably wasn't going to be able to avoid, was a serious discussion with Draigon and Kye about the bands, the binding ceremony, their home—wherever the hell that was. She grimaced. Somehow she had a feeling the conversation wasn't going to go smoothly.

With a sigh, she opened her eyes and took a sip of coffee. Admitted to herself as she did it that what she really wanted to do, what she needed to do in order to put this thing behind her was to find Holland and make sure she was okay. To make the offer of help one more time. If she could just do that…then she could walk away from this.

Footsteps sounded behind her. She turned and smiled, not surprised to see Kye a few steps away, naked. He glided to a stop and immediately reached for the shirt buttons, undoing them so the shirt spread, revealing her breasts, her belly, her cunt.

"I believe this is my shirt," Kye said, his cock stirring at the sight of his bond-mate. *Their* bond-mate.

The Ylan stones pulsed in anticipation of migrating to the bands on her wrists. Their vibration against his skin warning him that it was now too dangerous for him to mate with her.

To risk touching his bands to hers as they were intimate unless they were in the transport chamber and he and Draigon were taking her in the binding ceremony. Once she wore the Ylan stones there would be no hiding their true form from her, no hiding their thoughts or emotions from her.

"Are you saying you want your shirt back?" Savannah teased and Kye's heart filled with happiness, with relief that she'd put the events of the previous day behind her.

He reached out and stroked her side, loving the feel of smooth skin over sleek muscle. His cock echoing his thoughts, rising like an exclamation point between them. "Yes, I think it's safe to say I want my shirt back," he said, pulling her to him and taking her coffee mug from her hand, setting it on the windowsill so he could enfold her in a loose embrace. "But perhaps we had better eat first."

Savannah pressed against him, rubbed his cock with her lower body and sent fire through his shaft and up his spine. "Are you talking about food?" she asked.

Kye slid his hands down to palm her buttocks. "For starters."

"Hmmm, it might be a good idea. Especially if we're going to have a repeat of the marathon sex event we had last night."

Kye laughed, thrusting gently against her mound, his cock head beading with moisture as it rubbed over her flat belly. "I believe I'm up for it."

"I can *see* that. I can *feel* that."

He leaned down and captured her mouth in a brief kiss. Afraid that if he deepened it, he would soon be pulling her back to bed. But as much as he wanted to do just that, they needed to talk and he feared the conversation would not go well—despite her having agreed to go through the binding ceremony.

"I've got a question for you," she whispered, her expression piquing his curiosity and holding his trepidation at bay long enough for him to say, "Ask it."

"In the truck the other day, you said you'd never shared a woman before."

"That is true," he said, his mind racing, trying to determine the direction of her thoughts in case he needed to head them off. Failing.

"Draigon likes anal sex. And you like it. Obviously. Since we did that last night." She cocked her head, eyes sparkling though a trace of color was making its way across her cheeks.

"What you say is true. I enjoy taking you in that manner," he answered, hearing the caution in his own voice. Her smile telling him Savannah had heard it as well.

"So, now that the three of us are together, do you think you'd like to both fuck me at the same time?"

Kye stiffened and felt the heat rise in his face. Felt Draigon's amusement along the link they shared and knew the other man was awake and listening to the conversation.

When he didn't answer, Savannah gave a husky laugh and hugged him. "Forget I asked. From the expression on your face I'm guessing the answer is no, and I can guess why. It's probably a little bit too much male-male contact for straight guys. And from what I can tell, you're very straight," she said, rubbing against his thick erection, the conversation and her actions very nearly causing him to come.

He groaned and dug his fingers in her buttocks, stilling her movement before he coated them both with his seed. "Draigon and I will take you together during the binding ceremony."

"Speaking of which…" Savannah said, glad he'd brought it up though the fleeting expression on his face and the sudden nerves rippling through her gut told her maybe it would have been better to eat first, play some more and then tackle this subject. But rather than retreat, she plowed forward. "Want to tell me exactly what you and Draigon persuaded me to agree to?" She loosened her grip on him enough to lightly rub one wristband against his lower back. "I'm guessing that these things are your version of engagement rings. Right?"

"Yes," Kye said, glancing at the bed.

Savannah's attention followed his. Heat and love and desire settling in her cunt when Draigon rose and padded over to join them. His cock full, the tip already glistening.

She groaned when he pressed against her back, kissed along her shoulder in a repeat performance of the previous night. "It's not going to work this time," she said, making no effort to push either man away but resolved not to let them use her body against her. "We need to talk. About a lot of things."

Draigon's hand slid between her chest and Kye's, finding her breast and cupping it, sending spikes of fiery pleasure through her nipple as he rubbed against it in slow circles with his palm. "We have a lifetime for discussion. Once you agree to go home with us, we can join with you in the manner you were speaking to Kye about, and then we can leave."

Savannah closed her eyes, savoring the feel of them against her even as her heart skipped a beat before resuming in a thundering rush as her cop-mind processed *exactly* what Draigon was saying. The suspicions she'd had from the first—when she accused Kye of belonging to a cult—crashing in on her.

She took a deep breath. Forced a tiny measure of calm into her body.

They might not play fair when it came to getting her to agree to wearing their bands and going through a ceremony with them, but she didn't think they'd abduct her. She trusted them. And she trusted her own instincts.

"By home," she said, "I hope you mean—home to meet the relatives before coming back to Reno where Savannah has a job and a life and a large extended family. Not that I'm opposed to living and being a cop somewhere else, *after* we've discussed and agreed on it. But I don't intend to disappear off the face of the Earth with you guys. No matter how crazy I am about you."

Their sudden tensing told her she was on target. Their stillness reminded her of all the times she'd seen them with identical expressions, so completely focused inward they might as well be carrying on a private conversation. Or doing the Vulcan mind-meld.

She shook her head when the theme song from *Star Trek* segued into *The Twilight Zone*. She did *not* need this right now.

"Say you will come home with us," Draigon said.

"I'll come home with you," Savannah told them, unable to continue for several long moments because Kye's mouth covered hers, preventing it. But when the kiss ended, she added, "For a visit."

Her cell phone rang, halting further conversation. She pulled out of their arms and answered it.

"Look, I got to make this quick," The Ferret said. "Here's the address of that place I was telling you about. It hasn't come up yet and Becky hasn't volunteered it to Vaccaro and Kelleher."

Savannah scrambled for a pen and paper and wrote it down.

"You got it?"

She read it back to him.

"That's it. They're back. I gotta go." He paused. "Thanks for the save yesterday."

"Anytime," Savannah said, the line going dead, the memory of killing a man rushing in. But instead of threatening to overwhelm her, she found she could examine the event and then put it away in favor of focusing on a plan of action.

"That was Ricky," she said, wrinkling her nose in disgust as she looked at yesterday's clothing and decided they had time enough to buy or recover something clean before they did anything else. "He called to pass on the address of a place Becky had for clients who wanted privacy while they partied with her girls. It's a long shot, but I want to check it out."

Draigon's frown was immediate and earned him a small headshake from Kye, along with a warning. *Don't. You will not sway her. Consider this interruption a blessing. A chance to regroup and determine what to do next. What to say next. I have already mated with her so many times the Ylan stones now pulse in warning against my wrist.*

With a grimace, Draigon gave a slight nod. *Mine as well.*

"I thought your informant was now with Kelleher and Vaccaro," Draigon said, pleased he sounded so reasonable when his mate was very nearly driving him crazy with her disregard for danger.

"He is."

"Then why not pass the information to them and allow them to follow up on it? I thought you were now on administrative leave. Free to do what you want with your time."

Savannah shot him a glance. "I am. And what I want to do, besides get some clean clothes and some food, is to check out this address."

"Beloved—"

She held up her hand to stop him. "This is non-negotiable. If you would rather stay here or go back to the cabin—"

"I will do neither," Draigon growled, closing the distance between them, crowding her against the wall, his fingers digging into her upper arms in frustration. "I am trying to understand why you are not only willing to put yourself in danger but are willing to break rules you are sworn to uphold."

Fire flashed in her eyes. True anger. And for a split second, Draigon feared he had gone too far. Had driven a wedge between them.

His chest tightened and not for the first time he cursed the primitive nature of Earth, where the psi ability to communicate mind-to-mind had been suppressed and allowed to go fallow. Where all that he felt, all that he was, had to be communicated through body language or words alone.

Savannah sighed, relaxing against him and leaning her forehead against his chest. "Okay, those are fair questions."

She stroked his side and his cock responded by pulsing and leaking. The Ylan stones at his wrists echoing the warning Kye had spoken of. Vibrating, denser now in readiness for separating and migrating to the bands Savannah wore.

"Why are you willing to put yourself in danger? Why are you willing to break the rules over this?" he asked again, feeling calmer with her touch.

She exhaled, a burst of warm air against his chest. "First, I'm not sure this qualifies as dangerous. Based on what Kelleher said, and what The Ferret said, the blackmail scheme is either the girls operating solo, or them working with Becky or Steven Traynor, or both. And since Becky is now in protective custody, Kelleher and Vaccaro probably have everything they need to tie Traynor to laundering drug money. So I doubt Traynor's thinking too much about the girls right now. In fact, I wouldn't be surprised to hear he's suddenly out of the country and unavailable for comment. Now for your second question, that's a little trickier."

Draigon rubbed his cheek against her hair when she didn't immediately say anything. Enjoyed the closeness he felt to her, a closeness that was more than the touch of skin to skin.

"If we were strictly going by the books, then I know I should just call Kelleher or Vaccaro and let them check out the address. If this was just about Camryn and Ivy, then it'd be a slam dunk and I would have already passed on the information. But the problem is Holland. When I hauled her in the other day, there was some kind of a connection. Maybe it was one-way. Maybe I'm just kidding myself and it's too late for her." Savannah shrugged. "Maybe she just reminds me so much of Krista and me when we were her age that I'm seeing what I want to see. I don't know. But my gut tells me to find her first and do what I can to keep her from either disappearing on the street or ending up in juvenile hall."

"You intend to make her part of your family?" Draigon asked, his own emotions vacillating between pride and dismay.

Savannah laughed. "I'm winging it here, Draigon. One thing at a time." Her hands slid to his hips and she leaned into him, giving him a kiss. "Ready to get dressed and head out?"

His fingers tangled in her hair, pulling her face to his for a longer, deeper kiss. Finding humor in the knowledge that slowly but surely his bond-mate was corrupting him.

* * * * *

The address turned out to be a house built near a manmade lake. It was smallish, designed for privacy and coziness, and weekend stays instead of everyday life. Or so Savannah guessed, given that the majority of the neighboring houses had a nobody-home, this-is-a-rental feel and look to them.

"I'm going to knock on the front door," she said as Kye turned the SUV around in a driveway several blocks from the house. "Who wants to cover the back?"

There was the usual strange hesitation then Draigon answered. "I will enter through the back of the house. Kye will attempt to enter through the front door. You will remain in the car until we have secured the premises." His tone suggested he was not only serious but thought she'd go along with his suggestion.

Savannah shook her head. "No. The girls will recognize me. They may not be happy to see me, but my showing up won't scare them."

"As you wish," Draigon said.

Savannah turned in the seat next to him so she could read his expression. His calm answer making her suspicious. A suspicion that panned out a moment later when Kye drove by the house and kept going, telling her without words that he and Draigon were on the same wavelength.

"Would you like to reconsider my suggestion?" Draigon asked. Masculine amusement and superiority in his voice and scraping across Savannah's nerves.

Savannah closed her eyes and counted to ten. This was something she'd never contemplated when she fantasized about two men at once—how they might conceivably gang up on her!

Unfortunately she didn't have time to nip this problem in the bud. At least not right now.

"Okay, I'll stay in the car," she said, consoling herself with the knowledge—though in Holland's case she hated it—that the girls in question were used to strange men showing up and doing a hell of a lot more than making sure the place was safe.

Kye pulled into another driveway in order to turn around. Draigon cupped Savannah's cheek and forced her to meet his gaze. "Promise you'll stay in the car until one of us signals for you."

Savannah sighed. It was impossible to be pissed at him. Not when he radiated concern. Not when she saw love in his eyes, worry. "I promise."

He gave her a brief kiss and resettled in his seat. She put her hands on their thighs, squeezing. "You guys be careful, okay? There's no car out front, so it's possible no one's home." She sighed. "I can't believe I'm saying this, but I'd feel better if you had guns."

Kye covered her hand with his. "Do not worry. This is child's play for us."

"Child's play, huh?" But she didn't ask them to elaborate. And she didn't break her promise.

Even when Holland answered the door, Savannah waited for Draigon to appear and signal for her to join them.

"Something's happened to them," Holland said, arms wrapped around her body, shoulders hunching against the news she thought Savannah was bringing. "They're dead, aren't they? That's why they're not answering their cells."

Chapter Nineteen

ഇ

"Your sister and Camryn?" Savannah asked, heart wrenching at how vulnerable Holland seemed. How young, despite everything she'd seen and done.

Holland's arms dropped to her side. Surprise flashing in her eyes. Hope. Uncertainty. "You're not here because of them?"

"More because of you," Savannah said. "The blackmail scheme is about to unravel, Holland. The FBI is looking for you, your sister and Camryn. You can't hide out forever. You're smart enough to know that. I think there's room for cutting a deal."

Holland crossed her arms again, this time digging her fingers into her skin with enough force to leave tiny indentations. "I'd rather be locked up than go back into foster care."

"No you wouldn't."

"You don't know that!"

Savannah hesitated then nodded. "You're right. I don't know what your life has been like. I can guess, but I don't really *know*. The only thing I know for sure is that I'd like to help you."

"What's it going to cost me?" Holland said, expression becoming world-weary, too old, hopeless as she glanced at Draigon and Kye.

Savannah went with her instincts, the same as she'd done in the truck stop with The Ferret. She grabbed Holland's shoulders and gave her a little shake. "They're both mine and I don't share. Keep your eyes to yourself or you're going to piss me off royally."

Surprise replaced the jaded acceptance on Holland's face. Her mouth gaped for a second before she said, "Both of them? But you're a cop."

"Yeah and cops don't have a personal life. They're both mine but I'd appreciate it if you didn't spread the information around." Savannah paused for a second, before adding, "Which is why they're with me. I'm not on duty right now. I'm just following up on the offer I made you the other day. To help you get out of the situation you're in."

Holland dragged her hands down her arms, leaving red streaks where her nails touched. "There's no way out. I'd rather stay with Ivy and Camryn than go back into the foster care system."

Savannah glanced at Kye and Draigon, wishing they'd discussed possible outcomes if they found Holland.

Their relationship was so new. The phone call from The Ferret had interrupted the conversation about a binding ceremony and the exact terms of going home with them and they hadn't had a chance to get back to it.

She had no idea how they would feel about being responsible for a child who wasn't their own, and she was honest enough with herself to admit she wasn't ready to promise anything long-term when it came to Holland. She was just… Hell, she was just winging it, same as always. But she'd come this far and all she really needed was to buy some time. "Do you like horses?" she asked, grimacing at the prospect of arriving at her grandparents' homestead on the Bar None with Kye and Draigon in tow. But she needed a place to park Holland, one where she couldn't panic and run and one where there would be adult supervision.

"Horses?" Holland asked, looking at Savannah strangely.

"My family owns a ranch. You could stay there until things get sorted out."

"What about Ivy and Camryn?"

"We'd need to talk to them and see what they want to do," Savannah answered, avoiding the real question because she wasn't willing to lie to Holland. But there was no way either of the other girls was going to set foot on the Bar None.

Holland rubbed her arms. Her gaze flickering from the ground to Savannah's face, darting to Kye then Draigon before once again settling on Savannah.

Savannah pressed. "I told you the truth earlier, two FBI agents are in town looking for you. It's only a matter of time before you're caught and charged."

The silence lasted for several long minutes before Holland said, "Why do you even care?"

Savannah shrugged. "I don't know. I just do."

Holland squeezed her arms until her knuckles were white, finally loosening her grip and allowing the blood to return, offering a tentative smile. "I'll go with you."

"Do you need to get your things?"

"There's not much. We bailed as soon as we left the police station the other day."

Savannah was glad there was no anger in Holland's voice. Then again, a trip to the station probably seemed a hell of a lot better than having to service the pervert Camryn had sent into the room with Holland and the other girl.

Holland stepped back into the house and into the living room, stopping next to a couch that was also serving as her bed. She began stuffing clothes into a gym bag.

Savannah had thought to question Holland further when they were in the car, but now she hated to leave without searching the house. "Do you know where Ivy and Camryn are?"

Holland stilled, her shoulders hunching inward. Just a little. Not enough to notice except Savannah had been looking right at her when she did it.

231

Savannah walked over and knelt next to the girl. "You were afraid something had happened to them when you saw me."

"They left yesterday. They haven't come back and neither one of them is answering their cells." A whisper. "They always answer their cells. Not right away if they're working. But right after."

"Were they meeting someone?"

A slight nod. "I think so. But they didn't say." She looked up. Eyes haunted. "I didn't ask. I didn't want to go with them."

Savannah steeled herself against the image of Holland giving a blowjob to a man old enough to be her grandfather. "They were meeting a client?"

Holland reached for a pile of socks and put them in the bag. Then a shirt. And another shirt. Her movements slow, as though she was using the time to come to a decision. Finally looking up and meeting Savannah's eyes. "I think they were meeting Mr. Traynor."

"Is he the one telling your sister and Camryn which men to take back to the room with the camera?"

Holland's eyes glistened with tears and Savannah moved closer, unsure whether physical contact would be welcomed or repelled. "I don't know. Maybe, sometimes. Mostly it's Camryn and her brother."

"Can you identify Camryn's brother?"

Holland's gaze slid away from Savannah's. She ducked her head and swiped under the sofa, pulling out a stray sock as she answered, "No."

Savannah let it go for the moment. "Why do you think Ivy and Camryn were meeting Traynor?"

"Ivy gave me money so I could order pizza. When they were leaving I heard Camryn joke about how nice it was to have an insurance policy that covered drugs." Holland looked up and met Savannah's eyes again. "Camryn fucked him and he gave her drugs to party with. She called him her insurance policy."

Holland stood and looked around. "I'm ready."

Savannah got to her feet too, wondering if maybe Camryn was blackmailing Steven Traynor, wondering if Camryn knew about his connection to Dominguez and how easily he could supply her with drugs as a result of it. Then again, if she was blackmailing Traynor, he could have solved the problem by asking Dominguez to send The Psychos or The Cousins after her.

"Where do Camryn and Ivy go to party?" Savannah asked.

"To Alphonso's house. They always go there right after they get a *party pack* from Mr. Traynor." Holland tightened her grip on the gym bag, holding it to her chest like a shield as small tremors racked her body.

Savannah's heart wrenched as she easily imagined all the reasons Holland might be afraid, especially if drugs were involved. "We can get you settled at the Bar None. Then Kye and Draigon and I can come back and check out Alphonso's place. Do you have an address?"

Holland took a deep breath and shook her head. "I'll go with you."

Savannah started to say no then let it go. She didn't want to become Holland's jailer. She'd worked as a cop long enough to know some people never get clear of their problems, never get clear of the mess they make of their lives with bad choices.

According to the Social Services' report Kelleher had shown her, Holland had been running away from foster care since she was ten, always going to Ivy. Maybe the pattern was already too ingrained. Or maybe Holland needed a final confrontation with her sister to make the break.

"Okay," Savannah said. "Let's get out of here."

* * * * *

Alphonso's place was a tract house in suburbia. A landscaped yard with shiny, expensive cars in the driveway and lining the curb in front of the house.

Savannah glanced at Kye and Draigon, wondering what they were thinking. Since finding Holland they hadn't said a word. Then again, maybe they were concentrating on bodyguarding. Or maybe they were just biding their time, waiting 'til the situation played out and they were somewhere they could discuss things in private.

It worked for her.

"That's Ivy's car," Holland said, pointing to the silver convertible parked in the driveway.

"When were they supposed to meet Traynor?" Savannah asked, trying to get a fix on how long the people inside the house had been partying. Holland's answer making Savannah's stomach ripple with uneasiness when she realized Ivy and Camryn had gone out at about the same time the shootout with Psycho II would have started making the news.

They reached the front door, Kye and Draigon hanging back instead of insisting they go first. Savannah rang the bell. Several times. Then tried the door and found it unlocked.

Out of habit Savannah's hand went to where her gun usually rested in its holster. There was a moment of disorientation at finding it missing then she took a deep breath and opened the door. Yelling hello and not getting a response. Not hearing anything beyond the music. Hip-hop. The words so fast she couldn't make them out.

She yelled hello again then eased inside. Kye and Draigon fanning out. Moving in front of her. Holland pushing forward so Savannah was forced to grab the girl's arm in order to keep her from racing ahead. "You should go wait in the car while we check this out," Savannah said. Holland didn't answer, just tugged at her arm, trying to get Savannah to let her go.

There was the smell of pot. Just a hint of it in the hallway as they made their way toward the back of the house and the source of the music.

Savannah called out again. Worried someone in the house might be carrying a weapon and not wanting to startle or panic them—especially if they were high.

A few feet away from an open doorway the first whiff of voided bowels hit her. She stopped and tightened her grip on Holland's arm. "You need to either wait until we check this out or you need to go back to the car."

Holland made a gagging sound and nodded. Savannah had no choice but to trust her. She freed Holland's arm and surged forward, entering the party room a few paces behind Kye and Draigon. Taking in the scene with a glance that told her everything she needed to know.

Seven bodies.

Some of them curled in fetal positions. Some of them sprawled out.

On the floor. On the overstuffed sofa.

All of them still as death.

An assortment of drugs on the coffee table. Food. Bottles of liquor. Soda.

Vomit. Urine. Feces. The bodies' futile attempts to void themselves.

Kye was already crouched next to Camryn. He looked up at Savannah and shook his head. Draigon moved to Ivy but Savannah already knew they were the only three people alive in the room.

A sob sounded in the doorway. A gasping, retching sound and Savannah turned to intercept Holland before she went to her knees. "Let's go," she said. "I'll call this in from the car."

This planet grows more horrifying with each moment, Draigon said, both he and Kye lingering, allowing Savannah a head start as she hustled her new charge down the hallway.

This is no accident, Kye said. *But without knowing more about Traynor's habits, we cannot be sure that the death wasn't meant for him.*

It is more likely that he is behind the blackmail scheme and this is his way of eliminating those who might testify against him.

Kye nodded. *True. This would solve the problem of witnesses.*

If Traynor is responsible then Holland should be safe once Vaccaro and Kelleher have placed him under arrest. Even so, the Baraqijal clan-house is not without resources. Bounty hunters can be hired to protect Holland and her caretakers.

Kye's eyebrows lifted in response and Draigon grimaced in silent acknowledgment, adding, *You are right, I fear our stay here has just been extended. Savannah will not easily surrender Holland to the authorities or leave until she is settled.*

We will have to trust the humans to search the bodies and the cars and determine the truth of what happened here. Kye's expression hardened as he looked at the dead around them. *This is not our business to interfere in, though if opportunity presented itself, I would serve justice for what was done here and for what has been done to the girl.*

Draigon nodded. A tightness settling in his chest. Not because he disagreed with Kye, but because he *agreed* with him, and in agreeing gained unwanted insight as to how Adan could be such good friends with Lyan d'Vesti, a man whose willingness to bend and stretch the rules was well-known.

Savannah got to the car and dug out an FBI card from her pocket. Kelleher's. It wasn't standard operating procedure. But she wasn't on duty. And she figured she had a better chance of leaving before the cops got on the scene if she turned it over to the Feds and let them handle the jurisdiction issues.

This could conceivably go down as accidental death by overdose. But maybe if Kelleher and Vaccaro covered it, they'd find something here linking back to Traynor or Carlos Dominguez. In the meantime she had to keep Holland safe.

Savannah looked over to where the girl was huddling against the car door. Crying. Not huge sobbing bursts. But silent shudders that racked her body.

Fuck. This was the part she wasn't good with. Consolation. And for a split second Savannah was tempted to call in a Social Services counselor and turn this over to them.

Savannah took a deep breath and dialed Kelleher's number. "This is a courtesy call," she said when he answered, remembering their last conversation and adding, "not that you would have done me the same favor. I've got an address for you. Inside there are seven people. Two females. Five males. Cause of death is either going to be contaminated drugs or an overdose on super pure stuff."

"Camryn and Ivy?"

"Yes."

"You call it in yet?"

"You're my first call." Savannah hesitated a moment. "I have reason to believe Traynor was the source of some of the drugs."

There was a long moment of silence on the other end of the line, followed by a sigh. "You've got the kid?"

"I've been in contact with her," Savannah hedged.

"We're going to need to talk to her."

"Just talk?"

"What else?"

"Social Services, juvie."

"We're not interested in pursuing either of those outcomes."

237

"Once I call this in, it's out of my hands." Savannah took a deep breath and came clean. "Holland's with me. She went into the house when I did."

"Hold on a minute." There was muted conversation in the background. When Kelleher came back on he said, "The bodyguards with you too?"

Savannah looked up as Kye and Draigon opened the car doors and slid into the front seat. "Yeah, they're here."

"All four of you go into the house?"

"Yes." Savannah guessed where this was heading and volunteered the information. "Holland didn't touch anything. I touched the door handle, front and back, but nothing else." She frowned at Kye and Draigon, wondering at their delay in leaving the house. "I wasn't watching the guys."

"Does the kid know who's behind the blackmail?"

"I'll have to get back to you on that one. But I think you should check Camryn's background for a brother."

"Okay. Here's what I want you to do. Leave. Take the kid back to your apartment and keep her there. Vaccaro and I are on our way to the scene. For the record, a tip came in and we're checking it out. When we get there, we'll handle calling in the locals. Keep your cell phone on. We'll catch up to you later."

Relief poured through Savannah. She mouthed the words, "Let's go," to Kye, then turned her attention back to the conversation with Kelleher so she could pass on the address where Holland and the other girls had been staying.

She could hear the laugh in Kelleher's voice when he said, "Is that all? Or do I need to remind you that you're on administrative leave?"

"That's all." She couldn't resist saying. "For now."

"It'd better be."

"Did you figure out how Psycho II found us at the truck stop?"

"Best we can tell he got lucky and spotted Nowak, then followed him, hoping to catch him with Becky Traynor."

Kelleher signed off and Savannah studied Holland. The tears on the girl's face were dry now though her fists were clenched in her lap. She'd dug out her iPod and was listening to Keith Urban tunes. The volume turned up to form a musical no trespassing sign.

"Where to?" Kye asked.

"My apartment," Savannah said, still worried Holland would panic and bolt. But she didn't want to alienate Kelleher and Vaccaro. And she knew this was never going to end for Holland until all the other players were known and behind bars.

Savannah had no clue what she was going to do about Holland. At least not long-term. *Story of my life,* she thought. *Leap first. Worry about landing second.*

Movement in the front seat drew her attention to Kye's profile then Draigon's. Humor found her and she smiled. *Then again, there were definitely advantages to leaping first and worrying about landing later.*

When they got to the apartment Savannah directed Holland to the bedroom and watched as the girl set her gym bag down on the dresser, her expression lost in the mirror. Sad. Haunted.

Compassion pulled Savannah over to her. Made her reach out and gently remove an earbud. "You want to talk?"

Their eyes met in the mirror. Liquid blue and emerald green.

Tears trickled down Holland's face. "I hated her. I told her I hated her. I hated them both." A sob escaped from deep in Holland's chest, followed by another one, and another one.

She turned in to Savannah, accepted Savannah's hug, Savannah's whispered words of understanding, cried until she sagged and Savannah led her to the edge of the bed and they sat down.

"I just wanted it to be Ivy and me." Holland gulped in a shuddering breath of air. "When I was little, Ivy took care of me. I just wanted it to be like that again. Only better because I can take care of myself now."

Savannah sifted away from Holland, far enough to reach for the box of tissues on the night table and hand it to the girl before removing the other earbud and gently brushing the hair off Holland's face. "She was eight years older than you, wasn't she?" Savannah said, remembering Kelleher's comment when they'd met at the diner.

Holland nodded, rubbing at her wet cheeks. "Ivy would never have done any of this if it wasn't for Camryn. She did anything Camryn said to do. Anything."

Savannah had no way of knowing whether it was true or whether Holland just needed it to be true. "You mean the prostitution and the blackmail? The drugs?"

Another shuddering gasp for breath, followed by a tremor that shook Holland's entire body. "Yes."

"Were Ivy and Camryn doing the same thing in Vegas?"

"Yes." Tearful eyes met Savannah's. "I didn't know at first. But then one day Ivy took me to an apartment." Holland drew her knees up to her chest and wrapped her arms around them. "She made me a milkshake. Chocolate. Only she put something in it so I wouldn't care about anything." A sob escaped and Holland buried her face against her knees. Rocked. "Then Camryn got there. She had a man with her. Afterward...there were pictures and Camryn said that's what paid for *the life*. And Ivy agreed with her. Like always."

Sobs racked Holland's body, leaving Savannah heartsick, aching, feeling inadequate and helpless. Though the urge to try to alleviate Holland's pain was overwhelming.

Savannah rubbed Holland's back, whispered to her that she was safe now. Waited out the tears.

When Holland stopped crying, Savannah said, "The FBI agents are going to be here in a little while. They're going to ask you questions. But they're not interested in anything but your answers. They're not going to call in Social Services. They're not going to take you anywhere."

Holland met her eyes. "Then what?"

"We'll figure it out as we go along."

"I won't go back. I'll run before I go back."

Suspicion settled in Savannah's gut. Rage and nausea coiled with it. "Something happened in your last foster home?"

"I don't want to talk about it," Holland whispered.

Savannah let it go. Didn't press Holland for any more answers or try to stop her from putting the earbuds back in and walling herself off behind a barricade of music.

She stayed with Holland until the horror and worry and exhaustion finally took its toll and Holland curled up on the bed and closed her eyes. Then Savannah lingered until the girl's breathing was even. The sleep deep enough that there was no sign of thought.

Kye and Draigon wore identical grim expressions on their faces when Savannah joined them in the living room. And as though they were all three on the same wavelength, they met in the middle, Savannah glad to find herself between the two men. "Did you hear any of that?" she asked after several minutes of just savoring the feel of firm muscle and masculine heat.

"All of it," Draigon said. Anger vibrating through his voice.

"She will be protected and cared for from now on," Kye promised.

They pulled apart and Kye plopped down on Savannah's overstuffed couch. Draigon took the chair, but Savannah was too tense to sit. She paced the short distance to the window and looked out, then decided to put some music on.

The doorbell rang. "That's probably Kelleher or Vaccaro," Savannah said, getting there first since she was closer. Surprise flashing through her when she opened the door and found Fowler standing there.

"Can I come in?" he asked, his face drawn, stressed. GQ looks muted, but the kind of muted that pulls at a woman's heartstrings.

Chapter Twenty

ℰ

"Sure. What's up?" Savannah said, letting him in and closing the door. Not surprised when Kye and Draigon rose to their feet and came over to stand next to her, remaining at her side even after she'd made the introductions.

"You know those girls you've been asking around about?" Fowler asked.

Savannah guessed where the conversation was going and was touched that the Vice cop would swing by to deliver the bad news personally. For a split second she was tempted to let him off the hook and tell him she already knew about Ivy and Camryn, but she hadn't turned on the police scanner, hadn't heard from Kelleher or Vaccaro, so she didn't know what the status of the investigation was. "What about them?"

Something flickered in Fowler's eyes. Regret, maybe. Sadness. "Two of them are dead. I swung by the scene a minute ago when I heard it called in. Drug overdose."

He glanced around the room, lingering for a moment on the door to her bedroom before taking in the kitchen separated from the living room by a short counter. "It reminded me of those pictures of mass suicides. The ones where cult leaders talk their followers into drinking poisoned Kool-Aid. There were seven bodies at the scene." He speared his fingers through his hair as his gaze returned to Savannah, his distress obvious. "I figured you'd want to know."

"Thanks."

"You think I could get some water before I head out?"

Savannah nodded and moved to the kitchen. Her pulse spiking when Fowler stayed with her and they passed the partially open bedroom door.

Out of the corner of her eye she saw him glance in. "So you found the kid," he said, resignation in his voice. "She know about Ivy and Camryn?"

"I've got some bottled water. Black-cherry flavored. Would you rather have that?" Savannah asked, intent on avoiding his question, turning toward the refrigerator. Realizing a split second too late how casually Fowler had used the girls' names.

He grabbed her arm and pressed the barrel of a silenced gun against the side of her head.

"Stay right there," Fowler said to Draigon and Kye. Holding them at bay on the other side of the counter.

They slowly raised their hands. Though Savannah was sure Fowler knew they were unarmed.

"Christ, Holden, I did everything but buy you a ticket out of town. But you just couldn't leave this alone. I should have had Camryn take care of the kid. Slip her something and be done with it after she caught me changing out the memory chip in the camera a couple of weeks ago. I never wanted this to happen. The entire way over here I was praying I wouldn't find the kid here. I've had a tracer on your boyfriend's car since yesterday. I knew you'd been to Becky Traynor's playhouse. Then the call came in... Christ!" It was a near shout. Fowler's body practically vibrating against hers. Strung out with emotion.

Savannah's mind raced, trying to find a way for them to get out of this alive. And then it hit her. "You're Camryn's brother. The FBI is already looking for you."

He gave a bark of laughter. A terse sound. "Nice try. But Camryn was arrested in Vegas on some lightweight charges. They're the only prints in the system on her. I made sure the records reflect that she's an only child. Parents deceased. No known living relatives."

A cold sickness filled Savannah's stomach. Horror that she could have misjudged him so badly. Had considered him her one friend in Vice. "Did you kill Camryn and the others?"

"No. Traynor did that with one of his little party packs. And he'll get what's coming to him for it. In jail or out. I'll make sure of it." He hesitated. "I'm sorry about this, Holden. I really am. I liked you and that's the truth."

She knew in a heartbeat that he intended to pull the trigger and so she did the only thing she could. She dropped, hoping to take him with her, to pull Fowler off balance and split his attention.

Kye and Draigon lunged at the counter in the same instant Fowler released his hold on Savannah, his hand jerking upward. Getting off a shot.

Red blossomed across the front of Kye's shirt and he fell backward. Light caught on Draigon's wristband and then in surreal incongruity he lowered his hand. Retreated to the other side of the counter and gathered Kye into his arms.

"We will return to you," Draigon said, the red stones in his bands burning so brightly that Savannah blinked. Then blinked again with the realization that there was no one in the room with her. That only the blood on the counter and the tile proved what had just happened was real.

* * * * *

Draigon could feel Kye's life force fading. Could sense the frantic energy of the Ylan stones in Kye's wristbands as they tried to sustain him.

Without hesitation he used his own Ylan stones to transmute, to travel to the transport chamber in the Sierras, then to Belizair, to the bridge city Winseka, where the only known portal to Earth existed, and from there he used the last of the power and energy stored in his bands to go to the mountains, where the healers on Belizair lived.

245

"Follow me," an elderly Amato said in greeting, turning without another word and guiding Draigon through the ancient, twisting, underground passages, their walls deep tones of Ylan stone set in symbols and patterns that had once held significance for the Fallon.

Some of the tension eased from Draigon's chest and shoulders. The wings which had remained a collection of particles on Earth now opened slightly, relaxing.

Though Kye was still a dead weight in Draigon's arms, Draigon could feel Kye stabilize. As if death did not dare to enter this place where the Consort's veins lay exposed, opened, poured out in the form of the Ylan stone across the walls and ceilings, mixing with the ancient runes of the Fallon.

When he had studied the customs of Earth in preparation for claiming a bond-mate, Draigon had read the histories of how humans had once viewed his kind. How some of their places of worship contained images of winged men and women and children, angels, painted on their walls and stained in their windows.

There had been no time to visit one of the humans' holy places, but now, as he walked through the ancient caves of the Fallon, Draigon realized that this place of healing bodies was very much like the humans' place for healing souls. It radiated with peace and power, with echoes from the past, a connection to the very beginning of existence.

The healer entered a room, motioning Draigon toward its center and Draigon's breath caught at the sight of the altar within. It was made primarily of deep blue Ylan stones, but woven throughout were swirling ribbons of lavender containing a multitude of sparkling colors. The Tears of the Goddess.

Few had ever found them on Belizair. They were priceless—valued even by the Vesti, though because of their scarcity and not because of their religious significance. Until this moment, Draigon had seen only the Tears possessed by the priests and priestesses. Small stones, easily held in an infant's fist.

Without being told, Draigon placed Kye on the altar, hovering next to him, the memory of Savannah's anguished face assailing him as he looked at the Vesti who was his co-mate. The man who had found Savannah and kept her safe, whom Draigon had thought to resent and yet found he couldn't.

Kye's life force was weak, his breathing almost imperceptible, his dark suede-like wings draped over the altar, reminding Draigon of the bed-clothing on Earth. *He will be all right?*

The healer placed his hand on Draigon's shoulder. *It is up to the Goddess and her consort. Leave us now. My granddaughter waits outside to show you to a room. Your travels have left your Ylan stones drained. You may stay here while they are restored.*

* * * * *

Savannah cleaned up the blood, wiping it with a sponge, bleaching the counter and floor. *The Twilight Zone* theme song playing in her head along with visions of some secret government agency sweeping into her apartment to search for alien DNA.

Only the bands she wore on her wrists and Holland's presence in the bedroom had kept her grounded those first few moments after Kye, Draigon and Fowler disappeared. Now scenes from the past days crowded in. Subtle and not so subtle clues she'd picked up on but not recognized for what they were.

The hint of a familiar cologne—Fowler's—in her apartment the day she and Kye were here and found it had been carefully searched, probably by a different person than the one who'd trashed The Ferret's place.

Kye's disappearance without a trace the next morning. Draigon's sudden appearance a few days later. Both of their tracks going to a point and simply vanishing.

Draigon not knowing what fried chicken was. *Big clue there.*

Their not carrying guns despite being bounty hunters. She'd written that one off too.

Savannah moved to the window and looked out. Rubbed her chest with a suddenly shaking hand now that the business of destroying the crime scene was done. A sob forcing its way out. Oh god, what if Kye died?

Tears escaped and she closed her eyes. Willed the tears to stay put. The hope to remain. Tried to latch on to Draigon's promise that they would return. Not "I will return" but "*We* will return."

She combated the tears with deep breaths. Told herself that if they could disappear into thin air, then surely they had the technology to save Kye from a bullet wound.

She forced herself to think about the case instead. Seeing how the dots connected now. Fowler to Camryn. Camryn to Ivy and Holland. Camryn to Traynor. Traynor to Dominguez. Dominguez to The Cousins and The Psychos. Everyone accounted for but the missing Abrego brother—Psycho I, whose van Kye found abandoned in a garage near The Ferret's apartment building.

Fuck. Savannah leaned her forehead against the windowpane. In her mind's eye she replayed that first day together. The trip to The Ferret's apartment. Turning back toward Kye as they were on the sidewalk heading for the truck, asking him if he saw something, only vaguely noticing him lowering his arm to his side—the same way Draigon had done just after the flash that must have signaled Fowler's disappearance.

Savannah rubbed her forehead against the smooth glass. She hadn't even asked Kye why he thought a sniper might have been positioned in the garage. Though in her defense, after The Ferret's car blew up, a sniper wasn't out of the question. But to go days later and conveniently find a rifle case and registration papers...

Deep down she'd known. After the shootout with Psycho II, as they were getting ready to check into the hotel, when she'd been so worried and Kye had sounded so confident that they were safe from both of the Abregos—she'd had a brief, glittering moment when she wondered if Kye had found Psycho I in the parking garage and had done something to him.

But of course, she'd blown the thought off.

The phone rang and Savannah opened her eyes and pushed herself away from the window. Answered it, not surprised to hear Kelleher's voice saying they were on their way over to talk to Holland.

She went to the bedroom and found Holland awake, her face tear-streaked but no longer wet. Savannah sat on the bed and tried to feel sorry that she'd insisted they keep looking for Holland instead of taking off to parts unknown. Tried to tell herself that if she'd just dropped it, then Kye wouldn't have been shot.

But she couldn't regret trying to help Holland. She just couldn't. And in her heart, she didn't believe Kye or Draigon regretted it either.

Savannah took Holland's hand, almost expecting Holland to shun the contact and pull away. Holland held on instead. Her eyes meeting Savannah's. Trust there. Wariness. "That was one of the FBI agents. They'll be here in a few minutes. If you want to put this behind you, then you need to tell them everything. Including what you know about Camryn's brother. He's a cop, isn't he?"

Holland's hand tightened on Savannah's in response. "How'd you know?"

"Just a guess," Savannah said — one paid for in blood, but there was no way she could tell Holland the truth.

"I didn't know he was a cop until the day you took me to the station. I saw him there but he didn't see me."

Savannah closed her eyes. If only Holland had told her earlier — instead of denying that she knew what Camryn's brother looked like. If only...

Well, there was no point in thinking *if only*. There was only the here and now — and maybe the why Holland had held the information back.

I should have had Camryn take care of the kid. Slip her something and be done with it after she caught me changing out the memory chip in the camera a couple of weeks ago.

"Is Camryn's brother the one who handles the blackmail?" Savannah asked and Holland immediately looked away. Her voice a thready whisper full of shame when she answered, "He's the one who has all the pictures."

* * * * *

Draigon paced the visitor's sleeping chamber. Stretching his wings as he did so, relishing the movement, the ability to maintain his true form. His thoughts ricocheted between concern for Kye and worry for Savannah. His heart was heavy with the knowledge that when he had scooped Kye into his arms and transported in front of their bond-mate, he had perhaps ruined any chance they had to finish claiming her.

The threatened loss of Savannah troubled him far more than the fact he had violated one of the Council's strictest rules for those who traveled to Earth. His disappearance in front of Savannah had given direct evidence of the presence of those from Belizair, though few would fault him for his actions. Just as few would fault him for using the Ylan stones to destroy their attacker.

With a sigh Draigon sat down on a simply carved chair with a low back, forced his mind away from the turmoil of his thoughts in favor of reliving the time he'd spent on Earth in the company of Savannah. His body tightening as he remembered their first mating in the hot tub. His cock filling as phantom lips kissed over it. The need to be with her nearly overwhelming him.

Humor tugged at his heart when he remembered the drive to the cabin and how he'd been so enthralled by the sight of her breasts, by the wetness of her cunt that he'd lost control of the vehicle.

He laughed out loud, thinking about the times she'd teased him, prodded him into a lightness of spirit he was unaccustomed to.

He shook his head, revisiting how his confident resolve to remove her from her primitive, backwater planet had been relegated to failure within minutes of meeting her.

Draigon rose to his feet and resumed pacing. Grimacing as his cock pressed against the tight Earth clothing. The jeans he'd put on yet again in a silent hope that this would be the day Kye would be declared fit and they could return to Earth together.

The Ylan stones at Draigon's wrists were charged with energy. And yet the healers had not allowed him to see Kye yet.

He could not return to Savannah, not alone. Not without answers to the questions she would direct at him. Answers he was forbidden to give her under Council law.

Draigon sighed, defeat lingering at the edges of his worry. Savannah was the first of those carrying the Fallon marker to have family on Earth, a sense of belonging that couldn't be easily duplicated and the original erased.

There'd been no time to discuss her plans with respect to Holland. And both he and Kye had been grateful to dodge the discussion about the binding ceremony and returning home.

Movement at the doorway caused Draigon to break away from his worries. He glanced up. Anger and irritation flashing into him at the sight of Lyan. And yet instead of settling on him as they so often did, the emotions were fleeting, gone before he could say anything to antagonize the Vesti. "He is safe from death," Draigon found himself saying instead.

"May I enter?"

"Yes."

Lyan stepped into the room and offered his forearms in traditional greeting. "My thanks for saving his life."

Draigon closed the distance between them. Touched his bands to Lyan's. Their hands briefly gripping each other's forearms before they stepped apart. "He would have done the same for me."

"How goes it with Savannah?"

Draigon shook his head slightly. Realizing in that instant just how much his bond-mate had corrupted him. How much his love for her had changed him. Instead of disdain and anger for Lyan, he found himself wondering how the Vesti, known far and wide for stretching and bending Council law and managing to avoid serious sanctions, would handle the situation that he and Kye now found themselves in. "It grows more complicated each day Kye and I are with her," Draigon admitted, taking a seat and motioning for Lyan to join him.

Lyan sat, arranging the suede of his wings comfortably. "I will listen if you wish to share what has happened with her."

Draigon found it easier to show Lyan, to unroll the memories in a censored movie that ended with the events in her apartment. When he was done, Lyan shared images of his and Adan's pursuit of Krista. How he had also killed the man who threatened their bond-mate.

"It is a primitive planet and I admit to being glad we were able to convince Krista to return home with us," Lyan said. "And you are correct, your situation is more complicated than the one Adan and I found ourselves in, but I can see a way for you to be with your bond-mate—if you are willing to remain on Earth."

"Council law—"

Lyan held up a hand and Draigon halted. Surprise shuddering through him with the realization that he was willing to hear Lyan out.

"First," Lyan said, "your house is a respected one and you are an experienced bounty hunter whose talents would be of value to the scientists on Earth. Kye already serves the Council in such a way. And while Savannah's duties are not the same, she is a law-keeper whose knowledge and training could complement yours and Kye's.

"Second, Council law does not *require* that you bring your bond-mate to Belizair. It states only that she must *agree* to return home with you—which your bond-mate has done. And that once here, you must live in Winseka until the first of your children is born.

"And third, Council law states that our true forms can only be shown to our bond-mates in the transport chamber *prior to* transport. It says nothing about transport being mandatory once such a revelation is made.

"So it could be reasoned that you are free to complete the binding ceremony and mate with Savannah at other times in your true form, as long as you do so in the portal chamber—which is not such a great distance from the city your bond-mate calls home."

"The Council—" Draigon started to say, ready to elaborate and expand on the intent behind the Council rulings but halting in favor of examining Lyan's reasoning for flaws.

He found none.

All of Lyan's points were valid. And though Draigon hadn't shared the discovery of the human males carrying the Fallon gene sequence with Lyan, there was the added argument that Savannah's brothers and cousins might carry the markers as well.

Draigon had thought to claim Savannah and return to Belizair. He'd dismissed Earth as a backwater planet. Judged it as primitive. Resigned himself to a human bond-mate as though it was a terrible fate.

He was not one to doubt himself or his judgments, to question his decisions, but he had already been proven wrong, had already discovered parts of himself hidden under layers of restraint and freed by Savannah's teasing. The moment he'd seen Lyan and Adan's mate Krista and then his own, he had understood why his ancient ancestors were drawn to Earth and the humans found there. True, it was more dangerous than their world, but he had served in other equally dangerous places. And though they hadn't spoken of it, Kye seemed at ease on Savannah's planet.

With a clarity Draigon found hard to believe, Lyan's suggestion made perfect sense. His answer the obvious solution.

And as if sensing Draigon's growing acceptance, Lyan leaned forward and said, "The Council drags their feet, clings to decisions made in the past. They open the door leading to our future an inch at a time. But we cannot afford to remain mired and surrounded by rules that no longer make sense. Our presence on Earth must grow stronger and we must make alliances among the humans we have ties to. We must use those connections to expand our search for those with the Fallon markers. There are too many on Belizair waiting for a bond-mate to be found and it is taking too long to do so. If hope dies, then we die."

"I will speak to Kye," Draigon said, old habits lingering, making it impossible for him to tell Lyan that he was right in his arguments and conclusions.

"You will speak to me about what?" Kye said from the doorway, startling both his co-mate and his cousin, though the sight of Draigon and Lyan huddled together in conspiracy had very nearly made Kye question the state of his mental health if not his physical health!

The two men surged to their feet, greeting Kye with an embrace.

Lyan left once he assured himself Kye was well. Draigon replayed the conversation with Lyan, shocking Kye with his willingness to defy the intent of Council law if not the law itself. But humor quickly rushed in and Kye couldn't resist saying, "The humans have a saying that captures this perfectly. *It is easier to gain forgiveness than to gain permission.* Shall we return to Savannah?"

Chapter Twenty-One

ဆ

Savannah finished doing the breakfast dishes as her grandfather shuffled a deck of cards in preparation for a marathon session of Texas Hold-em. Relief and a measure of happiness filled her. Her grandparents had taken to Holland. Had treated her like family as soon as Savannah brought her back to the Bar None.

It was a start—to what, Savannah wasn't sure. But for the moment, Holland was safe and neither the police nor child services were looking too hard for her. It was one less thing for Savannah to worry about, which was good. Because right now she felt like her life was on hold.

"You joining us?" her grandfather asked as Savannah hung the dishtowel up.

The nearly non-stop games of poker had been a welcome respite from thoughts of Draigon and Kye. But Savannah was too restless to join her grandparents and Holland at the table. "No, I'm going to go outside for a few minutes."

She saw her grandparents exchange a glance. They were worried about her. But what could she tell them? *I fell in love with a couple of aliens? Or maybe they're supernatural beings. I don't know exactly what they are. But they protected me, fucked me, wanted to take me home with them—then one of them took a bullet for me and they disappeared, and the worst part of it is, I don't know if he lived or died, or whether I'll ever see them again. And even if I do see them again, I don't know how it's going to turn out.*

Savannah rubbed the wristbands. Finding comfort in the feel of them. Finding sanity in their existence. A physical proof that Kye and Draigon were real—though Holland's questions about their whereabouts had also been reassuring.

She walked down to the corral and leaned against the wooden fence, trying to internalize the tranquility displayed by a herd of ranch horses standing underneath several large trees. All of them still and calm, content, their only movement the flicking of their tails as they chased flies off sensitive skin.

No matter how crazy life got, how hectic and busy and frustrating, the Bar None was Savannah's refuge. She couldn't live here anymore—at least not in her parents' or grandparents' houses, but it was still home in a way, still more of a home than her apartment.

Savannah studied the wristbands. Again. She couldn't get them off. Not that she wanted to. But in all the time she'd examined them, she'd yet to find a release mechanism. In fact, they felt so much a part of her that she had a feeling she'd panic if they ever came off.

Sadness welled up inside Savannah. Confusion. Loneliness. Fear.

She could go for hours able to convince herself that if Kye and Draigon could disappear into thin air—and apparently take Fowler with them—then surely Kye couldn't be killed by a bullet. But then the doubts would start to slither in. Growing until sickness spread in her heart and soul. Until she was convinced he'd died. Until she was convinced she'd never see either of them again.

A sob lodged in her throat. Making breath impossible until she'd managed to wall off the grief.

She inhaled. A painful struggle against a tear-clogged throat.

In front of her three foals began playing. Trotting and cantering in graceful, poetic movement against a Sierra backdrop. Their coats glistening, sleek and shiny underneath a peerless blue sky.

The heaviness grew in Savannah's chest. If she had to choose, if going home with Kye and Draigon was permanent, could she give this up? Could she give up her family? Would she be able to tell her relatives where she was going? Even for Kye and Draigon she couldn't disappear into a black hole and leave the ones she loved to grieve and worry about what had happened to her.

Savannah sighed and closed her eyes. Rubbed the heels of her hands in small circles on her forehead.

Footsteps sounded behind her but Savannah didn't open her eyes or turn around. She'd known it would be only a matter of time before her brothers arrived and wanted to hear about the shootout she'd been involved in at the truck stop.

"Beloved," Kye whispered, his voice nearly stopping Savannah's heart, stunning her and trapping her in a moment of disbelief until she spun and saw him.

There was no single thought, only a cacophony of images and questions, emotion, as she hurled herself into his arms. Pressing kisses all over his face. Her fingers desperately struggling with his shirt, tearing at it to reveal unblemished flesh.

Tears coursed down her cheeks. A sob of happiness making it hard for her to speak. "I was scared you'd died," she managed, her fingers tangling in his hair, holding him as her lips and tongue assaulted his in a kiss that quickly merged into another, and then another, until her lungs burned with both emotion and the need for air.

She became aware of Draigon's presence but couldn't make herself release Kye. She reached out and pulled Draigon to them, her hand rubbing up and down his side as their lips met in kiss every bit as needy and desperate as the one she'd shared with Kye.

"You came back," Savannah said, weak with so many feelings that she was glad they were holding her, keeping her from sinking to the ground.

Draigon brushed his fingertips over her cheek and traced her lips. "Did you truly believe we wouldn't?"

"I didn't know what to think. You just disappeared."

Kye nuzzled against her temple. "You wear our bands. You agreed to a binding ceremony." He paused. "You agreed to go home with us."

Savannah's heart squeezed painfully in her chest. Raced so the blood thundered in her ears.

She wanted to delay the conversation, to lead them into the barn and make love to them, to bury worries of the future underneath a passionate present. But Kye's comment made it impossible. "I agreed to go home with you. But—"

Kye halted her with the quick press of his mouth to hers. "It is enough that you agreed. And eventually you will see our world. But for now, there is work here. A life here for all of us."

"For how long?"

Kye's expression grew somber. "All hope for our people is here and there is much you can do to help us."

The "aliens come to Earth to impregnate females" science fiction movies she'd watched as a teen tried to play on the screen of her mind. "By getting pregnant?"

Both Kye and Draigon smiled, masculine lips curving upward in anticipation. But before Savannah could say anything further, before she could become agitated, Draigon rubbed his hand over her belly, making her cunt clench and her womb flutter even as his words eased her. "Eventually, Savannah, but we are not anxious to share your attention with children. It is a decision we will make jointly when the time comes. Kye tells me birth control is practiced here. So we will wait. We will enjoy each other's company until you are prepared to return home with us." His face grew somber. "On this I can yield. But I cannot bear the thought of your putting yourself in danger each day."

Savannah stiffened. "You want me to quit my job."

Kye kissed his way to her ear, sending steel down her spine. Resolve. They'd used her body against her before—

numerous times — but she didn't want it to become the pattern that determined her future.

Savannah tried to pull out of their grasp and found it impossible. She opened her mouth to demand they release her, only to still when Kye said, "We do not intend for you to sit at home. We want you to work with us."

"As a bounty hunter?"

"Yes," Kye said and she didn't press him for details, though she could guess what bounty they were hunting.

Savannah closed her eyes. She'd become a cop because she wanted to make a difference. Because she wanted her life to *mean* something.

"Go through the binding ceremony with us," Kye said. "Learn who we really are. And if you decide you do not wish to work with us, we will accept your answer and do our best to keep you safe as you go about your work as a law officer." He nibbled her ear. "But I think you will find there are compensations to spending your days working at our side." He smiled against her skin. "Or beneath us. Or on top of us."

Savannah opened her eyes and gazed into his, seeing his teasing sincerity, his love. His optimism and hope. His confidence. Seeing much of the same when she turned her head slightly and looked at Draigon. Though Draigon was less sure, less at ease, and it made her heart smile, made her lean in and kiss him, a lingering exploration of masculine softness and hardness.

She loved them both so much. More than words could express.

They'd taken her by storm. Overwhelmed her body with a riot of passion. Intruded on her thoughts so time and time again she found herself thinking about them, wanting to share what was on her mind with them, revisiting the memories she had with them.

They'd filled the empty place in her soul. Claimed her heart. Completely. Totally. Irrevocably.

"Okay," Savannah said. "Okay."

Draigon's hand tightened on her side then left it to take possession of her arm, to bring the wrist with his band on it to his lips. "You will complete the binding ceremony with us?"

Savannah's heart flipped over at his vulnerable expression. "Name the time and place," she said, curling her hand so it cupped his cheek, unable to keep herself from lightening the mood by teasing, "As long as it doesn't involve Elvis, I'll be there for the ceremony. I draw the line at Elvis."

"Elvis?"

Kye laughed and sent the image of a dead singer to Draigon, along with a message, *I will explain it to you later. Or our bond-mate will. But for now I am in favor of returning to the transport chamber.*

As am I.

Draigon leaned into Savannah, wishing he could pull her completely into his arms but understanding her need to cling to Kye. Accepting it. Finding he had no jealousy or anger in his heart. Finding instead a nearly overwhelming love for this remarkable human woman who was their mate and would one day give them children. "Beloved, will you leave with us now?"

She glanced at the house a short distance away, for the first time wondering if her grandparents and Holland had seen Draigon and Kye's arrival and the heated kisses that had followed. "I can't just disappear."

Kye laughed. "Unlike the day Draigon appeared as you were demonstrating your roping skills, we came here by car."

Savannah's eyebrows drew together. "How did you know where to find me?"

"You will understand after the binding ceremony," Kye said, bending to press kisses along her neck and shoulder, lingering over the place he had repeatedly bitten her. "Tell your family you will return later today and introduce us to them."

Savannah hesitated only a second before nodding and pulling away. "I'll meet you at the car."

* * * * *

The trip to the transport chamber in the Sierras was agonizing for Draigon. The delay almost unbearable. And by the time they climbed out of the car, his body was coated in a sheen of sweat, his cock hard and full, aching and pulsing with both need and protest.

By the Goddess and her consort, Savannah's sensual torture as they'd traveled had very nearly reduced him to begging and pleading and "spilling his guts" as she'd claimed was her intention when they refused to answer her questions, though spilling his seed was closer to the truth. And Kye was in no better shape.

There was no need for conversation between them. No need to read each other's thoughts or emotions or intentions. To coordinate their actions. He and Kye were of one mind as they grasped Savannah's wrists and drew her through the foyer where most shed their Earth clothing, taking her directly into the chamber.

She gasped in surprise and wonderment, whispered, "This is beautiful," with such awe that the fever in Draigon's blood cooled enough that he could prevent himself from stripping and taking her to the floor in a wild rut. And once again, as though the connection to Savannah had attuned them to one another, Kye reached him telepathically, saying, *I feel like tumbling our mate onto the bed and fucking her until she passes out with exhaustion. But I would also have us build a memory that we can all savor.*

We are of like mind, Draigon said, releasing Savannah's wrist and shedding the much-hated Earth clothing as Kye did the same. Anticipation, love washing through him. A happiness he couldn't contain and didn't want to as he turned toward Savannah and gained her attention.

Savannah gave a husky laugh. The chamber with its skylight and its exquisite blossoming plants, the elaborate floor pattern of crystal stones, the huge bed on a low platform — all of it faded against the sheer beauty of Draigon and Kye as they stood naked in front of her. Their cocks rigid, their bodies hard muscle. Their expressions identical portraits of masculine determination, though she would never confuse the two of them or want them to be any different than who they were.

Kye. Humorous, uninhibited, playful.

Draigon. Serious, reserved, full of hard-to-reach places.

Savannah reached for her shirt, intending to peel it off but Draigon and Kye took her wrists, preventing her from doing it. "Oh no, beloved," Kye said. "This is for us to do."

They kissed the bands at her wrists again before releasing her. Kye moving around to her back as Draigon knelt before her. Both of them tormenting her with kisses and strokes, with nibbles and sucking bites as they slowly removed her clothing. Continuing their attention long after what she had been wearing lay heaped on the floor.

Savannah arched as Kye fondled her breasts. Moaned when he tweaked her nipples while Draigon's tongue made a foray into her slit then swiped upward, circling and teasing her clit so the hood pulled back and revealed the tiny, ultrasensitive head. She whimpered when he struck it, flicking it, rubbing it with his tongue before taking it into his mouth, sucking it even as his tongue continued to caress and swirl over and around it. All of it exquisitely timed to Kye's manipulation of her tender areolas.

Her fingers dug into Draigon's hair. Holding him to her as her lower body writhed, rubbed and pumped against his mouth. The need for release building until she came in a white-hot flash that left her shaking, strung-out, her cunt spasming, clenching and unclenching, desperate to close around their cocks.

"Payback is hell," Savannah managed, "not that this will stop me from asking you questions in the car again."

Kye laughed, his palms gliding over her nipples. "Draigon and I look forward to it."

Draigon rose to his feet. The position making it easy for Savannah to grasp his cock, to brush her thumb against the silky, wet head. "I'm going to die if you guys don't fuck me soon. I think I've mentioned it before. You two have turned me into a nympho with a serious sex addiction."

"As long as the addiction is limited to us," Draigon said, covering her hand with his, a groan escaping when she abandoned the tip and stroked up and down his shaft.

Savannah kissed him, tasted herself on him and found it darkly erotic. Felt her own arousal trickling down her inner thighs. The fullness of her cunt lips making it impossible to close her legs. And then Kye's hand was there, further preventing it. His palm against her mound, her clit stabbing into its center as his fingers burrowed into her channel and her inner muscles reacted, clamping down, holding him, releasing him only to hungrily grip him again.

I cannot last much longer, Draigon said, stepping back from Savannah.

Nor can I.

Kye forced himself away from Savannah's body. Coming around so they were both facing her. "We would have you see us as we truly are before we join completely with you."

Savannah tensed but didn't look away from them. Her stomach flip-flopped and her pulse spiked. She'd wondered if what she saw was what they really looked like. "I'm ready," she said, bracing herself. Praying she wouldn't react negatively and hurt their feelings.

The stones on their wristbands seemed to swirl and come to life. The air behind their backs shimmered as though thousands of molecules were suddenly gathering in one place. Behind Draigon, the phantom mist sparkled like a glittering, gauzy fabric. Behind Kye it was a deep brown cloud. Until finally the particles became solid forms. Wings.

Savannah laughed. Filled with joy. Awe. Love. Humor.

"Wingman and Batman. I don't know how I do it, but damn I'm good when it comes to nicknames."

She stepped into them. Made Draigon shudder as she ran her fingers over his red and gold-veined feathers. Made Kye do the same as she stroked the velvet suede of his dark chocolate wing and whispered, "I thought you two were gorgeous before, but now... I just want to wrap myself up in you and stay there."

Draigon took her hand in his. "I believe Kye and I can accommodate you."

Kye took her other hand and they led her to the bed, stretched her out between them and resumed their earlier assault, using their hands and mouths in a coordinated attack that left her breathless, pleading, shivering by the time Kye rolled to his back and took her with him, pulled her onto his cock, his soft wings spread out like a glorious dark brown comforter, his hands going to her buttocks, opening her for Draigon.

She gasped when Draigon's fingers rimmed her back entrance, her channel clamping down on Kye's cock in a fist of feminine heat when the oil they'd used on her before spread across her tight hole, lubricating her, sending fiery lust radiating outward, inward, so she groaned, pumped against Kye, felt the oil trickle downward, sensitizing every place it touched, reaching her cunt, his penis, and making them both pump and strain.

Kye's cock jerked with a dark, unfamiliar pleasure as Savannah's channel tightened when Draigon began pushing into her, his penis stroking Kye's through the thin barrier separating them. *Hurry!*

Draigon groaned in response. Pushed deeper. Said, *Position her wrists*, and Kye threaded his fingers through

Savannah's so their bands touched, lifted their arms above their heads so Draigon could join his hands to theirs, his bands to theirs when he was finally fully seated. Their cocks both inside her. The three of them joined completely.

For a shimmering moment they held still. Fought against the demands of their bodies and the feverish need to move.

They savored their first complete coming together. But all too soon Savannah's internal muscles rippled against cocks pulsing in time to the crystals on Draigon and Kye's bands— Ylan stones ready to migrate, their power intensifying the connection, making it impossible for Draigon and Kye to remain still any longer, to do anything but finish what they'd started, to thrust and counterthrust, to claim their bond-mate in a wild rush of passion and love and release. A shattering climax that left them slick with sweat, melded together and yet completely open to each other, mind-to-mind, heart-to-heart, soul-to-soul. So intimately connected that at first Savannah thought the feelings rushing through her, nearly overwhelming her with their intensity, were an outpouring of her own love, a reflection of how much she'd come to need Draigon and Kye. But then Kye's voice sounded in her mind, sent her heart thundering again when he said, *We need you as well, Savannah. Never doubt it.*

She met his gaze and remembered all the times she had seen Kye and Draigon standing together in a curious silence. Almost as though they were talking to one another without saying a word. Now she knew differently. *You can read each other's minds,* she said. Not sure how to direct her thoughts.

We open and close our thoughts at will, Draigon said.

Fuck! Savannah said, jerking at hearing his voice though she should have anticipated it.

He laughed in her mind. A husky masculine sound as his hips pumped slowly, his cock now against the crevice of her ass. The feathers of his wing a sensuous teasing along her side. *If you desire a fuck then I am certain Kye and I can rise to the occasion.*

Savannah's heart flooded with a fresh wave of love. Draigon's quick humor and playful response making her laugh.

Kye pressed a kiss to her lips. *This is our binding day and we would not disappoint our mate in any way.*

She shivered, aware of his cock full and ready again, slick against her belly. Of Draigon's penis, now equally engorged, pressed against her buttocks.

She had a million questions and yet the urge to join completely with them pulsed through her like a unifying heartbeat. A call that originated from the bands on her wrists and couldn't be refused.

Savannah glanced at the bracelets then, her cop mind processing what she was seeing, recognizing why they'd insisted she accept the bands, why this was called a binding ceremony—even if she didn't immediately know how some of the stones from Draigon's and Kye's wristbands could have shifted to hers.

We will explain in as much detail as you desire. Later, Kye said, his hands going to her hips, urging her to shift, to claim his cock again.

Savannah didn't resist his urging. Her fingers stroked the soft underside of his wing as his penis slid home. *We'll talk on the way to the ranch. I promised Grams we'd be back in time for dinner,* she said, waiting until Draigon had also joined his body to hers before teasing, reminding them of an earlier conversation, *so now would be a good time to prove you don't need to eat Prairie Oysters in order to go the distance and keep your bond-mate sexually satisfied.*

Kye laughed while Draigon muttered something about primitive, backwater planets. But then both of them were touching her, not only with their hands and lips but with their emotions, their thoughts. Filling her with more than just their cocks. Giving all of themselves even as their voices whispered in her mind, promising to protect and pleasure her as was their right, their duty. Their privilege.

Epilogue

෨

Jeqon d'Amato contemplated the results of the DNA matching with a mix of hope and uncertainty. He was a scientist, but he did not exclude the possibility that the Goddess's wisdom and vision were at work. Reshaping Belizair in a way that was more pleasing to *Her*.

Once the Fallon had been a great race of winged shapeshifters. But arrogance and jealousy, pride and prejudice had destroyed them, splintering them into a multitude of races that were lesser than what they had once been, scattering them until only the Amato and Vesti remained on Belizair.

The first of the human women bonded to both a Vesti and Amato male were close to giving birth, the much-anticipated event the reason he had the Council house and laboratory in San Francisco to himself.

The others had already gone to Winseka, preferring to be ahead of the births than to risk missing them. And now that he had the results of the DNA matching, he would join them soon.

Jeqon was not alone among the scientists in wondering what abilities the children of these matches would have. The tests they were able to perform on samples obtained from the fetuses showed the distinctive markers of both races—the presence of the genes responsible for the feathered wings of the Amato and the suede, bat-like wings of the Vesti.

Since all of the women carried twins, many concluded there would be one Vesti infant and one Amato infant. And since the wings would not manifest until after birth, when the wristbands were put on and a portion of the parent's Ylan stones migrated to the children's bracelets, there was no way to prove or disprove, to know for certain what these children would be.

Jeqon thought perhaps the children would be *more*. He thought perhaps they were the first small step in the return of the Fallon. He prayed to the Goddess and her consort Ylan that it was so.

It had taken the threat of extinction to redirect the attention of the scientists to Earth. To make them consider the gene pool there among the humans who were the descendants of the Fallon. And in doing so, they had found hope for the unmated males. For Belizair itself.

Jeqon moved to the window of the Council house and looked out at the San Francisco bay, wondering if the discovery of the two human males carrying the Fallon gene sequence offered the unbonded women of Belizair a true hope or a false one. If it offered his sister Zantara a chance at happiness or a pathway to more despair.

The Ylan stones in his wristbands hummed against his skin, resonating with energy, an indication his sister would soon arrive on Earth. He folded the paper containing the results of the DNA matching and put it in his pocket as he turned from the window and made his way to the transport chamber, praying to the Goddess for guidance as he did so. For forgiveness. For a setting aside of the anger between Zantara and him.

The Hotaling virus had done more than threaten those on Belizair with extinction, it had raised old hostilities and torn apart families. He and Zantara had never been as close as some siblings, but they had been on friendly terms — until the virus struck.

Their society was one that valued free choice, free will, but even so, women who bore and raised children were revered. And to be unable to do so...

Zantara was not alone in finding herself without hope, struggling with despair and feelings of worthlessness, anger.

Bitterness. Jeqon could understand these feelings, had tried his best to console her, to offer what hope he could. But in her pain she had struck out at him for his friendship with Komet d'Vesti of the Araqiel. In her pain she had inflicted heartache and misery on others, had insisted Adan's eldest brother, Zeraac, who she had pledged herself to, be tested and then when he was found to be sterile, had cast him aside—only to turn around and go to their uncle in protest, to try to set aside the mate-bond when Komet and Zeraac claimed the human female Ariel and took her to Belizair.

Jeqon stopped outside the transport chamber, the resonance vibrating through his wristbands telling him the portal sequence was nearing completion. He braced himself, prayed once again for guidance from the Goddess and the Consort. Wondered again if *Her* hand wasn't at work, recasting the Amato and Vesti. Reweaving the fabric of their world, strand by strand. Mate-bond by mate-bond.

The doors opened and Zantara stepped out. Her eyes meeting his. Glistening with tears as she stepped forward and extended her arms, touched her bands to his in a traditional greeting. *I have made my peace with Zeraac and gained permission from the Council to serve as one of their agents here. To seek out unwanted children carrying the Fallon gene, and should any be found, to help raise them until they are old enough to be matched and taken to Belizair of their own free will.*

Joy poured through Jeqon, her words the very omen he had prayed for. *You have arrived at the perfect moment. Draigon, Kye and their human bond-mate, Savannah, have found a young female named Holland who has the Fallon marker.* He paused then switched to the spoken word, "She is not an infant or child. She is thirteen Earth-years and her life has not been an easy one."

Zantara did not hesitate. "Tell me where I need to go."

Jeqon gave her the coordinates and watched as she returned to the chamber. The bands on his wristband humming to life as she transported.

270

Only when the vibration had stopped did he return to the laboratory and pick up the telephone. Smiling when Draigon answered after enough rings to suggest he might have been occupied, his growled hello confirming it.

"Zantara is on her way to assist with Holland," Jeqon said. "I have not shared this information with her, but the human male named Kelleher is a match for her."

Also by Jory Strong

ᔕ

Carnival Tarot 1: Sarael's Reading

Carnival Tarot 2: Kiziah's Reading

Carnival Tarot 3: Dakotah's Reading

Crime Tells 1: Lyric's Cop

Crime Tells 2: Cady's Cowboy

Crime Tells 3: Calista's Men

Crime Tells 4: Cole's Gamble

Death's Courtship

Ellora's Cavemen: Dreams of the Oasis I (*anthology*)

Ellora's Cavemen: Jewels of the Nile III (*anthology*)

Ellora's Cavemen: Seasons of Seduction I (*anthology*)

Ellora's Cavemen: Seasons of Seduction IV (*anthology*)

Elven Surrender

Fallon Mates 1: Binding Krista

Fallon Mates 2: Zeraac's Miracle

Fallon Mates 3: First Sharing

Fallon Mates 4: Zoe's Gift

Familiar Pleasures

Spirit Flight

Spirits Shared

Supernatural Bonds 1: Trace's Psychic

Supernatural Bonds 2: Storm's Faeries

Supernatural Bonds 3: Sophie's Dragon

Supernatural Bonds 4: Drui Claiming

Supernatural Bonds 5: Dragon Mate

The Angelini 1: Skye's Trail

The Angelini 2: Syndelle's Possession

About the Author

8>

Jory has been writing since childhood and has never outgrown being a daydreamer. When she's not hunched over her computer, lost in the muse and conjuring up new heroes and heroines, she can usually be found reading, riding her horses, or hiking with her dogs.

Jory welcomes comments from readers. You can find her website and email address on her author bio page at www.ellorascave.com.

Tell Us What You Think

We appreciate hearing reader opinions about our books. You can email us at Comments@EllorasCave.com.

Why an electronic book?

We live in the Information Age—an exciting time in the history of human civilization, in which technology rules supreme and continues to progress in leaps and bounds every minute of every day. For a multitude of reasons, more and more avid literary fans are opting to purchase e-books instead of paper books. The question from those not yet initiated into the world of electronic reading is simply: *Why?*

1. *Price.* An electronic title at Ellora's Cave Publishing and Cerridwen Press runs anywhere from 40% to 75% less than the cover price of the exact same title in paperback format. Why? Basic mathematics and cost. It is less expensive to publish an e-book (no paper and printing, no warehousing and shipping) than it is to publish a paperback, so the savings are passed along to the consumer.

2. *Space.* Running out of room in your house for your books? That is one worry you will never have with electronic books. For a low one-time cost, you can purchase a handheld device specifically designed for e-reading. Many e-readers have large, convenient screens for viewing. Better yet, hundreds of titles can be stored within your new library—on a single microchip. There are a variety of e-readers from different manufacturers. You can also read e-books on your PC or laptop computer. (Please note that Ellora's Cave does not endorse any specific brands.

You can check our websites at www.ellorascave.com or www.cerridwenpress.com for information we make available to new consumers.)

3. *Mobility.* Because your new e-library consists of only a microchip within a small, easily transportable e-reader, your entire cache of books can be taken with you wherever you go.

4. *Personal Viewing Preferences.* Are the words you are currently reading too small? Too large? Too... ANNOYING? Paperback books cannot be modified according to personal preferences, but e-books can.

5. *Instant Gratification.* Is it the middle of the night and all the bookstores near you are closed? Are you tired of waiting days, sometimes weeks, for bookstores to ship the novels you bought? Ellora's Cave Publishing sells instantaneous downloads twenty-four hours a day, seven days a week, every day of the year. Our webstore is never closed. Our e-book delivery system is 100% automated, meaning your order is filled as soon as you pay for it.

Those are a few of the top reasons why electronic books are replacing paperbacks for many avid readers.

As always, Ellora's Cave and Cerridwen Press welcome your questions and comments. We invite you to email us at Comments@ellorascave.com or write to us directly at Ellora's Cave Publishing Inc., 1056 Home Avenue, Akron, OH 44310-3502.

COMING TO A BOOKSTORE NEAR YOU!

ELLORA'S CAVE

Bestselling Authors Tour

UPDATES AVAILABLE AT

WWW.ELLORASCAVE.COM

Cerridwen, the Celtic Goddess of wisdom, was the muse who brought inspiration to storytellers and those in the creative arts. Cerridwen Press encompasses the best and most innovative stories in all genres of today's fiction. Visit our site and discover the newest titles by talented authors who still get inspired - much like the ancient storytellers did, once upon a time.

Cerridwen Press

www.cerridwenpress.com

Discover for yourself why readers can't get enough
of the multiple award-winning publisher
Ellora's Cave.

Whether you prefer e-books or paperbacks,
be sure to visit EC on the web at
www.ellorascave.com

for an erotic reading experience that will leave you
breathless.

LaVergne, TN USA
21 December 2010
209702LV00002B/85/P